THE ISLAND IN THE MIST

C.G. MOSLEY

D0834896

SEVERED PRESS
HOBART TASMANIA

THE ISLAND IN THE MIST

CHAPTER 1

The year is 1511...

The merciless sheets of stinging rain continued to pelt Macuya's face and there seemed to be no end in sight. He ran through the jungle aimlessly and it seemed that the only thing forcing him onward was the sheer desperation he felt. Several days earlier, he made one of the most agonizing decisions of his life when he left his tribe to escape the invading Spaniards. The Taínos were forced into slavery almost immediately and Macuya had seen too many of his brethren die during the rebellion. The Taíno were skilled warriors, but their weaponry was clearly inferior to the swords and crossbows wielded by the Spaniards. Macuya had been in the thick of many of the battles with their invaders. He had seen a lot of spilled blood and almost all of it belonged to the Taíno. The pride and bravery that initiated the rebellion soon turned into pure fear, and fear will push a man to do extraordinarily desperate things. Macuya took one of the tribe's fishing boats and escaped the brutality of the Spaniards via the Atlantic Ocean. He had taken boats into the ocean many times before, but he had never ventured far enough to lose sight of his island home. He did not know what was waiting for him in the depths of the ocean, and worse yet, he did not know how long it would be before he found land again. The only thing he was sure of was that facing the terrors of the sea would be better than facing the certain death the Spaniards were eager to deliver.

The trip, for the most part, was uneventful. Food was not a problem due to the fact that Macuya was a very skilled fisherman. Water, on the other hand, ran out very quickly. The scorched, prickly feeling in his throat was almost unbearable by the time the sun rose and fell the fourth time. Sparkling water surrounded him in every direction as far as the eye could see, but he knew drinking it would certainly hasten his demise. All of the time alone provided another tremendous burden he hadn't thought a lot about. Macuya suddenly felt guilty for leaving his tribe behind. He had originally justified his actions by telling himself that he was a terrible chief and that his leadership had led many to their unnecessary deaths. Leaving the island and the people who had followed him seemed to be the last kind thing he could do for them. Once he was gone, they would be forced to surrender to the Spaniards and the killing would end.

Now that he was alone with nothing but the sea and his thoughts, he began to feel uncertain about his decision. *What if the killing doesn't stop?* It was a terrible thing to consider, and it certainly wasn't doing him any good thinking about it now. But the question would not stop burning in his head. He wondered what his people would think when they first realized that he had vanished. He hoped that betrayal would not enter their minds, but if the Spaniards continued to murder them, then it certainly would. That thought made him shudder. He shook his head in an attempt to clear his thoughts, and suddenly the burning sensation in his throat came roaring back. Just thinking about water seemingly made his mouth dry up more as his body continued to beg for it. As the sun fell for the fifth time, he prayed to the gods that when he went to sleep he would awaken in the spiritual world.

The next morning, when the realization that the gods had ignored him set in, Macuya had finally reached his breaking point. He struggled to make his sun-blistered legs move, but when they finally did, he stood up in the boat. He looked to the heavens and screamed contumaciously to the gods above. After his tirade, he fell back into the boat and sobbed. His body was so dried up he was unable to even muster tears. Trying to cry with no tears was an awkward feeling and Macuya rubbed his eyes in a useless attempt to create moisture. When he removed his hands, something caught his eye in the distance. He crawled to the bow and ignored the pain on his sunburnt hands and knees. There was a tiny gray object on the horizon in the direction the ocean current was taking him. At first, he decided it was a cruel trick that the gods were playing on him as punishment for the tongue-lashing he'd spat at them moments earlier. He lay back into the boat and exhaustion forced him back into a deep sleep.

Hours later, a sudden jolt awakened him and he sat up, wide-eyed and surprisingly alert. The first thing he noticed was that the sun was gone. The sky was cloudy and the air felt cool and damp. The boat had apparently continued to travel toward the gray object he had seen before he fell asleep. It was not a trick by the gods, but a blessing instead. It was a beach! He looked back and a good distance behind him there seemed to be a wall of mist. It was so thick he could not see beyond it, and it was thick enough to block out the sun. He used what seemed to be the last ounce of strength he had left to jump onto the cool sandy beach and rejoice at the turn of good fortune. After a few moments spent thanking and apologizing to the gods, Macuya began to walk further inland in search of water. He quickly found a small stream and he dropped to his knees, eventually dunking his head into the water. He took in gulps of the cool freshwater and every cell in his body seemed to soak every drop up like a sponge. He could literally feel his arms and legs come back to life, and he felt relief as his mouth, tongue, and throat were finally wet again.

Once it was clear to him that he was going to live, Macuya wondered if there were any other tribes on the island. If there were, he needed to avoid them until he had a chance to observe them. There was a good chance they would kill an outsider like him immediately. However, he also knew of gentler, peaceful tribes that may offer him food and shelter. He decided to travel further inland and search for signs of humanity. The jungle was lively and vibrant with colorful flowers and birds alike. There were plenty of coconuts, berries, and fruits to eat. This observation was comforting to him as he also realized that there was a possibility he wouldn't find anyone. He quite possibly could be all alone on the island, and the more he thought about that, the more it scared him. He accomplished what he had set out to do: he escaped from the Spaniards. Part of him was proud of that, but another part of him was fearful that he would never see a human being again for the rest of his life. He pondered that for a long moment and decided if that was what the gods had in store for him, he would embrace it. He alone created the scenario he found himself in. He would shoulder the consequences that derived from his decisions.

He had not walked long when he heard something (or someone) rustling in the bushes. He stared into the brush for a long moment as he thought about what to do next. The plants shuffled around once more and it was easy to see that it was not a person. It had to be an animal of some kind. Carefully, he took both hands and parted the dense vegetation, fully expecting a bird to fly out and startle him. Instead, what he found was something he had never seen before. A large lizard stared back at him. It stood just above Macuya's knee and seemed harmless. He had been around nature long enough to realize that just because something looked harmless, didn't mean it was so. He slowly let the surrounding plants spring back to their original shape and the lizard was once again hidden from view. The lizard was much larger than any he had seen on his native island. He wondered how many other animals existed on this island that he had never seen before. The further Macuya ventured into the jungle, the more it slowly began to thin out. Eventually, the jungle completely ended and a wide-open valley stretched out a great distance in front of him. The sight in the valley made his jaw drop.

There were herds upon herds of giant lizards. The other one paled in comparison to some of the ones he was seeing now. Some of them he estimated were the height of ten men. They all seemed to be grazing peacefully among one another, and they reminded him of the cows he'd been around back home. Some of them had large horns protruding from their heads, and some of them looked like larger versions of the lizard he met in the jungle. Some walked on four legs (like the horned ones) and some only walked on two. The fear he initially felt when he spotted them quickly turned into awe. He watched another herd gracefully move over to a large pool in the middle of the pasture and they all began to drink at once. The different herds seemed to be oblivious to one another, and it was unlike anything Macuya had ever seen before.

Suddenly, he noticed their behavior begin to change. It seemed as if all at once, they stopped grazing and drinking. They raised their large heads at attention. It was as if they all heard him at once. He looked around to see if anything else triggered the reaction, but found nothing. He slowly crept back into the jungle's shadows, but stayed close enough to continue watching. It quickly became obvious that they weren't paying any attention to him at all because they continued to stand deadly still.

Finally, almost in unison, the giant lizards scattered in all directions. Macuya gasped as he watched another large lizard tear through the trees on the opposite side of the clearing. It roared loud enough to make his bones rattle. The sound was terrifying and the animal's open mouth was full of jagged teeth. He cowered down low behind a fallen tree even though he knew the lizard wasn't even aware of his presence. The only thing it had on its mind was devouring one of the many animals grazing in the clearing.

Its two large muscular legs propelled it after the herd that was closest to it. It was the four-legged horned lizards, and most of them had a large enough head start that there was no chance of the monstrous lizard catching them. There were a few, however, that weren't so fortunate. The massive lizard sunk its teeth into the hindquarters of one of the stragglers and it bellowed in pain. A couple of the horned lizards turned back and charged at their attacker. One of them punched its horns into the two-legger's right thigh, and the lizard roared in what seemed to be mostly anger, not pain. The other one charged at its left side, but this time, the two-legger was ready. It dodged the attack and bit down hard on the horned lizard's back. It bellowed louder than the other one had and fell over, motionless.

The remaining horned lizard seemed to realize the odds were not in its favor. It quickly turned to run, but the two-legger bit into its tail, stopping it abruptly. The horned lizard scraped and clawed the ground, frantically trying to pull itself free of the two-legger's death grip. The struggling finally paid off as the horned lizard jerked free, but a chunk of its tail was now missing. Blood poured from the gaping wound and the animal wailed as it rushed to catch up with the herd. Macuya looked on as the dust cloud from the one-sided fight began to settle and the large two-legged lizard feasted on its kills. The gruesome scene changed his thought process dramatically. Suddenly, the possibility of stumbling upon a hostile tribe didn't frighten him much anymore.

Nightfall was approaching quickly. Macuya saw a flash of lightning and he heard thundering in the distance. The heavy mist continued to hover around the island, but he sensed that a squall was approaching behind it. The variety of giant lizards that inhabited the island seemed to sense the squall also as evidenced by the moans, bellows, and roars that the animals made throughout the late afternoon. Macuya felt a hint of despair as he scrambled to find some sort of shelter for the night. He needed something that would keep him dry and, more importantly, protect him from the carnivorous lizards that were nearby.

was similar to what he felt the day before when he drank from the stream, but this was different. A rejuvenating wave of energy flowed through his veins that made his muscles pulse and his body shake. The awkward feeling scared him at first, but there was no pain involved. Instead, it was extremely pleasant. He soon felt that he was ten—no fifteen years younger! He looked down into the pool of water, and as the ripples settled, he was amazed to find that he even looked fifteen years younger! A strange sound from the shadows of the cave walls startled him, and he whipped his head around to see what was there. He saw small figures moving toward him in the darkness. The figures stood almost chest high and he slowly began to back away. One stepped into a beam of light that illuminated a red-and-white feathery head.

Macuya blinked in amazement at the sight of yet another strange animal on the island. This animal seemed like the lizards he'd seen before except portions of its body were lightly covered in feathers. The very large eyes were more forward facing on this animal and they were locked menacingly onto Macuya. Soon, he heard others approaching from other directions; the situation was quickly turning uncomfortable. The animals began making noises that closely resembled the bark of a dog. Macuya turned to run, but he was met by more of the strange feathery animals approaching from the entrance. The one immediately in front of him crouched down and positioned itself similar to the way a cat would when it was ready to pounce. Macuya stood still a moment and patiently watched to see what the animal would do next. It glared at him with its large yellow cat eyes and it barked at him again. He took a step back, and as he considered his next move, the animal suddenly sprung forward at him. Macuya's combat experience and newfound youthfulness proved worthy as he quickly dropped to the ground, narrowly missing the attack. The other animals were taken aback by the intelligence of their prey and they seemed confused. Macuya took advantage of their bewildered states and sprinted past them all and out of the cave.

Once outside, he used his memory and good instincts to try and run in the general direction of the beach, and more specifically, the boat. His heart raced and his head constantly swiveled in all directions as he scanned the landscape ahead for more carnivorous lizards. He occasionally did see a few, but he never stopped running. He decided if any of them were a threat to him, the last thing he should do is stop to find out. He just kept running. It had been a long time since he had been able to run so far for so long without becoming winded. He wondered how long the effects of the magical water would keep his youthfulness and stamina boosted to the level he currently felt.

Relief set in when he jogged to the edge of the familiar large valley he had crossed the day before. The numerous herds of plant-eating lizards were still there, just as they had been before he witnessed the giant two-legger chase them all away. He crouched down in the shadows of the trees and scanned the horizon carefully for the monstrous lizard. He consumed a few berries while he watched and waited. When he was satisfied that it was safe to cross, he darted into the open. Occasionally, he looked right to left, but for the most part kept his attention on the wood line straight ahead. Suddenly, a flock of birds ahead of him and to his right scattered in all directions out of the trees. Macuya's heart sank when the large two-legger charged into the open field. It stopped momentarily and flung its head upward. The lizard's mouth opened and unleashed a deafening roar, purposely making its presence known to the hundreds of animals grazing across the field. Macuya began to pray that the gods would help him sneak by yet again, and he realized that he was so frightened he was praying out loud. The gods seemed to listen because the two-legger paid him no attention. It seemed to enjoy chasing the weaker lizards and the challenge that came along with it. Natural curiosity made him want to stay and watch the incredible predator work, but he focused on the task at hand.

Macuya kept his full attention on locating the beach as soon as possible. The roar of the two-legger echoed behind him, but he ignored the loud sound. His ears were straining to hear a much calmer and gentler sound, the ocean. Soon, he began to think that he was traveling in the wrong direction. He didn't remember the trek between the beach and the valley being as far as it now seemed.

He finally stopped running and tried to listen intently. For a moment, he heard nothing, but just as he was about to resume running, he heard the familiar surf directly to his left. Overcome with relief, he continued onward until he finally stumbled out onto the white sand. At first, the boat was nowhere to be seen and he feared that the tide had taken it away. Fortunately, after a few moments, he spotted it a great distance up the beach. The cool sand was a welcome change for his sore and swollen feet as he ran toward his escape. When he reached the boat, his first instinct was to immediately push it into the water and paddle away from the island as quickly as possible. Then he noticed the empty water bags lying in the boat. If there was any chance of surviving the ruthless sea, he had to fill the water bags before he left. He wasted little time rushing back into the jungle and filling the bags at the nearby stream. Before he left the stream for the final time, he drank all that his body would allow him to consume. He drank so much that his belly ached, but he ignored the pain. It was absolutely crucial to hydrate his sour though as one tribe leader in particular turned everything into disarray.

Juan had begun to trust the one called Macuya a great deal, and he seemed to be the most intelligent of them all. Through him, the Taíno were becoming more and more compliant and there seemed to be less and less beatings. Then one day, seemingly out of nowhere, the rebellion started.

Led by Macuya, the tribe united and suddenly lashed out against the Spaniards. The Taíno were skilled in combat and very deadly with spears and poisonous darts. They had countless other deadly weapons made from stone, and he'd never met a single Taíno that was reluctant to use any of them. Juan lost several very good men in the early goings of the rebellion. However, at no time did he ever fear that he would be unable to regain control of the situation. Because no matter how skilled the Taíno warriors were at combat, and no matter how barbaric and deadly their primitive weapons were, there was one thing that the Spaniards possessed that completely threw the odds in their favor. The crossbow. It was powerful, it was deadly, and it was completely unstoppable against a primitive tribe of people. For all the Spanish blood spilled across the landscape of Puerto Rico, the Taíno blood exceeded it ten-fold. The rebellion was short-lived, and within a matter of weeks, the entire tribe had resumed their work in the fields and mines. There was, however, one curious occurrence near the end of the rebellion that puzzled Juan relentlessly. Macuya, whom he'd become quite well acquainted with, vanished from the fighting altogether. At first, he decided the Taíno chief must have been killed in battle. All of his men were ordered to search for the remains of Macuya and they were promised a handsome reward for him, dead or alive. When nothing turned up, Juan turned his attention to the tribe, and he questioned the ones that were easiest to communicate with. Juan and his men soon learned that many of the Taíno were angry and accused their leader of deserting them. None of it made any sense, and just when Juan had decided he would never know the answer to the puzzle, an incredible thing happened. A one in a million shot occurred when one of the Spanish merchant ships found a small Taíno fishing boat adrift a few hundred miles away from Puerto Rico. Inside, they found Macuya in surprisingly good condition for someone who had been in the open sea for many days.

The merchant ship arrived in Puerto Rico in the early morning hours, and as soon as Juan finished his breakfast, he requested that the guards bring Macuya to him at once. Juan continued to stare out across the vast Atlantic Ocean as he waited and pondered what it must have been like all alone in such a harsh environment. In a way, he could understand why Macuya chose such a hopeless escape of the island. Macuya was a true soldier and a real soldier would choose death above being captured by the enemy in almost every circumstance. He understood why he would choose to face the unknown of the ocean instead of the possibility of execution by the hand of the Spaniards. What he could not understand was why he deserted his people the way that he did. And how did he manage to fair as well as he did after being so long at sea? These were questions that he would not be able to find out unless he asked Macuya directly.

A ruckus behind him shattered his thoughts. He turned and saw Macuya being led toward him by two guards. His second-in-command, a gruff middle-aged man named Roberto, followed. When the guards got within a few feet of Juan, they stopped abruptly and yanked the shackles on Macuya's arms and legs, tightly removing all the slack. Roberto walked around them and respectfully removed his hat which revealed his thick, graying hair. He put an arm around Juan and led him a short distance away from Macuya.

"Governor, the translator has spent all night with him and we've found out a few details about our prisoner," Roberto said quietly.

"What sort of details?" Juan asked.

"It seems that Macuya felt he was doing the tribe a favor by leaving. I believe he gave it a lot of thought before he acted on it."

Juan's eyes widened. "He thought he was doing them a favor? By leaving them?"

Roberto nodded. "Yes, he believed that if the tribe had no leadership, they would be forced to surrender."

"He was right about that," Juan chuckled, revealing a mouthful of tobacco-stained teeth. "That answers one question. I'm also curious to know how he fared as well as he did. His face seems smoother and more boyish. His color is very healthy for someone who spent four days in the sea."

Roberto nodded again, and took a moment before he spoke. "Yes…we asked him about that too."

Juan waited for a response as Roberto rubbed the back of his neck, still collecting his thoughts.

"Go on," he replied impatiently.

"From what he is telling us, Macuya did not spend the entire four days in the open sea. He told us that at one point during his voyage he fell asleep. Later, he awoke to find his boat shipwrecked on an island and he spent a great deal of time there."

Juan's eyes lit up. "An island? Are we aware of this island?"

CHAPTER 4

Puerto Rico, Spring of 1985

Angus Wedgeworth slapped the back of his neck in a desperate attempt to rid himself of some sort of biting insect that would not go away. He wiped the remains of the crushed insect on his pant leg. He was dressed in a very expensive grey suit, but since he owned nearly a hundred suits, (many of them also grey), soiling this particular one mattered very little to him. Suits, much like every other thing he owned, could be easily replaced. Angus was a self-made millionaire and he savored every minute of it. However, the minutes, unfortunately, were beginning to wind down.

Having recently celebrated his seventy-fourth birthday, Angus had fallen into what he could only assume was a mild case of depression. He couldn't be sure, simply because in all of his seventy-four years, he'd never experienced what depression felt like. Money brought him nothing but happiness throughout his colorful life. Over the years, he'd watched other millionaires and countless celebrities make appearances on primetime talk shows, and with tissue in hand, proceed to tell the world how lonely they feel and how terrible being rich and famous really was. Angus rolled his eyes at those pathetic individuals and vowed he would never turn into one of them. Up until this part of his life, he never had. Actually, to him, this wasn't even the same thing.

The root of the anguish he now felt was nothing more but the realization that he was nearing the end of his life, and as much as he loved his money, the thing hardest for him to accept was that he couldn't take it with him. He kept the selfish feelings to himself, and although he knew how incredibly shallow his thoughts would sound if he made them known to others, he quite frankly didn't care. It was he and he alone that started the very first Wedgeworth Furniture Store in his hometown of Hattiesburg, Mississippi almost forty-five years ago. Success came easy for him, and in less than a decade, a total of fifty-eight Wedgeworth Furniture Stores popped up all over the contiguous United States. After two decades, that number steadily increased to a whopping one-hundred and fifty stores. Before he reached the age of forty, he easily reached a celebrity status of sorts. His face in the Wedgeworth Furniture television commercials became almost as recognizable as the colonel of the Kentucky Fried Chicken fast food chain. The end of his life was something he never thought about, and now it was apparent that death didn't discriminate between the rich and the poor. Unfortunately, money could not buy eternal life, but if it did, he would willingly give every cent he had to have it.

Angus shook his head and did his best to rattle the depressing thoughts out of his mind. Hours earlier, he'd made an appearance to see the grand opening of the first Wedgeworth Furniture Store in Puerto Rico. It was quite an accomplishment for him, and it was hard to contain his pride. The success he enjoyed never got old, and he rewarded himself frequently.

Now he stood before a massive street market filled with hundreds of less fortunate people struggling to make a living. They were selling everything from homemade jewelry to figurines carved from stone, and there were even women braiding hair for a small fee of ten dollars. Angus looked over his shoulder where his white stretch limo was parked nearby. His personal bodyguards, Travis Mills and Frank Turner, watched him closely as they always did. Travis was a tall, large-framed man, and he was balding. His appearance alone intimidated most. He was forty years old and remained one of the few people Angus considered a friend. Travis had been employed by him for twenty years, and there was no one better at what he did than he. Frank had worked for him roughly ten years and was handpicked by Travis. Angus had always allowed Travis to manage Frank so he knew very little about the younger man. Frank shaved his head and his thick, black eyebrows slanted in such a way that made him always seem angry. The unusual thing about Frank was that he never spoke. Angus never bothered to ask why, and he wasn't sure if Travis had ever heard him speak or not. Eventually, Angus just assumed the young man was mute. Both men normally wore jeans and tight T-shirts, but since they attended the grand opening also, today, they wore black suits. The black sunglasses both men wore completed the package and most people who didn't know better would swear they were in the secret service.

Over the years, Angus had gained a healthy amount of trust in Travis and Frank. He'd tested their loyalty on more than one occasion. Once, Angus discovered that his personal chef, a heavy middle-aged man named Jacob Fleming, had been stealing money from him. He'd never been so furious in all of his life, and upon the discovery, he demanded that Frank and Travis bring the thief to his office at once. Minutes later, they returned with the frightened chef. Angus ordered them to shut the door and lock it. He wasted no time confronting his thief and demanded a confession. Jacob, of course, denied the entire thing for fear of losing his job or worse, spending time in jail. Angus was certain

Angus eyed the young man for a long moment. The kid seemed to be telling the truth. He looked down at the homemade medallion resting in his palm and thought back to the early days of his furniture business. It was very similar circumstances because he made almost all of the furniture on his own. He longed to have those days back again. The memories weighed heavily upon him again, and before he knew it, his eyes were watering up. He struggled to fight back tears as he realized what was happening. *Of all times to break down! Of all times to let it all get to me! Not now, not in front of this kid!* He quickly turned his back to the young man and did his best to regain composure. He glanced over toward Travis and Frank. He wasn't surprised at all to see them walking towards him with concerned looks on their faces. He gently waved them off and turned back to face the boy.

"Okay, kid, you got me. You're a heck of a salesman. I'll give you seventy-five for the medallion. You tell your grandfather that one of your customers complimented you on your sales ability." The words he spoke were nothing more but an attempt to cover up the sudden wave of emotion that cut through him like a hot knife in butter. He fumbled around his jacket pocket in search of his wallet. When he found it, he retrieved some cash and handed it to the boy.

Armando carefully took the money and stared at Angus with wonder. "Thank you, sir, I hope you enjoy the medallion. I will tell my grandfather what you said."

"Thanks, kid," he said, and he turned away to escape the pitiful situation before it got worse. Before he even took a step to leave, what he feared would happen suddenly did.

"Sir, if you don't mind my asking, is something wrong?" the boy asked innocently.

Angus stopped walking immediately and spun around to face the genuinely concerned boy.

"I'm fine, young man, why do you ask?"

"You just seem...saddened."

Angus stared at Armando for another long moment and actually contemplated pouring his heart out to this stranger. He couldn't keep his thoughts and concerns bottled up forever. It would almost certainly do him good to let it all out, and who better to tell it to than this kid who really had no idea who he was? He stepped slowly back toward Armando and pulled the gray fedora from his head. He plopped the hat down on the table and fell back onto an old wooden chair next to the boy.

"Okay, kid, just remember you asked for this," he said with a nervous laugh.

Armando nodded and reassured him it was alright.

"I just turned seventy-four years old," he began.

"Happy birthday to you, sir," Armando said.

"Thanks, but listen to what I have to say before you interrupt. It's not really a joyous time for me. I'm undoubtedly nearing the end of my life, and it's absolutely eating at me."

"You have no idea how much longer you will live, sir," Armando interrupted again. "People are living longer and longer, and for all you know, you may live to be one hundred."

Angus shook his head. "No, not me, kid. I figure I'll probably make it to eighty or eighty-five at the most and that'll be it. If I'm lucky, I've got ten more years left in me." He paused and glanced over at Armando who was still shaking his head in disagreement. "Trust me, kid, I've just got a feeling. I've had a long good life, and I've had anything and everything you could ever ask for. I'm a selfish man, Armando; I have no problem admitting it. I've enjoyed my life, and I'm not ready to die any time soon. There is so much more I'd like to do." Tears began to well up in his eyes again and Armando patted him softly on the back.

Armando felt pity for the wealthy old man who was now sobbing in front of him. He was just about to speak again when two large men dressed in black suits ran up from seemingly out of nowhere.

"Mr. Wedgeworth, are you okay?" Travis asked.

Angus laughed a moment before he spoke. "Travis, I'm fine, me and my new friend Armando here were having a nice discussion about life and I got a little choked up."

Travis eyed the young man closely, but said nothing. Armando didn't like the way he stared at him. Frank stood nearby, but remained silent while Travis investigated.

"You and Frank head back to the limo, I'll be right behind you," Angus said as he stood up from the rickety chair. When Travis didn't move, Angus patted his shoulder and said, "Go on now, I promise I'll be right behind both of you. Let me say goodbye to my friend here." Travis finally nodded and motioned for Frank to follow him back to the car.

Armando watched the sharp dressed men walk away and suddenly felt relieved. The two men appeared intimidating, but he supposed they were the old man's bodyguards. *They're supposed to look that way,* he thought. He dismissed it and turned his attention back to the old man.

"Are you going to be alright, sir?"

Angus nodded. "Yes, I suppose I will. Death will eventually catch up with us all. Maybe one day, there will be a way for people to live forever; it's just a shame I will never get to see it. I would pay handsomely for that sort of thing. Oh well, thank you for listening to me babble about all of this, kid. It was very therapeutic for me to get it all off my chest." He stood and began following Travis and Frank back to the car.

Armando thought to himself about what the old man had just said. There was no doubt he was a very wealthy man and eternal life was obviously something he had become obsessed with. So obsessed, he would be willing to pay a large sum of money to acquire it. A few times during their conversation, Armando considered revealing a well-kept family secret to the old man. Over four hundred and fifty years ago, his great-great-great-great-great-great-grandfather discovered the legendary fountain of youth. He drank from the fountain and felt its power take over his body. It was he who made Ponce de León aware of its existence. He spent a large portion of his life in prison until he escaped somewhere around his one hundred and fiftieth birthday. Today, his grandfather had reached the age of five hundred and fourteen years old, but still looked as if he were no older than twenty-two. Armando often wondered if the fountain of youth still existed somewhere, but his grandfather insisted that searching for it would lead to certain death. His grandfather believed that the fountain of youth was a curse, not a blessing. He seemed almost miserable living day after day with no end in sight.

His grandfather was by no means immortal. He could get sick, and he could be killed any number of ways just as any ordinary man could. He just did not ever age. His body and all of his organs remained young. Armando, unfortunately, knew that suicide was becoming a concern for the family as their dear grandfather seemed more and more depressed as the years clicked by. He knew his grandfather would certainly disapprove of him telling this strange old man the secrets of his past; however, if the old man was willing to pay for information about the fountain of youth, maybe it would be worth it. Maybe his grandfather would be less inclined to be angry if it was to make the lives of their family much better than it presently was. If he was going to say something, he knew he had to make up his mind quickly. Angus was almost to the limo.

"Sir! Please, wait!" Armando shouted.

Angus stopped beside the car and looked back at the young man. He was surprised and puzzled all at the same time. Armando quickly ran to him. "Wait," he said, now trying to catch his breath. "I do know of a way to get what you want."

"What are you referring to, kid?"

"Eternal life."

Angus perked up. "Quickly, get in the car," he said, almost shoving Armando into the limo.

Once inside, Angus wiped sweat from his brow with a handkerchief and offered Armando a cold drink. The boy was momentarily awestruck as he realized he was sitting inside of a limousine, something he never dreamed he'd get the opportunity to do. He ran his fingertips across the soft leather seats and breathed in a pleasant vanilla aroma that washed throughout the car's interior.

"Alright, kid, what are you talking about?" Angus was genuinely interested in what Armando had to say, but he did his best to sound skeptical. The young Puerto Rican told what he knew about his grandfather and the fountain of youth. Angus suddenly didn't have to pretend to be skeptical. He found himself very skeptical of the story his new friend told. The fountain of youth was nothing more than folklore. At this point, it wouldn't have made much difference to him if Armando had told him that his grandfather also owned a ranch full of unicorns. He stared out the window as he mulled it all over, then he glanced back over to Armando. The young man was smiling and wide-eyed. He apparently did not pick up on the fact that Angus wasn't buying a single word of his story.

"Would you like to meet my grandfather?" he asked excitedly.

At this point, Angus couldn't help but laugh. "Are you serious? Do you actually think I believe that load of manure you just told? Kid, I take back what I said about you being a good salesman." Angus's friendly attitude suddenly expired as he leaned over and opened the car door. "Get out of my car," he commanded.

Armando boldly leaned over and pulled the door back shut. "Sir, I am not lying to you. I speak the truth. Come speak to my grandfather and you will see for yourself."

Angus stared at him, trying to sort it all out again in his head.

"Sir, please believe me!" Armando pleaded.

Angus deeply wanted to believe the young man. *What would it hurt to go meet his grandfather?*

"Okay, kid, tell me how to get to your grandfather," he said.

Armando's smile widened even more and he slapped his knees happily. He reached over to grab the seat belt when Angus grabbed his arm firmly. His eyes were not as bright as they once were.

"You better not be toying with me, boy. I have little patience for games," he said fiercely.

Armando felt his pulse quicken and suddenly wondered if this was a good idea after all.

"I am not playing games," he replied softly as he yanked his arm away. "You will see when you meet my grandfather."

Angus slowly leaned back in his seat, but his icy gaze held strong on the young man.

***

The limo arrived at the house much faster than Armando's bicycle would have gotten him there. The bike ride usually took between thirty and forty minutes, but in slightly less than fifteen, they had arrived. Angus peered through the tinted glass at the worn-out shack Armando called a home. Many of the shingles were ripped off or peeling away. *Probably hurricane damage from the past*, he figured. The wood siding was an awful light green color and the paint was flaking off all over. Many of the windows across the front were cracked, but amazingly none were broken out completely.

"You're telling me in five-hundred years, your grandfather *still* has not figured out how to get a decent home?" Angus asked grumpily.

"We've never had much money, that's one reason why I decided to reveal his secret to you," replied Armando. "You said you'd pay a lot of money for eternal life."

That single statement infuriated Angus as he suddenly realized what was happening. *This kid is playing me for my money*, he thought. As Armando reached for the door handle, Angus quickly slapped his arm down and clutched the boy's throat tightly. He leaned forward and pushed the young man back against his seat. Armando was surprised at just how strong the seventy-four-year-old man was. He struggled to breathe, and now more than ever he regretted bringing the old man to his home.

"You're trying to steal money from me, aren't you?" Angus growled. "There isn't any fountain of youth. You're lying, aren't you?"

Armando tried desperately to pull the boney hand from his throat. He shook his head and struggled to answer Angus's question. The grip loosened slightly.

"No!" he rasped. "I'm not lying to you! Please take your hands off me!"

Angus held on for a few more seconds then finally released the young man. "I may be old, but I'm very independent, kid. This is one old man that won't be taken advantage of. I pray for your sake you're not lying to me."

"I'm not! I swear it!"

Angus opened the car door and Armando bolted out. He considered running away but quickly realized that it would be useless when he found Travis and Frank already waiting for him outside. Angus stepped out of the car behind him and slammed the door.

"Let's go see Grandpa," he said gingerly.

As they reached the battered front door of the house, Armando stopped abruptly and turned to face his hostile guests.

"You must give me an opportunity to speak to my grandfather first. He's probably going to be angry with me for revealing his secret to you. I need to explain to him that you're willing to pay us for the information. My hope is that he will understand when he realizes this is a chance for his family to have a better life. Please give me the chance to talk to him," he pleaded, nearly tearful now.

Angus was becoming unsure of things the more they went along. At first, he thought Armando was trying to get in the house alone so he could lock the doors and call for help, but the look in the boy's eyes suggested something different. He was on the verge of tears much like any boy would be if he suddenly came to the realization he'd made a terrible mistake and told something he shouldn't have. He now seemed to be more fearful about how his grandfather was going to react than of what Angus and his bodyguards could potentially do to him for lying.

"We're going to follow you into the house, but I will allow you a moment to explain things to your grandfather. Just be snappy about it," he said.

The boy nodded, then immediately twisted the knob and barged into the house. Angus followed with his bodyguards close behind. Armando walked toward a hallway and quickly glanced back at the other three, signaling for them to wait where they were. Angus stopped, but listened carefully as he heard a conversation begin in Spanish. He couldn't understand a word that was being said and thoughts of trickery crept back into his mind.

"We have no idea what they're talking about; they could be planning something," Travis said, obviously thinking the same thoughts.

"Easy, Travis. We'll give him his moment with Grandpa like we promised. You know as well as I do that they're not going anywhere fast," Angus responded calmly.

He studied the interior of the house just as he had done when they drove up on the outside. The interior was dusty, most of the carpet ripped and frazzled. There was very little furniture in the room they were in, only a couch and two wooden chairs. Angus briefly considered taking a seat on the couch but changed his mind as he saw a small mouse take refuge underneath it. He couldn't imagine what living in these conditions would be like. The once-muffled conversation down the hallway became noticeably louder, and Angus could clearly make out the voice of another man. The other man sounded very young; there wasn't a hint of anything in the voice that indicated he was a grandfather. Angus was about to storm down the hallway when he caught himself. He shook his head when he remembered that Armando had told him his grandfather had the body of a twenty-two year old. The talking finally stopped and the only sound now was footsteps approaching down the hallway. Armando returned to the living room with another man who looked only slightly older than him. The man was much more muscular than Armando; his eyes were full of life and at the moment, full of anger.

"Grandfather, tell them about the fountain of youth," Armando urged.

His grandfather shook his head angrily, his bronze face turned red with rage. "You brought these strangers to our home. You tell them what they want to hear," he answered, poking a finger in his grandson's chest.

Armando paced across the floor a moment and tears began to stream down his face as the realization of his betrayal fully set in. He knew he'd gone too far, but there was no turning back now. The three men who now stood in his home could harm them if they wanted to; he had to tell them the story.

"This is my grandfather, Osvaldo," he began, weeping. "He was once the leader of a Taíno tribe back in the early 1500's. At that time, he went by the name Macuya. When Ponce de León and the Spaniards invaded this island, my grandfather fled to the sea. He landed on a mysterious island and discovered the fountain of youth. He drank the water and has remained young ever since." He paused to wipe the moisture from his eyes. "That's all I know, please leave us now; I changed my mind about the money. I don't want it!"

Osvaldo tried his best to remain distant, but finally embraced his remorseful grandson. Angus, Travis, and Frank looked on, unsure what to say next. Angus eventually broke the awkward silence.

"So why did you change your name?"

Osvaldo continued to hug his grandson tightly as he glared at Angus.

"I grew bored with it." His words were clearly sarcastic. "Now leave my home."

Angus crossed his arms and shook his head. "That's not a very nice way to treat your guests."

He made eye contact with Travis. "Grab the boy," he commanded.

As Travis approached, Osvaldo pushed his grandson behind him. "Don't come any closer," he said in a threatening tone. When Travis kept walking, Osvaldo prepared to rush at him when he suddenly heard Armando cry out to him from behind.

"Grandfather, stop!"

Osvaldo forgot about Travis as he whipped around to see what the matter was. He had been so worried about Travis, he never saw Frank slip behind him and grab Armando. Suddenly, he felt completely helpless and could only watch as Frank held a handgun tightly against his grandson's head. Osvaldo stared into Frank's eyes and did his best to read the quiet man's intentions. It was clear that the he had used guns to hurt people before, and he certainly wouldn't hesitate to use one on Armando to get what he wanted. He knew there was very little he could do now and he didn't struggle at all when Travis wrapped his arm around his neck and squeezed tightly. Osvaldo felt the room spin around him and before he knew it everything began to fade to black. The last thing he saw before he slipped out of consciousness was the look of horror on his grandson's face. He tried to speak, to tell him it was alright, but it was too late. He was out like a light.

CHAPTER 5

When Osvaldo awoke, he found his hands bound tightly behind his back and he was lying face down on a damp concrete floor. He attempted to get up and immediately realized his feet were bound together also. His mouth was gagged, but it didn't stop him from attempting to cry out for help. He yelled with all his might but the gag did its job, keeping the volume of his cries low enough to prevent anyone nearby from hearing them. The room was dark except for a few beams of light coming in through a glass window that had been painted over many years before. Some of the paint had chipped off, allowing a small ray of sunlight to pierce sharply into the darkness. Judging by the small size of the windows and the fact that they were installed almost at ceiling level led him to believe he was being held captive inside a basement. He felt no pain, probably because the old man and his two henchmen had been careful not to hurt him while he was unconscious. He figured it had everything to do with the fact that he still had information they wanted. They wanted to know where the fountain of youth was and, unfortunately, they didn't realize that he genuinely had no idea how to find the island. He wondered where Armando was and did his best to convince himself that his grandson was fine. Worrying about that now would do him more harm than good; he had to remain calm. He turned his attention back to the twine that bound his hands and feet. He had to find a way to get free! As he tried desperately to pull his wrists apart, he felt the twine cutting deeper into his skin. It seemed that the more he struggled, the tighter it got.

"Stop struggling, it's useless. You're just making it worse," a familiar voice called out from the veil of darkness.

The voice startled Osvaldo and he immediately recognized it to be the old man. He tried to curse his captor, but the only sound that came out was muffled and distorted. The old man grabbed a chair and dragged it across the concrete floor as he walked toward Osvaldo. The sound of metal grinding against concrete echoed loudly and it made his skin crawl. When Angus got within a few feet, he stopped and sat down in the chair. Osvaldo tried desperately to see the old man's face, but it was useless in the thick blackness of the room. Angus eventually leaned over and one of the beams of sunlight shone directly on his face. That was the only part of the old man he could see and it was an eerie sight seeing total darkness except for the old face shining brightly before him. Angus reached down and carelessly ripped the gag free from Osvaldo's mouth. He took a moment to open and close his mouth in an attempt to work out some of the soreness before he spoke.

"What have you done with my grandson?" he asked.

Angus stared at him a moment, then held up a small glass to his lips and took a drink. Osvaldo figured he'd brought the drink in with him; he had just been unable to see it. There apparently wasn't much left in the glass because as soon as Angus chugged it down, he threw it over his shoulder and it shattered all over the floor.

"You're grandson is just fine…for now," he replied menacingly.

Osvaldo felt a mixture of fear and fury all at the same time. He thrashed about once more, trying unsuccessfully to break free again.

"Where is he?" he asked softly, but firmly.

"He's nearby, but that's not really important right now. What *is* important is for you to tell me the truth. Is there or isn't there a real fountain of youth?" Angus asked.

Osvaldo didn't say anything at first. He couldn't decide what the best answer should be. He figured he could easily tell the old man that his grandson made the entire thing up. Angus would be extremely angry, no doubt, but he just might let them go. On the other hand, he'd already proven that he had no problem using violence to get his way. He may become so furious that he killed them both just to make himself feel better.

The other option, of course, would be to tell the truth. He could tell Angus that the fountain of youth truly did exist, but then he'd almost assuredly hold them longer while the desperate, obsessed old man launched a search for it. After he thought a few seconds, he decided to deny everything.

"My grandson did a very bad thing to you," he began. "He made a poor choice to lie to you in an effort to get money from you. I assure you that if you release us—" Angus abruptly kicked him hard in the face. Osvaldo felt his nose break and he yelped in agony. So much blood poured from his nose that he began to feel lightheaded. He wasn't sure if was from blood loss or the violent blow he took to the face. The blood ran into his mouth, and he couldn't speak at first because he was too busy spitting it all back out. Angus's voice began to thunder above him, and he did his best to stay conscious long enough to hear what he had to say.

"Do you think I'm a fool?" he yelled. "The first hole in your story is that you don't look a day over twenty-five years old. You just said yourself that Armando is your grandson. Explain to me how a man your age can be the grandfather of a seventeen-year-old boy?"

Osvaldo closed his eyes and the realization of his mistake set in. *I should've denied he was my grandson!*

Angus continued. "Furthermore, with the help of your dear grandson, I did a little research while you were napping. We got our hands on a few history books, and as it turns out, there once was a chief named Macuya listed in all of those books. Armando continued to plead with me to believe him. He really wants me to believe that you are Chief Macuya." He paused and chuckled. "You know, I think I'm actually starting to believe that kid."

Osvaldo continued to spit blood and he decided he wouldn't speak now even if he could. There was nothing more to say. He and Armando were in serious trouble and there was nothing to do now but cooperate. The old man before him was clearly deranged. There was no reasoning with someone in Angus's mental state. Eternal life meant so much to him that the possibility of finding it had totally consumed him and clouded his judgment. There would be no convincing him that it didn't exist now. The only thing left to do was conjure up every memory he could of that harrowing adventure he'd lived almost five hundred years ago. He had to try and remember every detail to feed the old man's obsession. Suddenly, a chill swept across him as something he'd tried to block out throughout his entire life slammed into his mind like a freight train. There was one part of the equation that he'd never even gotten the opportunity to explain to his insane captor. As hard as it was going to be to find the mysterious island, that was probably going to be the easy part. Actually getting to the fountain was going to be the hard part. He remembered the monstrous reptiles that called the island home. He learned later in life that the giant lizards were called dinosaurs. He decided at that moment that he would help Angus in any way he could to find the island, but he vowed he would not set foot on it when it was found. If the old man killed him, so be it. That would certainly be better than being eaten alive.

CHAPTER 6

Mississippi Museum of Natural Science in Jackson, MS. Two months later...

Jonathon Williams carefully held up the recently reconstructed *Basilosaurus* vertebrae and breathed a sigh of relief that the tedious job was finally complete. He gently placed it in a holding tray with the other vertebrae, and as he gazed down at them, the feelings he had could only be described as bittersweet. He'd received a phone call a couple of weeks earlier from Peter Reinhart, an amateur paleontologist that frequented the museum just for the occasional opportunity to speak with him. At first, the enthusiasm of the middle-aged dino hunter was a breath of fresh air for Jonathon. He appreciated the man's passion and his genuine interest in his branch of science. There were many times that Peter popped in with curious looking fossils, usually shark teeth, that he casually asked Jonathon to identify. Jonathon always obliged, even at times when he really didn't have the time to do so. One day, on a typical Thursday afternoon, Jonathon's office phone rang and he answered it only to hear a frantic voice on the other line. It was Peter, and he'd apparently discovered something pretty impressive. It had been a scorching, dry summer and many of the lakes and rivers across the state were drying up in vast numbers. It wasn't the first summer the state of Mississippi had experienced with that sort of heat and it certainly wouldn't be the last. When the water in the rivers had all but dried up, many times it uncovered astonishing treasures. At least, they were considered treasure to the paleontology community.

Roughly thirty-five million years ago, the state of Mississippi and many other states across the south were covered in ocean. The oceans were shallow, but they were full of aquatic life. The *Basilosaurus* was a prehistoric whale that thrived in the shallow seas. When all of those oceans dried up, countless *Basilosaurus* skeletons were left scattered across the southeast. In the nineteenth century, the fossils of the *Basilosaurus* were found so frequently that they were regularly used to make furniture. They were still plentiful in the twentieth century and had become so popular that four years earlier, the state of Mississippi decided to make it the state fossil. Alabama did the same a few years later. Occasionally, very complete specimens were found when the summer heat dried up the rivers. Peter spent a lot of time on the rivers during this time with hope that he would find some uncovered remains of *Basilosaurus*. Almost two weeks ago, he finally did. His excitement got the best of him as he wasted no time retrieving his tools and he began carelessly chipping away at the almost rock-hard clay encasement surrounding much of the skeleton. He'd already damaged many of the vertebrae when he finally made the decision to call Jonathon.

It aggravated Jonathon that Peter didn't contact him before the damage had been done, but he never let him know it. After all, amateur paleontologists were responsible for many of the greatest finds in history. They were valuable to the science and the last thing he wanted was to form a reputation as a scientist that despised them. Suddenly, the phone began to ring. He instantly thought of Peter. *I plainly told him I'd call him when I was finished*, he thought. He shook his head and snatched up the phone.

"Peter, I told you I'd—"

"Hello, Jonathon," the soft, feminine voice interrupted.

It was his girlfriend Lucy, and she sounded as if something was wrong. She usually didn't call him at work and her voice was a lot softer than usual.

"What's wrong?" he asked.

"We need to talk…soon. When can you meet me for lunch?"

He glanced over at the clock on the wall. It was only a few more minutes until twelve. "I can leave right now if you'd like. Where do you want to meet?"

"Meet me at that place you took me to a few weeks ago," she responded.

He didn't respond because he didn't have any idea what place she was referring to. He closed his eyes and struggled to remember.

Lucy sensed his memory lapse. "That place that makes the deli sandwiches. I think its downtown."

"Oh yes," he said, remembering. "I'll meet you there in half an hour."

She never said another word, just hung the phone up abruptly. That wasn't like her and he had a feeling he knew what was up.

***

When Jonathon arrived, Lucy was already there waiting for him at a table outside. It was a very pleasant day; the sun was hidden behind gray clouds and the temperature was considerably cooler than it had been a few days earlier. He strolled over and kissed her on the cheek. She didn't pull away, but there was a coldness about her that he didn't like.

"Have you ordered anything yet?" he asked.

"No. To be honest, I'm not hungry at all. I just need to talk to you in person," she replied, her lips trembling a bit as she spoke.

"Sweetheart, what's wrong?"

Suddenly, her eyes watered up and tears began to stream down her soft cheeks. "It's over, Jonathon. I don't want to do this anymore."

He wasn't surprised with what he was hearing. He knew all along that she was going to say something like that. He just sighed and nodded.

His response seemed to anger her.

"Do you not have anything to say to me?" She wasn't trying to hide her emotions at all, and actually she'd become a little loud. Jonathon slowly peeked around in both directions and felt his face redden when he noticed all the people around them were now watching them.

"Sweetie," he whispered. "I don't know what to say. I had a feeling this is what you wanted to meet about. I really don't want to lose you, but I don't know what the solution for all of this is either."

"I've been more than patient with you. I've poured every ounce of myself into this relationship. I've tried so hard to prove to you how much I love you," she sobbed. Now her makeup was streaking all over her face.

"I know that, and I love you too. But, I'm just not ready to make the kind of commitment you want me to make."

Lucy shook her head and tried desperately to prevent more tears from flowing. She finally placed both of her elbows on the table and held her head in her hands. Her long, curly brown hair cascaded down her arms and hid her face from view. "I just don't understand why," she said. "I just don't get it. If you love me and you only want to be with me, then why not marry me? We've been together for eight wonderful years."

Jonathon sat quietly a moment, not sure how to respond. He genuinely felt bad for Lucy, and he felt guilty for putting her through all of this. To be honest, he didn't understand why he felt that way either.

"I guess it's just a guy thing," he said, finally. "You know we're all afraid of that kind of commitment. Lucy, it's not fair for you to let something like this tear you up this badly. It's certainly not fair for me to try and keep you around when I obviously can't give you what you want right now. I want you to know that I'll always be around if you need me."

He waited for her to say something, but she remained silent.

"I don't want you to keep hurting, so I'm just going to leave. I love you, and I'm sorry," he said. He rose from the table, took a moment to give a disapproving glare at all the onlookers surrounding them, and then escaped as quickly as he could.

***

A sharp knock on the heavy wooden door woke Angus from the afternoon nap he was enjoying in his office. The large leather chair was as soft as a pillow, and it seemed to swallow him up when he sat in it. It was perfect for napping.

"Come in," he called out groggily.

Travis let himself in and was followed by a tall, slender man dressed in denim shorts and a polo shirt. He also wore hiking boots and sunglasses. They both sat down in the two large leather chairs across from Angus's wide wooden desk. Angus's chair squeaked loudly as he adjusted from the leaned back position he was in before they knocked on his door. He sat upright and rolled the chair up closely to his desk.

"You have good news," he said with hope in his voice.

Travis smiled and the other man nodded. "Yes, sir, we have great news. I think we found it," he replied.

"The Puerto Rican said it was a relatively small island with a shroud of mist surrounding it, right?" the other man asked.

"That's correct, Eric...tell me you found it," Angus answered.

Eric grinned widely and that was all the confirmation Angus needed. He stood up from his chair and rushed around to hug both men. "Thank you, thank you so much," he said happily.

"You're welcome, sir, but there is more that you need to know," Eric replied, cautiously.

Angus stopped himself.

"Oh yes, of course. Please tell me everything," he said as he made his way back to his chair behind the desk.

"First off," Eric began. "The island was extremely tricky to find. It seemed like I flew all over the Atlantic these past two months looking for your island, and I was just about to decide it didn't exist when I spotted something odd. At first, it appeared to be smoke, or steam coming from an underwater volcano. I thought back to what the Puerto Rican said about mist around the island; it turned out that he was right. The mist that covers it serves as a great camouflage against the ocean. From the air, it's very hard to see, and I would guess the same would hold true from a ship. It would be hard to spot on the horizon because then it would be camouflaged with the clouds. It's in the heart of the Bermuda Triangle, and before I go any further, let me tell you I ain't a very superstitious person."

Angus nodded. "No, of course not."

"However, there is some really strange stuff about that island you should know before you explore it."

"Like what sort of strange stuff?" Angus asked, curiously.

"Well, for starters, the day after I discovered it, I set out early to take another look at it. But the funny thing is, it wasn't there. I double-checked my coordinates and I'd almost decided that my eyes had played tricks on me the day before. That is until I headed back and spotted the island again. I jotted the coordinates down again, thinking I'd just made a mistake, but when I returned the next day, it was gone again," he replied.

Angus said nothing; he just sat quietly, wide-eyed.

Eric pulled out a map and unfolded it across Angus's desk. "The only way for this to make sense is for me to just show you," he said. "The three corners of the Bermuda Triangle touch Miami, San Juan, and Bermuda. I drew the triangle on this map to show you just how central this island is."

Angus nodded, and took note that part of the triangle touched San Juan, Puerto Rico.

Eric continued. "You'll also notice that I drew several red 'X's to form a circle within the triangle. Next to each 'X,' you will also see that I've written a date. Over a course of one week, this is the path that the island moved."

"Whoa, wait," Angus interrupted. "Did you say it *moved*?"

"Yes, I know it sounds crazy but this island moves every day."

"But that's not possible," Angus argued.

"I understand that, sir, I wouldn't believe it either if I hadn't witnessed it with my own eyes."

"That's amazing," Angus said softly.

"The good thing is that I've noticed it makes the same movement every week. It moves in this circular pattern exactly the way I've drawn it out. Fortunately, that will make it easy to find again. I don't have any explanation for why it does this, except we should all take note that it lies in the heart of the Bermuda Triangle. I've read a lot about the possibility of other dimensions. I wonder if maybe this island is on the edge of another dimension. We've all heard supernatural stories about the Bermuda Triangle."

"Another dimension? Fascinating. Well done, Eric," Angus said, clearly interested but unafraid of the strange phenomena. "I'm very impressed that you found it. The camouflage and the constant movement is probably why it's never been discovered before now."

"I agree," Eric replied. "Keep in mind, I had plenty of time to look. I constantly searched for this island for nearly two months. I had about decided you were wasting your money, but as long as you continued to pay me, I was going to keep looking."

"I appreciate your efforts." Angus turned his attention back to Travis. "How soon do you think we can put a crew together and explore the island?" he asked.

At this point, Travis became restless in his seat. "Sir, there is one more twist that you need to hear."

"Well, by all means, spill it," Angus said impatiently.

Travis glanced over at Eric. "Go on, tell him," he urged.

Eric nodded, and then let out a sigh. "Well, as you already know, the island is covered in a thick mist. It's not just the sides, the top is covered also. From the air, I couldn't see the ground at all. To be absolutely sure there was an island beneath it, I had to make a risky decision to fly within the mist. I say it was risky because for all I know, there could be mountains everywhere, and it would be easy to fly straight into one when I came through the other side."

"That does sound dangerous," Angus agreed.

"I circled a few times and finally found a spot I felt comfortable entering. I dropped down as slowly as I could until I popped through. At first, all I saw was jungle, but then I reached a huge clearing near the center of the island. That's where I saw them," he said thoughtfully.

"Saw *them*? What did you see?" Angus asked.

"Dinosaurs. There were dinosaurs everywhere. It was the most incredible thing I've ever seen."

"Dinosaurs? Are you absolutely certain of that?"

"Mr. Wedgeworth, I've never been more certain of anything in my life. It was definitely dinosaurs. My plane was very low, just above the treetops. When I came upon the open clearing in the center of the island, there was no mistaking what I saw. There were countless herds of them. All different kinds too."

Angus sat silently and fidgeted with his fingers as he thought to himself. "Osvaldo hasn't mentioned anything to me about dinosaurs," he said, finally.

"Well, sir, I suggest you ask him. I know what I saw," Eric replied flatly.

***

Osvaldo wondered what was going on when Frank showed up suddenly and yanked him up the stairs to another room he'd never seen before. He was forced to sit down in a wooden chair. Frank then used a plastic tie strap to fasten Osvaldo's wrists to the back of the chair. Osvaldo wondered if he really seemed that threatening to his captors for them to take such measures in keeping him restrained.

After a few minutes, the door swung open and Angus entered. He grabbed an office chair with wheels and rolled it over to where Osvaldo was sitting.

"Osvaldo, I appreciate you coming up here to meet me on such short notice," he said in a nauseatingly polite tone.

"If you really appreciate it, you will untie me."

Angus looked at Frank. "His hands are bound; it is really necessary to bind him to the chair also?"

Frank said nothing, although he was secretly annoyed that now he was going to have to cut off the tie strap he'd just put on. He pulled out a pocketknife and cut it loose. Osvaldo leaned forward and let his arms rest on his back. It felt much better than having the wooden back of the chair between them.

"Thank you, but releasing my hands would be nice too," he said.

Angus laughed. "Now you're pushing your luck, Grandpa. I have something I need to ask you."

"I have something I need to ask you too," Osvaldo shot back.

"Okay, you first," Angus replied with obvious interest.

"Where is Armando?"

"He's nearby, don't you worry."

"I want to see him," Osvaldo said.

The old man shook his head. "I'm afraid that's not possible. At least not yet. If you continue to cooperate with us you will eventually see him again. If you don't, well…"

"What do you want?" Osvaldo asked angrily.

"Tell me about the dinosaurs."

Osvaldo suddenly felt his heart race. He clenched his jaw just to keep it from dropping to the floor. *If he knows about the dinosaurs, then he's found the island*, he realized. He was aware of the fact that Angus had been searching for it for two months now, but he never dreamed he'd actually find it. It had been five hundred years since he discovered it and no one, to his knowledge, had ever found it since.

"You found the island," he said in a whisper.

"Yes, I found it. Are there dinosaurs on it?"

"Yes," he admitted reluctantly. "There are enormous dinosaurs on the island."

"Then why haven't you told me anything about them?" Angus asked, a hint of rage was in his voice.

"I never thought you would find it, honestly. I just figured after all of these years it didn't exist anymore."

Angus stood up and struck Osvaldo squarely across the jaw with the back of his hand. "Is there anything else you're withholding from me?"

It was a hard hit, but Osvaldo hardly noticed it. He was still in shock that the old man had actually found the island.

"No…there isn't anything else," he said.

"Good, you go back to your dungeon and get some rest. You and Armando will be accompanying us on a little expedition after we make our preparations to leave," he snarled as he began to walk out of the room.

"No! Armando cannot go with you! I will cooperate with you, just please leave Armando here!"

Osvaldo was pleading, and it was the first sign of weakness Angus had observed since they'd kidnapped him. He stopped and turned back toward him.

"I'm afraid Armando has to come along. You're the only one who knows where the fountain is. Let's just suppose we arrive at the island and you refuse to help. Think of Armando as sort of an insurance policy. It's actually very simple. You'll cooperate, or we'll hurt your grandson," he answered.

Osvaldo was on the verge of tears; his eyes were full of pure terror.

"No! I will cooperate, I swear it! I don't want my grandson anywhere near that island, it is extremely dangerous! Please!"

Angus left the room and walked down the hallway back to his office where Eric and Travis waited. He hardly noticed Osvaldo's loud, frantic screaming that echoed all around him.

CHAPTER 7

The bright light from the refrigerator illuminated Jonathon's now scruffy face and he retrieved a carton of orange juice. He filled a small glass he'd gotten out of the cabinet and proceeded to chug the cold citrus drink right where he stood. He couldn't get Lucy off of his mind. He figured most men would drink alcohol to drown their blues away, but he absolutely hated the bitter taste of it. Orange juice and Hawaiian Punch were going to have to do the job for him.

He wandered to the living room and flicked the switch on the wall to brighten things up a bit. The room wasn't very extravagant, but it wouldn't be hard for someone to figure out what he did for a living just by looking around. He had lots of specimens lying around. Actually, the majority of what he had was teeth and ancient clam shells. Unfortunately, that was pretty much all there was to be found in his part of the country since it had once been an ocean. Because of his lack of animals to study, he'd become quite the expert on the *Basilosaurus* and it was what most people in the profession knew him by. That wasn't to say that he didn't have any experience with other dinosaurs. He'd been on lots of digs in the Badlands of Montana and North Dakota, and as he thought about it, he decided he should plan another trip there in the near future.

On his way to the television, he pulled off his fedora and tossed it on an old wooden rack in the corner of the room. The hat rack was next to a large trophy case. The trophies inside gleamed brightly. Jonathon gazed at them a long moment and thought of his father. When he was a small boy, his father taught him the art of knife throwing. It was something his father had done for many years professionally. Jonathon had fond memories of his father performing knife throwing shows for his school and countless birthday parties over the years.

The most terrifying part for him was the most anticipated part for the audience. His father would introduce a beautiful woman to the crowd and he would then have her stand in front of a large piece of plywood. He then bound the woman's hands over her head so she would be unable to move. After allowing plenty of tension to build with the audience, his father would then stand twenty feet away and throw a total of six knives. Each blade stuck in the plywood with a loud *thud* on either side of the woman's torso. Of course, the crowd always gave a roaring applause, but Jonathon always breathed a sigh of relief. For him it was more than just a show. The woman bound to the wooden wall was his mother. Thankfully, his mother managed to escape years of the act without suffering from any major injury. The only incident that ever drew blood was a minor nick to her thigh. However, it was enough to get his father's attention because shortly thereafter, he gave up the knife-throwing show for good. Today, Jonathon's mother and father were both alive and well, enjoying the sunshine of south Florida.

Jonathon picked up on his father's talent and became very skilled with a knife in his own rite. He didn't have a knife show, but he did compete in knife-throwing competitions a lot as a teenager. He competed, and most of the time, he won. He had the trophies to prove it. Jonathon rarely carried a pocketknife with him when he was on a dig, but he almost always kept a large hunting knife on his belt. Most men feel safe if they're carrying a gun, but for Jonathon, the knife was all he needed. It was a useful tool on digs, and he could be deadly with it if he ever had to be.

He turned the television on and plopped down on a large leather couch that was way past its prime. He carelessly kicked his feet up on the coffee table, knocking magazines and books off in the process. Lucy wouldn't leave his mind and he cared little about anything else. Rex, his golden retriever, jumped up on the couch with him and rested his furry head on his lap. The dog seemed to sense that its master was feeling a little blue.

"I'll be alright, boy," he said as he scratched Rex behind the ears.

The local news was on, and though he didn't really feel like watching it, he didn't feel like getting up to change the channel either. As it was, he'd turned it on just in time to catch the news of the world, and he was pleased to see that the new Soviet leader, Mikhail Gorbachev, had made good on his promise to begin the withdrawal of troops in Afghanistan and Mongolia. Immediately following that story, they began a discussion about the upcoming Christmas season.

"It's July, for Pete's sake," Jonathon said aloud.

The young man reporting the story began to talk about the soon-to-be hot gifts of the season. Among them was something called a Nintendo game console that had apparently already become wildly popular in Japan. Finally, they got to some local news, and just as Jonathon was beginning to drift off to sleep, he heard something that jarred him awake. The anchorman announced that he'd given an exclusive interview to Angus Wedgeworth, the local millionaire who owned the famous Wedgeworth Furniture store chain. This demanded Jonathon's attention because he knew Angus personally and had for many years. The old man had a reputation of being crotchety and very hard to deal with. He was always looking for tax write-offs and he frequently donated large sums of money to the museum. Occasionally, he would pay the museum a visit, and it always irritated Jonathon how everyone seemed to roll out the red carpet for the man. He clearly had an ego problem, and Jonathon believed the visits were nothing more but a reminder to all of the employees that he personally paid a lot of their salaries.

Jonathon appreciated the donations just as much as the museum curator, but he still saw the man for what he was: a snobby, selfish Scrooge who cared about no one but himself and his money. Angus always made a point to stop in his laboratory and pretend to be interested in his work. Jonathon always did his best to smile and answer his questions as politely as he could when on the inside he wanted to smack the old man's cocky grin off his face. After a few minutes, he would abruptly leave and visit the entomologist, or the zoologist, or whoever was next down the hallway. Then he would leave and things would return to normal.

The interview began with Angus being congratulated on the first Wedgeworth Store to open outside of the United States in Puerto Rico of all places. The old man smiled and seemed to be genuinely proud of the accomplishment. Jonathon could certainly respect that; he knew Angus had humble beginnings. He just wished he could've remained humble himself. The interview trudged on to mention that he'd recently celebrated his seventy-fourth birthday and Jonathon couldn't help but notice this seemed to make the old man a bit uncomfortable. He thanked the newsman and tried to direct attention back to his stores. Then, shockingly, the newsman asked him if he'd given any thought to who would be the heir of the furniture store when the time finally came for him to give it all up.

Jonathon thought it was a tacky question, even for a sleazy man like Angus. However, the old man seemed unaffected by the question and answered very matter of factly that he had no intentions of leaving the store to anyone. The newsman laughed the reply off, clearly thinking it was a joke. When he pressed on, Angus reiterated very firmly that his company would always be run by him. Then he smiled widely and declared that he planned to live forever so there was no reason to make plans to leave his fortune to anyone. Still thinking it was a joke, the newsman laughed heartedly again.

Jonathon remembered feeling a slight chill up his spine when Angus made the bold statement. There was something about the way he said it that made him believe he meant it. *The man is completely off his rocker*, he thought. As he drifted off to sleep, he hoped he wouldn't have nightmares about the old man living forever and terrorizing him for the rest of his life.

CHAPTER 8

The next morning, Jonathon awoke with a splitting headache. The orange rays of light from the rising sun shone brightly into the living room and did nothing to help the excruciating pain in his skull. He sat on the edge of the couch a moment and closed his eyes tightly, hoping some of the pain would subside. It did slightly, and he walked slowly to the medicine cabinet in the bathroom to take a couple of Tylenol. He didn't have any nightmares about Angus, fortunately, but he did dream endlessly about Lucy. There was no question in his mind that he couldn't let her go easily and the first thing he needed to do was call her. He pulled on his trademark cargo pants and slipped on a red, loose-fitting IZOD shirt. He then grabbed his hat and reached down for the phone. It rang for what seemed like an eternity but Lucy never answered. She usually slept late during the summer, and it was probable that she had a rough night too. She, unlike him, drank alcohol and loved it. He pictured her hung-over from a night of endless drinking and probably suffering from a headache much like his own.

The stress of the whole ordeal was most likely the culprit for his own aching head as he was a classic example of a worrier. He worried about anything and everything. He worried about everything from dying early to losing his job unexpectedly and now it was possibly losing the woman he loved forever. Rex darted to him as he sensed his master was about to leave. Jonathon gave him a swift pat on the head and headed out to his jeep. The Tylenol hadn't quite kicked in yet and the sunlight was getting brighter. He quickly fumbled around the console for his sunglasses and felt instant relief when he put them on.

Twenty minutes later, he entered the museum and was quickly greeted by the curator, a sixty-something-year-old man named Martin Webb. He was dressed in his usual suit and tie.

"Morning, Marty," Jonathon said, surprised.

"Good morning, Jonathon. You're running a few minutes late, aren't you?" said Marty anxiously. He wasn't upset that Jonathon was late; something else seemed to trouble him.

"Yeah, I've got an awful headache. I'm a little slow this morning. What's wrong with you? You seem tense."

"Yes, I am somewhat tense I guess," he chuckled. "It's just that Angus Wedgeworth arrived as soon as we opened our doors this morning."

Oh great...just what I need today, Jonathon thought, trying desperately to hide his displeasure. For a split second, he wondered if he was still sleeping and having the nightmare he predicted would happen.

"Why is he here so early?" he asked.

There was a steady stream of employees arriving for work, and Marty gently grabbed Jonathon's arm and led him into the gift shop for more privacy. His beady eyes darted around nervously.

"I was curious about that also. I asked him to come chat with me in my office and he declined. He said he only wants to speak with you."

Jonathon was taken aback.

"With me? What does he want with me?"

Martin shrugged. "I have no idea, he wouldn't tell me. He said he wants to talk to you. When I noticed you weren't here yet, I offered to let him wait in my office. Once again, he declined. He said he'd rather wait in yours."

"That would be hard to do since I lock it up," Jonathon replied with a grin.

"Well, actually, I let him in."

"Marty! You know I don't like people snooping around in there when I'm not here," Jonathon grumbled.

"Yes, I know, I know," Marty replied, holding up his hands. "But you know how much money he pours into this place. He paid for a lot of that equipment you have. Who knows, he may be here to make a donation specifically for your work."

Jonathon's heart fluttered a little. He hadn't thought of that possibility. Then he remembered who they were talking about and his headache flared up again.

"I won't take any money from him. He can donate to the museum so it can be evenly distributed or I don't want any of it," he said firmly.

"Don't be stupid," Martin scowled. "If he offers money, you darn well better take it and put it to good use. You're always saying you want to spend more time doing fieldwork. Use it for that."

Jonathon wanted to argue about the issue further, but Martin all but pushed him out of the gift shop.

"Go on, he's waiting for you."

He reluctantly made his way to his office and was surprised to see the door closed.

"No telling what he's into," he muttered to himself as he twisted the knob. Angus was relaxing in his office chair with his feet propped up on the desk. He was reading a book on dinosaurs of the Cretaceous Period and didn't seem to notice him enter.

"May I help you?" Jonathon asked finally, trying to sound unfazed by the unexpected visit.

Angus slapped the book shut and quickly sat upright in the chair.

"This is a fascinating field of science, Mr. Williams," he said cheerfully.

"Yes…I think it is."

"My favorite dinosaur throughout my entire life has always been *Stegosaurus*. It is one of the most recognizable dinosaurs right up there with the *T-rex* and *Triceratops*."

"Yes, that's right, it is," Jonathon agreed.

"I was just reading your book here and it came as a surprise to me that *Stegosaurus* didn't even live in the same time period as *T-rex* and *Triceratops*."

"Yes, sir, it's a common misconception. The reality is that millions of years separated them from each other. *Stegosaurus* was alive during the late Jurassic Period."

"How fascinating," the old man replied, and he truly did seem interested.

Jonathon wondered where this newfound interest suddenly came from.

Angus gazed around the office at the charts and pictures of different species of dinosaurs. There was a long awkward silence and Jonathon wondered if he'd forgotten he was there again.

"What can I do for you today, Mr. Wedgeworth?"

"Oh please, don't call me Mr. Wedgeworth. My name is Angus. Call me Angus."

"Okay…Angus. How can I help you?"

The old man beamed at the question. "Actually, I think we can help each other quite a bit."

"And how is that?"

Angus turned and grabbed the office chair he'd been sitting in. He rolled it across the floor and moved it behind Jonathon.

"Trust me; you're going to want to sit down for this."

Jonathon wished the man would get to the point, but he played along and sat down.

"Mr. Williams, how long have dinosaurs been extinct?"

"That's not fair, if I have to call you Angus, you call me Jonathon," he quipped.

"Okay, Jonathon, please answer the question."

"They've been gone around 65 million years. Why?"

Angus laughed merrily. Jonathon looked on, very confused.

"I don't understand. What is so funny about that?"

Angus suddenly quit laughing and turned serious. He drew his face close to Jonathon's.

"What if I told you that dinosaurs are still alive today?"

Jonathon raised an eyebrow. *Its official, he's lost it.*

"I'd say that's not possible," he replied calmly.

"Jonathon, it's the truth. They are alive today and I have the proof."

He still didn't believe it and was beginning to feel very uncomfortable.

"Come on...you don't *really* believe dinosaurs are alive today, do you?"

Angus nodded.

"On this planet? You believe they are alive on this planet?"

Angus nodded again.

"Don't take my word for it, see for yourself," he said as he grabbed a file folder off the corner of the desk and handed it to Jonathon.

Inside the folder were four photographs. The pictures were apparently taken from an airplane, and at first, it seemed that they were of some animals grazing in a large field. He couldn't quite make out what the animals were at first, but suddenly the realization of what he was looking at grabbed him and he felt slightly dizzy.

"Is that what I think it is?" he asked softly.

"It is exactly what you think it is," Angus replied.

"This is a herd of *Gallimimus* dinosaurs...and are those... *Triceratops*?" he asked, his voice rising from excitement.

"Well I thought those looked like *Triceratops*, but I honestly had no idea what *those* were," he said pointing to the herd of *Gallimimus*. "That's why I've come to you, to identify them."

"Where did you find these?"

"A pilot that works for me found them on an island in the Atlantic Ocean. Naturally, they were just as shocked as you and I are. They immediately took some pictures."

Jonathon reached over to his desk and opened the top right drawer. He dug around in its contents until he pulled out a small magnifying glass. He studied the photographs carefully. They certainly appeared to be authentic.

"Who else knows about this?" he asked.

"No one, just you. I want to explore this island, and since you're pretty much the only paleontologist I know, I would like for you to come along."

Jonathon dropped the magnifying glass and stared at the old man for a long moment.

"Of course, I'll be willing to pay you," Angus said, confused about the silence.

Jonathon continued to stare, almost in a trance. He had become so enchanted with the photographs and the possibility of seeing real live dinosaurs that he almost forgot who he was talking to. Dinosaurs were extinct, and the more he thought about it, the more he had a hard time believing what he was hearing. Everything just seemed too good to be true. Angus Wedgeworth was one of the last people on earth he trusted and he wasn't about to begin acting differently now.

"Mr. Wedgeworth," he began.

"Angus...call me Angus."

"Oh, yeah...sorry. Angus, I can't do this," Jonathon said, handing the photographs back.

The expression on Angus's face was one of pure astonishment.

"What do you mean?" he asked.

"There are plenty of other paleontologists across the country that are far more qualified than me. If this is a real photograph and you plan on exploring this island you better take someone who knows what they're doing. This could be a very dangerous undertaking. I don't want that kind of responsibility."

Angus didn't like the way Jonathon seemingly questioned the photograph's authenticity.

"You don't believe the pictures are real?" he asked, trying to sound hurt.

"I didn't mean to imply that I don't believe you," he answered. "However, you must understand that this just seems too good to be true."

Angus nodded.

"I didn't believe it at first either, Jonathon. I finally had to take a plane and fly low over the island to see it with my own eyes before I accepted it. I'm not asking you to believe the pictures, but I am asking you to believe *me*."

Jonathon still believed it was all some sort of trick, but he didn't let Angus know it.

"I believe you," he lied. "But I'm still not the right guy for this job. Most of my experience has been with marine paleontology. You need to find a paleontologist at a large university to help you."

The old man was secretly becoming quite agitated with Jonathon's refusal to assist him. He was just about to begin one more attempt to persuade him when something caught his eye on the wall over Jonathon's shoulder. It was a photo of Jonathon and a young woman. Angus thought hard and vaguely remembered meeting the woman a few months ago on one of his visits to the museum. She was Jonathon's girlfriend, and if he remembered correctly, she was a paleontologist also. She was wearing a Mississippi State University sweatshirt. *A paleontologist at a large university...good idea*, he thought. He decided he'd wasted enough time with Jonathon. Suddenly, he held out his hand. Jonathon shook it.

"I'm really sorry I can't help," he said.

"I'm sorry you're being so foolish," Angus quipped. He turned abruptly and disappeared out of the office. Jonathon sat in his office chair and took a deep breath, glad that the ordeal was finally over. He couldn't help but wonder if he was being foolish, but it was only a small part of him that felt that way. Knowing what he knew about Angus, the chances were very good that he had made a wise decision. Martin suddenly appeared in the doorway.

"Well, what happened?" he asked, taking a seat on the edge of the desk.

"You'll never believe it," Jonathon said, chuckling.

"Try me."

"He wants me to take off with him to an island that he is convinced is inhabited by dinosaurs."

Martin smiled, and his eyes widened.

"Are you serious?"

"Yes, he brought pictures and I will admit they looked awfully real."

"Well, what did you say?"

"I said no of course!" Jonathon replied, surprised that he even asked.

Martin laughed.

"Well, why would he make up a story like that?"

"I don't know...I'm confused about that too," he answered, leaning back in the chair. "Although, you know he's getting pretty old. He may be losing his mind."

"I would laugh, but I know you're not joking. True, he is getting pretty old, but he still seems pretty sharp to me. You sure you shouldn't check it out?"

Jonathon shook his head without hesitation.

"No, I don't trust that guy. If I took off somewhere with him, you'd probably never hear from me again."

"Oh come now," Martin scowled. "Do you honestly think he's going to take you off somewhere and kill you?"

Jonathon didn't reply, he just stared at him.

"Jonathon! Don't be ridiculous. He may be arrogant and selfish, but I don't think he'd intentionally harm someone."

"All I know is I don't trust him, and I'm not flying away somewhere with someone I don't trust."

Martin grabbed his shoulder firmly. "I don't blame you for that. You did the right thing."

"Thanks. Listen, I think I'm going to take off around lunch. I've got to go take care of something this evening."

***

The first place Jonathon went when he left the museum was the nearest florist. He bought a dozen yellow roses (Lucy's favorite) and the most expensive bottle of wine he could find. Jonathon had given it a lot of thought and decided there was no way he was going to stand by and let Lucy bow out of his life. After a lot of careful consideration, he decided that there was no doubt she was the woman he wanted to spend the rest of his life with. After he bought the wine, the next stop was the jewelry store. He finally conceded that Lucy was completely right. There was no reason after eight years that they shouldn't take the next step and get married. The timing was right, and he was going to buy the most expensive engagement ring his salary would allow. He decided that even if he proposed and she said no, he wouldn't give up until he won her back.

Roughly an hour later, he stood at the base of her apartment building. The sun set below the trees behind him and the sky turned violet. It had just turned seven-thirty, and there were speckles of dim stars beginning to appear across the sky. He climbed the stairs to reach the third floor. The bottle of wine was under one arm, the yellow roses in the other. Up until the moment he stood before her door, he'd felt fine. He'd been calm, collected, and eager to see her. Now things had changed dramatically. His stomach rolled and he felt nauseous. There was no doubt about it; his nerves were getting to him. They were punishing him relentlessly; he'd never been so scared in all of his life. *No turning back now*, he thought and he tapped the door twice with the bottle of wine.

He could hear footsteps on the other side, and as they grew louder, his heart raced faster. The door swung open, and Lucy was more than surprised to see him. Her long, brown hair was in a ponytail and she wore a small T-shirt and athletic shorts. She spotted the roses and a slight smile lit up her face. She stood silent a moment, not sure what to say.

"May I come in?" Jonathon asked.

"What?...Oh! Of course," she said, stepping aside.

Jonathon walked in and set the wine on the kitchen table. She followed, and he offered her the roses.

"You got me roses?"

He nodded. "They're certainly not for me."

She laughed nervously and took them. "They're absolutely gorgeous." She snatched some flowers that were already sitting in a vase at the center of her table and replaced them with the roses. "Thank you, Jonathon."

"You deserve them after what I put you through yesterday," he said.

She waved him off. "No, don't say that. I shouldn't try to force you to do something that you don't want to do. That was selfish of me."

"No, Lucy, I—"

"Jonathon, let me finish," she interrupted. "I've given this a lot of thought. What I did to you yesterday was wrong. I shouldn't have called you to meet me and then ambush you the way that I did. I'm sorry about that, and I really hope you'll forgive me."

"But you didn't do anything wrong," he countered.

"Jonathon, please."

He really wanted to argue the issue further, but the look in Lucy's eyes suggested it would only ignite another fight between them. That was the last thing he wanted to do now. "Okay," he surrendered. "You are forgiven."

"Good. Then that's that. I think it's best if we just become friends now," she said flatly, walking toward her bedroom.

Jonathon stood still a moment, unsure if he heard her right. "Wait a minute…What did you say?"

She reached her dresser and pulled a drawer open, then she paused to face him. "I'd rather be your friend than nothing at all. If we keep going this direction, we're going to end up hating each other. It may not be tomorrow, it may not be five years from now, but one day, we'll hate each other. I just can't bear the thought of that, so I think it's best if we end the romantic relationship and just become friends," she said again as she grabbed a shirt out of the drawer.

Jonathon shook his head, trying desperately to process what she was saying. To make matters more confusing, she placed the shirt she'd just grabbed into a suitcase that was open on the bed. It was full of clothes, books, and some of her field gear was lying nearby waiting to be packed.

"What are you packing for? The next semester of college doesn't start for another couple of weeks."

"I'm not packing for work, silly. This is for something else. I should be back in time to teach."

He looked on as she continued to toss clothing and other items into the suitcase. It almost seemed that she'd forgotten he was even there. He thought about retrieving the ring, nestled away deep in his pocket, but decided to hold off as things seemed to be spiraling out of control.

"So where are you going then?"

"I can't talk about it," Lucy said firmly. She suddenly stopped, realizing how rude she sounded. "Sweetie, I'm sorry. I've just got a lot on my mind. I've got to catch a plane at seven in the morning. I don't have a lot of time."

Jonathon did his best to contain the mixture of confusion and aggravation that begin to well up inside him. "In the morning? You're leaving in the morning?"

"Yes, it was sort of spur of the moment."

"Are you going on a dig?" he asked, frantically trying to pry information out of her.

"You could say that," she answered.

A terrifying thought crept into his mind. *Surely Angus hasn't gotten hold of her.*

"Lucy, you haven't spoken to Angus Wedgeworth today have you?"

She immediately stopped dead in her tracks and looked him in the eyes. "How did you know that?" she asked, astonished.

"Lucy, you can't go with him. You don't know him like I do."

"Wait a minute, back up and answer my first question," she demanded. "How did you know I talked to him today?"

"Because he visited me this morning. I've got a pretty good idea that he gave you the same little presentation he gave me."

"You think so, huh?" Lucy crossed her arms and leaned against the wall. Her lips were pursed tightly together and her cheeks began to turn red. Each reaction was a clear suggestion that she was becoming agitated.

"I know so," he replied. "He showed you pictures and promised you a chance to come face to face with real live dinosaurs, didn't he?"

She stared at him a minute, now very visibly angry that he knew about Angus's visit. "Well, I'm going, and you're not changing my mind," she said, zipping the suitcase up. "There is no way that I can pass up an opportunity like he is offering. Frankly, I'm surprised that you did."

Jonathon felt his blood pressure rise, but did his best to stay composed. "You're smarter than this. You know full well that the odds of dinosaurs surviving millions of years on a deserted island are pretty much slim to none. Think before you take off with someone you hardly know."

"If I didn't know better, you almost sound jealous. He's a seventy-four year-old-man, Jonathon. I assure you he's a little too old for me," she said. She sounded almost playful, but he recognized it for what it was. Cruel sarcasm.

Jonathon could feel the tension building in the room. He had to try a different approach. "Lucy, I don't want you to go with him. I'll be worried sick if you do."

Her mood suddenly turned sympathetic and grateful. She strolled over to him and took both of his hands in hers. She looked him in the eyes. "Jonathon, I don't want you to worry about me. I promise you that everything will be fine, and if I begin to feel uneasy about this, you'll be the first one I call to rescue me."

Jonathon looked away and shook his head. "That's not good enough. I don't want you to go with him, period."

She sighed and jerked her hands away, placing them on her hips. "I'm a grown woman. You can't tell me what I can and can't do. Give up, Jonathon, I'm going."

He opened his mouth to plead with her further but thought better of it. There was no way he was going to change her mind. "Fine, do what you want," he growled.

He stormed out of the apartment without saying goodbye. As he stomped his way to the jeep, he began to feel a knot form in his stomach. There had to be some way he could talk her out of it. For a moment, he contemplated marching right back up to her apartment and trying again, but he knew it was useless. The only thing he could do now was drive home and sleep on it

When he finally did return home and settle into bed, although he was very tired, he was unable to fall asleep. All he was able to do was think about Lucy and all of the horrible things that could possibly happen to her. After about a full hour of tossing and turning, he finally leaned over his nightstand and turned on the lamp. He retrieved a backpack from the closet and threw a couple of pairs of pants and shirts in it. He glanced over at some of his field tools and decided there would be no need to bring them. There would be no need for any of it. What he did need, however, was something for protection. He didn't own any guns and never had any desire to. Now, for the first time in his life, he wished he did. What he did have was the large hunting knife he kept on his belt when he was out on digs. It was a very handy tool to have as he he'd used it for everything from opening a can of baked beans, to skinning and cleaning fish. He zipped up the backpack, and then placed the knife and holster on top of it. He set the alarm clock next to his bed so that he would wake up early enough to beat Lucy to the airport. If he couldn't talk her out of coming back with him, then he was going to go with her. He rolled back into bed and found it was much easier to fall asleep this time.

CHAPTER 9

Jonathon arrived at Jackson-Evers Municipal Airport around five o'clock the next morning. Exhaustion overwhelmed his body due to the fact he'd probably only slept a total of three hours the night before. He knew that her flight left around seven, but what he wasn't sure about was what time she would actually get there. He decided to sit in the jeep, banking on the chance that he would see her pull into the airport. If he saw no sign of her by six, he would go inside and begin searching for her. The sun wasn't up yet, and the darkness teamed with his exhaustion to make it very difficult to stay alert and awake. Every so often, a plane would fly low overhead, and it helped keep him awake for a while. But soon, even the roar of jet engines in the dawn sky did very little to keep him conscious. He leaned forward in his seat and rested on the steering wheel. His eyes never left the entrance to the airport. There was a good bit of traffic entering in and out, and if he wasn't careful, her small red sedan would sneak past him. His eyelids grew heavy and he shuffled in the seat to get his blood flowing. He drummed the steering wheel with his fingers for so long that they actually began to hurt. The pain didn't bother him; actually, it helped to keep him awake. A glance at his watch showed five forty-five and there was still no sign of her. He longed badly to be back in his warm bed, sleeping deeply.

***

A loud pounding on his door startled him. Jonathon opened his eyes widely and looked outside to see who was harassing him. It was Lucy. She was wearing a yellow button-up blouse and cargo pants similar to the ones he had on. Her hair was no longer in a ponytail and she, unlike him, looked well rested. She didn't look happy to see him.

"What are you doing here?" she hissed.

Jonathon held his arm up and looked at his watch. It was six-thirty. He'd fallen asleep. He opened the jeep door and rolled out. "Coming to stop you, of course," he mumbled.

She snorted and turned away from him abruptly in the direction of the terminal entrance. "Good luck," she snarled.

He quickly reached back in the jeep and grabbed his bag then jogged to catch up to her. "You're either staying here, or I'm going with you. One way or the other, I'm not going to let you recklessly endanger your life."

"Go home, Jonathon."

Lucy struggled to get her suitcase up the steep stairs that led to the doorway into the terminal. Jonathon slid his arm through the strap on his bag and let it dangle behind him as he reached for her suitcase. She batted his hand away.

"In case you didn't know it, it's now 1985. Women can take care of themselves now. I can manage just fine, thank you," she growled. Suddenly, the suitcase handle slipped from her grasp and tumbled end over end down the steps.

"I can see that," Jonathon muttered in response as he chased after the suitcase. "Let me help you."

"You just want an excuse to follow me," she said.

Jonathon didn't answer.

"Fine," she huffed. "But I'm still leaving, and you aren't going to change my mind."

She entered the airport with Jonathon in tow and they immediately spotted Angus Wedgeworth sipping coffee in the lobby. He was dressed in his usual suit. Jonathon watched the old man squint as he eyed him and his face lit up when he realized who he was. He rushed out to greet them.

"Good morning, Lucy," he said, grabbing her small hand and patting it gently between his own. "I must say it is a surprise to see you, Jonathon," he said cheerfully.

Jonathon cut to the chase.

"You're not taking Lucy."

Angus stared at him a moment, then laughed. "Take her? You make it sound as if I'm kidnapping her. She agreed to come on her own. I made an offer to her just like I made an offer to you. You said no, she said yes. End of story."

"No, not end of story," he replied, obvious anger in his voice. "Find someone else. I'm not comfortable with you taking her."

Angus looked over at Lucy. "My dear, he is speaking as if he owns you. It sounds like you are his property," he chuckled.

She shook her head. "He's just a little over protective is all," she answered, and then looked to Jonathon. "Sweetie, that's enough. I appreciate you helping me with my bag, but I have got to be going now." She leaned forward and kissed him on the cheek. "I'll let you know as soon as we return."

"If you return," he replied.

Her face reddened as she was clearly becoming agitated again. She opened her mouth to speak, but Angus cut in unexpectedly.

"Jonathon," he began. "I assure you that Lucy will be well taken care of. You don't have anything to worry about while she is with me."

Jonathon rolled his eyes, unconvinced.

"However," he continued. "If you would like to join us and keep an eye on her for your own peace of mind, I will be more than happy to provide you with another ticket. I just so happen to have an extra," he smiled as he pulled a slip of paper from his inside coat pocket.

For a split second, Jonathon considered telling him to shove the ticket somewhere very unpleasant. There was no doubt that Angus had an extra ticket because he knew there was a good chance Jonathon would show up at the airport. It was a well-planned trap, and it worked flawlessly. He eyed the old man staring back at him, knowing full well he was aware that he was mulling it all over in his head. Angus knew he'd hooked him.

"I would love to join you," he said finally, his words thick with sarcasm.

"Very well," Angus replied. "The plane is waiting."

***

Jonathon hated flying. A fear of heights had haunted him his entire life. Once the plane leveled off, he eased his grip on the seat's armrest only slightly and worked up the nerve to peek out of the window. The sight of the puffy clouds below the plane with the morning sun shining brightly overhead was beautiful and terrifying all at the same time.

"How long is this flight?" he asked Lucy nervously.

"We'll be in Atlanta in about thirty-five minutes," she replied calmly. She knew of Jonathon's fear of heights. She reached out and gently grabbed his now sweaty hand. Although she was angry with him for following her to the airport, she couldn't ignore the fact that his intentions were good. He genuinely cared about her, and the sheer fact that he was putting himself through the plane ride was evidence of it.

"Where do we go from Atlanta?" Jonathon asked, seemingly relieved that the flight wouldn't take long.

"Once we land, we'll board Mr. Wedgeworth's private jet and fly down to a small airstrip near Miami. At least that's the way I understood it," she replied.

"Oh great, we're going to land and then go right back into the sky again?"

She nodded. "Sorry. You didn't have to come," she reminded him playfully.

Once back on the ground, Jonathon was pleasantly surprised at how quickly they were ushered through Hartsfield-Jackson International Airport to a small hanger outside where Angus's private jet awaited them. The plane was sleek and beautiful. The white paint looked practically brand new, and the light blue stripes that zigzagged own the fuselage gave the plane a speedy look. The tail fin had a large blue "W" displayed proudly on both sides.

The door was open and a man in his forties hopped down the steps and greeted them.

"Afternoon, folks, my name is Eric Gill. I'll be your pilot today," he said proudly.

Jonathon sensed the guy was cocky. He figured most pilots were, but something about the guy's smirk and his perfectly combed dark hair bothered him. Angus stopped near the steps and motioned for them to climb aboard. Lucy smiled brightly and eagerly climbed into the luxurious plane. Jonathon spotted Eric eyeing her closely. Once she passed him and entered the plane, he leaned backward and watched her walk down the aisle. Jonathon rolled his eyes. Lucy was a very pretty woman; he was used to seeing other men gawk at her. There was a time when he was amused by it. Now, with their relationship hanging in the balance, it only sickened him.

"Gorgeous plane," he said as he got within arm's length of Eric.

"Yes, it is," he agreed. "This is a Gulfstream III, brand spanking new."

Eric held out a hand and Jonathon shook it reluctantly.

"Nice to meet you, I'm Jonathon," he said, trying to be polite.

"Nice to meet you too, Jonathon," Eric said, still shaking his hand. Suddenly, he leaned over close. "Listen," he whispered. "Who's the brunette?"

Jonathon clenched his jaw. "My girlfriend," he growled, pulling the brim of his hat down. Eric was taken aback, but did his best to disguise it. "Oh, I see," he said calmly. "Sorry."

Jonathon turned away and sat down next to Lucy. "He seems like a nice guy," she said when he sat.

Jonathon didn't respond.

"Something wrong?" she asked.

"No...everything's just swell," he replied gruffly.

Someone approached him from behind and put a firm grip on his shoulder. Jonathon looked back to see a large balding man, with dark eyes looming behind him.

"Travis Mills," the man said, holding out a bulky, callused hand. Jonathon looked at the hand and cautiously offered his. Travis squeezed it tightly as he shook it and stared Jonathon in the eyes.

"I'm Mr. Wedgeworth's bodyguard," he said. "I heard that you are a last minute guest on our little expedition."

"Yeah," Jonathon answered.

"We're not gonna have any trouble out of you, are we?"

Jonathon felt his blood pressure rise, and he was contemplating asking Travis what his problem was when Angus intervened.

"Travis," he said, almost in a fatherly tone. "Be kind to our guests. I invited Jonathon along. He's a good man and no one for you to be concerned about."

Travis kept his gaze steady on Jonathon.

"That's good to know," he said. "I'm sure we'll get along just fine." He winked at Lucy mischievously and plopped back down in his seat. Another younger man sat behind Travis and Jonathon assumed by his appearance that he was a bodyguard too.

"He was kind of a creep," Lucy whispered. "The other one is named Frank, he doesn't say much. They both seem angry all the time."

Jonathan turned toward her and smirked. "Yeah, good thing you're not all alone with these guys, isn't it?"

She smiled sheepishly, getting his point. As much as she didn't want to admit it, she was quickly becoming relieved Jonathon came along. Something about the way Travis winked at her bothered her.

Minutes later, the Gulfstream was airborne and they were above the puffy clouds again. The plane was considerably smalle,r and it seemed much harder for Jonathon to feel comfortable. Turbulence rocked and shifted the tiny plane around the sky, and when he peered out the window and saw the wings shaking, his stomach began to roll.

"I think I'm going to be sick," he moaned and he fanned himself with his hat.

Lucy noticed his observation and laughed. "We're going to be fine, airplane wings do that," she said reassuringly.

Jonathon closed his eyes and didn't open them again until he knew they were descending to the small airstrip near Miami.

CHAPTER 10

The Gulfstream touched down a few minutes after five o'clock. Eric brought the plane to a stop near a small hanger at the end of the runway. He opened the door and they all clambered out into the bright Florida sunshine. Jonathon placed his hat back on his head and pulled the brim down low to shield the bright sun. The building they were near was red, trimmed in white, and looked more like a barn than an airplane hangar. There were a few prop planes inside it and those were the only other aircraft he spotted on the property. There was another shed roughly fifty yards from them that housed an old fire truck and a tractor. Another building next to it was apparently used as the airport office. There was nothing but open pastures on either side of the runway. A gravel road ran parallel to the runway and disappeared behind some large oak trees. Once outside the Gulfstream, Jonathon walked out toward the runway and surveyed the land around him. He caught Angus creeping up beside him out of the corner of his eye.

"Let me guess, you own all of this," he said glancing at him.

Angus grabbed him by the neck; once again, he seemed fatherly. "Yes, I just bought it six months ago. It's not much now, but I've got plans for a few improvements."

He took a deep breath. "Fresh air. It seems that it's getting hard to come by now."

Jonathon shrugged. "Yeah, there's plenty of it out here," he replied, wondering what that had to do with anything. The old man stood beside him silently as if he wasn't sure what to say next. It soon occurred to Jonathon that Angus was simply trying to make conversation. A desperate attempt to make peace. He couldn't oblige him...at least not yet. He looked back at the plane where Eric, Lucy, and the two bodyguards were unloading the baggage and preparing to take it toward a van near the airport office. Poor Lucy was struggling to carry his bag and her bulky suitcase at the same time. She dropped his bag, and when she bent over to pick it up, he noticed Eric and Travis smiling lustfully and whispering as they stared at her behind. He shook his head. *I really don't like those guys.*

"Why don't you trust me?" Angus suddenly asked.

Jonathon stirred up some dust with his boot. "Don't take it personally; I don't trust a lot of people."

"I don't buy that. You don't trust me and I'm fine with that, but I would just like to know why."

"Well, Angus, I've heard a lot of stuff about you. Bad stuff. And before you ask, yes I believe most of it," Jonathon replied, still staring out across the pasture.

Angus nodded silently. "Well, regardless of what you've heard, I swear to you that there *are* dinosaurs alive and well on an island that has remained virtually untouched for millions of years. I want you and Lucy to be a part of that. You will soon see that I'm not lying to you."

"I'll believe it when I see it," he replied. The truth was, Jonathon really was beginning to believe it. He'd overheard Travis and the other bodyguard speaking about dinosaurs on the plane and Angus seemed to be telling the truth. He couldn't put a finger on it, but something still seemed wrong. It was just a vibe that he felt. He didn't trust Angus, and he didn't know if he ever could.

"I will earn your trust," Angus said, seemingly hearing his thoughts. "When we arrive on the island, you'll be so impressed you'll probably even apologize for some of the rude things you've said to me."

Jonathon wasn't sure if the old man was joking or serious, but he laughed anyway. "Just know that I'm watching you and those three apes you've got working for you. Don't try anything funny with me and Lucy or I swear I'll kill all four of you."

His words were cold, and they seemed to get the point across because Angus was clearly taken off guard. He opened his mouth but no words came out. Jonathon casually walked away and left Angus standing alone, shocked.

He made his way over to the van, but Lucy and the others weren't there. All of the bags were already loaded, and he figured the only place they could've gone was the office. It was a one-story steel building painted blue with only a few windows. A large metal sign next to the door confirmed his assumption that it was indeed the airport office. He went inside and was surprised at how cool it was when he entered. He heard voices and laughter down a hallway and he followed it to find Lucy, the bodyguards, Eric and a couple of other people he hadn't met yet. One was an older man sitting at a table, probably in his late fifties or early sixties. For his age, he was very athletic looking and seemed very strong. His hair was blonde and he had a full beard. He was dressed like a man prepared to go on a safari. He had on a tan button-up short sleeve shirt, and tan shorts. A large tan bush hat adorned his large head. The man looked very familiar, but he couldn't place where he'd seen him before.

The other individual sitting on the edge of the table really got Jonathon's attention. It was a young woman, probably early twenties, and she was stunningly beautiful. Her hair was a deep red; it was long and full of body. She wore a tight-fitting teal tank top and gray shorts, cuffed at the bottom. He had a feeling she had to wear a lot of sunscreen to protect her cream-colored skin, and the candy-apple red lipstick she wore accentuated her pouty lips. She looked him straight in the eyes when he appeared at the doorway and gave a slight smile. For a second, he forgot all about Lucy…until she spoke.

"Jonathon, there you are!" She walked over to him and took him by the arm. "I want you to meet someone," she said, leading him toward the safari man. "This is Silas Treadwell." She said his name in such a way that she expected Jonathon to recognize it. He didn't and his expression gave him away.

The safari man shifted in his chair and laughed. "Dear, I'm afraid he doesn't know who I am," he said.

"Jonathon," she said, surprised. "You don't know who he is?"

He crossed his arms and stared at the man a moment. "I'm sorry, although you do look vaguely familiar, I can't place where I've seen you," he said.

The room erupted in laughter, and suddenly Jonathon felt like he was in the middle of some sort of joke. Lucy continued to stare at him, surprised.

"Jonathon, Silas has a national television show. You've never seen it?"

"I don't watch a lot of television," he confessed.

"You've never heard of the television show *Wild World*?" she asked, seeming to hope that he would remember.

"Actually, I think I do remember hearing of that show," he lied. "I'm sorry, I just don't watch it. As I said, I don't watch a lot of television of any kind."

Silas stood up from the table and shook his hand. "That's quite alright. It's actually refreshing to meet people every now and then that haven't heard of me," he said. "I visit different regions of the world and hunt all sorts of animals, especially dangerous ones."

"And now you want to hunt some dinosaurs," Jonathon blurted out.

Silas chuckled. "Not exactly, at least not yet. I've known Angus a long time. I wouldn't call us close friends, but we're acquaintances. He called me and asked me to join him. My experience with wild animals may come in handy. I'll get some of the credit for the discovery and the eventual plan is to bring *Wild World* to the island to give the public the first glimpse of it. Can you imagine how the world will react?"

"Yeah, I'm sure they'll eat it up," he answered grumpily as he walked over to a refrigerator in the corner of the room. He was thirsty. Inside the fridge, he found a variety of sodas to choose from. He reached in and grabbed an orange-colored can.

"Jonathon doesn't believe that we're going to find any dinosaurs," Lucy explained. "He's seen the pictures and everything, but he still doesn't believe."

Silas smiled widely. "Really? You don't believe."

Jonathon opened the soda can and took a swig. He nodded his head as confirmation.

Silas walked over to him.

"That's great, because the truth is, I don't either."

Jonathon grinned and suddenly felt a great deal of relief to know he wasn't the only one who was skeptical.

"You two will get along nicely then," Angus announced as he entered the room.

"I've seen them with my own eyes," Eric said. "Travis and Frank have seen them too. They are real and you two will see soon enough."

The redhead approached Jonathon and held out her hand to introduce herself. Jonathon took it and wanted to hold on to it for a while, but forced himself to let go.

"Hi, I'm Annie," she said cheerfully.

"Hello, Annie. What about you? Do you think there are some real dinosaurs hiding out in the Atlantic?"

She nodded and smiled, revealing a mouth of perfect, pearly white teeth. "I kind of have to."

He raised an eyebrow. "What you do mean you *have* to?"

"Because Uncle Angus says he's seen them. I believe him," she answered, her green eyes sparkling.

Jonathon glanced at Angus who approached and put an arm around his niece.

"Uncle Angus, huh?" he said.

"I'm afraid so," Angus answered. "Annie is a freelance photographer, and I've hired her to photograph our expedition. She will, no doubt, have a Pulitzer Prize winning photo to take home soon."

Travis walked over to Lucy. For the first time, Jonathon noticed his incredibly large arms. His biceps seemed to be on the verge of ripping the sleeves apart on his shirt. He placed one of the massive appendages around Lucy. "What about you, sweetheart? We know where everyone else stands. Do you believe there are dinosaurs or not?" He held her against his body tightly and Jonathon resisted the urge to say something...for now.

"She's with us, Travis," Angus said. "She's just as excited as the rest of us."

"I have no reason to doubt Mr. Wedgeworth," Lucy said, pulling away from Travis. "Although, I understand Jonathon and Silas's reluctance to believe," she added.

The smirk on Travis's face disappeared when she pulled away from him and walked over to Jonathon. He focused his steely eyes on Jonathon, but he did his best to hide his anger and said nothing.

"Well, there's one thing I know for certain," Silas said, apparently growing tired of the discussion. "You're never going to change my mind if we just sit here debating everything. What are we waiting for? Let's get going."

CHAPTER 11

As it turned out, the small airport they arrived at was much closer to Fort Lauderdale than Miami. Travis drove the van along a strip of highway that ran parallel to the beach. Angus sat in the passenger seat next to him. The bench seat behind them is where Lucy and Annie sat. They had been chatting ever since they left the air strip, and Jonathon wondered if Lucy would be so friendly with Annie if she knew how much he'd been distracted by her good looks. The seat behind them is where Silas and Jonathon sat. He had hit it off with the older man pretty quick and he considered himself lucky to have found an ally. Silas wanted to know everything he could learn about dinosaurs in the short amount of time he had before they arrived at the island. He quizzed Jonathon relentlessly about all the different types of dinosaurs and their behavior. Not surprisingly, the game hunter wanted to know everything he could about *Tyrannosaurus rex*. That particular dinosaur clearly interested him most as it did almost everyone. After all, tyrannosaur was the most famous and fearsome of all the carnivores that had been discovered. The last seat in the van is where Frank sat. He remained silent as he always did, but he seemed to be listening to everything that was being talked about in the van. Frank looked just as menacing as Travis, but Jonathon didn't seem to feel nearly as threatened by him. Nevertheless, he was nowhere near trusting him either. Eric Gill remained at the airstrip where he would await their return. The fact that he wasn't coming along was a much-needed relief for Jonathon. Eric had shown a lot of interest in Lucy, and Jonathon was going to have a hard enough time keeping an eye on Travis.

Jonathon gazed out across the vast Atlantic Ocean and thought again of the real possibility that there were dinosaurs living and breathing somewhere out there. He'd tried desperately to hang on to the belief that this was all some sort of trick, but it was becoming very apparent that they were indeed going to be boarding a ship soon. As much as he wanted to continue to believe that Angus was up to no good, he couldn't find any evidence to support it. They'd been treated very well and everything seemed to be happening exactly the way they were told it would. Travis had been the only part of the entire trip that was unpleasant, but even he was tolerable. He found himself feeling anxious and even a little excited about what was ahead. However, if they did arrive at an island inhabited by dinosaurs, extreme caution would have to be exercised. He wondered if stubborn Angus would truly listen to his advice as he said he would. It bothered him even more when he thought of the monumental task of getting Travis to heed his warnings. *You're getting ahead of yourself*, he thought. *Wait until you see a dinosaur first.*

The entire drive from the airstrip took about forty-five minutes, and it suddenly occurred to Jonathon that he hadn't eaten anything.

"Angus, I'm starving. Is there going to be any food on this ship?"

Angus turned in his seat and nodded. "Yes, forgive me, I suppose I should supply some sort of itinerary for all of you. First off, you may eat whenever you like once we're aboard. There is plenty of food in the lounge, so help yourself." He looked down at his watch. "It's almost six o'clock now and the trip will take roughly seven hours. We'll probably shove off around seven. We should arrive near the island around two a.m. We'll drop anchor and allow everyone to finish up with a good night of sleep. Just hang on a few more minutes, Jonathon, we're almost there."

Just as he'd promised, a few minutes later, the van came to a halt at a small marina. It didn't take long for Jonathon to figure out which ship they would be taking before Angus had a chance to tell him. There was a medium-sized fishing boat near the end of the longest pier. Every other boat was considerably smaller and would not be practical for the trip they were taking. There were a couple of sailboats, one of them being boarded by a young family, and a yacht. As Angus led them to the fishing boat, Jonathon noticed the name of the yacht. *Wedgeworth I* was the name of the ship and he wondered if there was possibly a Wedgeworth II somewhere. As they arrived at the fishing boat, a forty-something-year-old man met them on the pier. He wore an Atlanta Braves baseball cap with tufts of curly salt-and-pepper hair popping out around the edges. His narrow eyes had crow's feet etched at the corners, obvious evidence of the countless years the man had spent squinting over the mirrored surface of the Atlantic Ocean. He wore a plain white T-shirt and blue jeans. His shoes looked almost as old as the man who wore them and looked similar to some sort of military combat boot.

"Welcome," he said. "I'm Charlie Blackstone, your captain. This is my ship, *Bethany*. Come on aboard and make yourself comfortable. The first mate and I will retrieve your bags."

Behind him, the ship was painted almost solid black, except for a red strip around the hull. The name *Bethany* was scribed in black on the red stripe. Jonathon figured the ship was about seventy-five feet long and figured it was being used as a charter fishing ship. Angus was probably paying a pretty penny for their excursion. Captain Blackstone waved a hand toward a ramp that led in a slight incline onto the ship's deck. A tall, lanky man jogged down the ramp and stood alongside the captain.

"This is the first mate, Denny," Captain Blackstone said quickly, and then both men made their way to the rear of the van where Travis was opening the door.

Jonathon led the group onto the deck. The ship's bridge blocked out the sun and cast a large shadow across the deck. Just below the bridge, Jonathon noticed a doorway that led below. *Bethany* had more room below her deck than she appeared to have from the view outside. The largest room (the lounge) consisted of a small fridge, a table and four chairs, a sofa, television, and radio. A small hallway branched off from the back of the room and three cabins flanked each side. The cabins were very cramped, about eight feet by eight feet, and each contained a bunk bed. The end of the hallway led to two more doors, Jonathon was unsure what was beyond them. He hoped and assumed at least one of them concealed a bathroom. He went into one of the cabins and thought about how the sleeping arrangements would be. Annie apparently was thinking about it too and she swiftly declared her and Lucy were sharing a room.

He glanced over at Silas and grinned. "Do you snore?"

"No, do you?"

Jonathon shook his head.

"I guess that means we're bunking together," Silas said, opening the cabin directly across from Lucy and Annie's.

"That's cool, as long as I get the top bed," Jonathon said.

Travis snuck up on them and tossed their bags onto the floor of the cabin they'd just claimed.

"You ladies have fun," he said jokingly, and for a second, Jonathon was beginning to think the big lug wasn't so bad. Then the next thing that came out of his mouth ruined all that.

"Lucy, you sure you don't want to bunk with me, sweetheart?" he asked.

She rolled her eyes. "In your dreams."

He stared at her and smiled. "I'll make you feel things you've never felt before."

She put her hands on her hips and Jonathon knew the look in her eye. He saw the storm brewing and knew if Travis knew what was good for him, he'd abort the romance mission now.

"Let me tell you something," she began.

Too late, pal, you just screwed up big time, Jonathon thought.

"I don't appreciate nasty little comments like that. I haven't heard comments like that since high school. I'm not interested in pigs like you and I never will be. The best thing for you to do while we're on this boat is avoid me. Don't talk to me and don't look at me. Do you understand me?"

She took a deep breath and released it gently, apparently trying to regain her composure. Travis stood still for a long moment, dumbfounded. Annie held her hand over her mouth in a desperate attempt to contain laughter, and Silas quickly made his way back on deck to avoid the awkward situation. Travis glanced over at Jonathon who was unable to hide his amusement. Finally, he turned away from them all and retreated back to the deck. Once he was completely gone, Annie released her laughter and she was so loud Jonathon was sure Travis could hear her.

"That was great," she said, giggling.

Jonathon walked over and put a hand on Lucy's shoulder. "Are you alright?"

"I'm fine," she said. "Actually, I feel much better."

He looked back toward the deck. "You didn't have to be quite so...so...mean. Did you?"

Lucy was appalled. "What? Are you kidding me? I can't believe you're taking that creep's side."

Jonathon held up his hands. "No, that's not what I'm saying at all. I just mean that guy isn't used to being embarrassed like that. He might try to retaliate."

"So let him. I can't believe you think I should just take that crap from him. I can't believe that you didn't get involved. The way he's been acting toward me is completely inappropriate," she fumed.

"That's exactly what he wanted me to do. He's just looking for a good excuse to bust me in the chops. He's just using you to get to me, that's all."

Fortunately, Annie agreed.

"I think he's right, Lucy. Travis clearly doesn't like him."

She shook her head, unconvinced. "I'm not so sure. The way he looks at me makes my skin crawl." The thought made her shiver as if a chill ran through her.

Jonathon put an arm around her in an attempt to comfort her. "I'll speak with Angus about it. Don't worry about him. I promise I won't let him harm you."

He meant what he said, but he was afraid Lucy didn't believe him. He desperately hoped that he would never have to prove it to her.

***

Immediately after the confrontation with Lucy and Travis, Jonathon's appetite disappeared. It wasn't until about an hour after their departure that the hunger returned. Fortunately, Angus had the lounge fully stocked and food was something that they wouldn't lack on the trip. The ship rocked back and forth, and Jonathon had to grab the back of a chair with one hand to steady himself while he searched the fridge. He decided on a ham and cheese sandwich and grabbed a small bag of potato chips off the counter. As he sat at the table, Travis walked through the room alone. When he saw him, Jonathon immediately stopped chewing his mouthful of sandwich expecting another confrontation. He didn't get one. Travis never even looked his way as he disappeared into the hallway and closed the cabin door. Silas appeared shortly after and plopped down on the opposite side of the table.

"You save anything for me?" he asked, eyeing the sandwich.

Jonathon nodded. "There's plenty to eat. Nothing extravagant, but plenty to snack on and keep us going."

Silas rummaged through the cabinets and the fridge then finally settled on a sandwich also.

"Travis say anything to you?" Jonathon asked.

Silas had just taken a bite out of his sandwich. "No," he mumbled through the mouth full of food.

Jonathon smiled and allowed him to finish chewing.

"Not a word," he said finally. "He's just sort of walked around on the deck. I did see him walk over and speak to Frank briefly, but I couldn't hear what was said. Lucy and Annie were up there too, drinking beer and talking, but Travis never even looked their way. He never even approached them. Why? Did he say something to you?"

"No. He just walked by right before you got here. He didn't say a word, didn't even look my way."

Silas wiped his mouth with a napkin and chuckled. "Lucy really put him in his place. He's making it worse by acting like a baby about it."

Jonathon leaned back in his chair to relax. He took his hat off and twirled it around on his finger as he thought. "I wish she hadn't said anything," he said.

"Why is that?"

"That guy's hurt people before. I can see it in his eyes." Jonathon tossed the hat up and let it land on the table in front of him. "And when I say hurt, I mean physical hurt. I believe he's had a lot of experience doing it too."

"Well, you know he *is* a bodyguard," Silas said, tilting his head slightly. "I'm sure he has knocked a few people around in his time."

"Yeah, but I think he's gone beyond that. I've just got a bad feeling about him."

"Nah...you're just saying that because you boys got off on the wrong foot."

Jonathon shook his head in disagreement. "I just hope he stays away from Lucy and doesn't try to retaliate."

"Okay, okay, we'll agree to disagree," Silas said. "There is something I gotta ask you. It's bugging me."

Jonathon leaned forward and put his arms on the table. "Sure, what's on your mind?"

"What's the story with that knife you carry around on your belt?"

Jonathon glanced down at his hip and pulled the large knife from its sheath. He laid it on the table between them. The ivory handle looked brighter than usual under the overhead lights.

"Let's just say that I'm pretty good with a knife. I can do things with a knife a lot of people can't."

Silas cocked his head to the side. "Like what?"

Jonathon picked the knife back up and held it tightly in the palm of his hand. Suddenly, he tossed it straight up into the air. It twirled end over end at a high rate of speed. He reached out and grabbed it before it fell onto the table. "I used to compete in a lot of competitions when I was a kid."

"What sort of competitions?"

"Knife-throwing competitions. I won just about every one I ever entered."

Silas crossed his arms and leaned back in his chair. "So you can throw a knife pretty much wherever you want to," he said, genuinely interested.

Jonathon nodded. "It just came natural to me. My old man used to have a show…a knife-throwing show. He used to do shows for schools, birthday parties, and the town we lived in would hire him to do a show at the annual fall festival each year. He was quite the celebrity where we lived."

"I imagine so," Silas said. "So you're basically saying that you carry that knife around for protection. It's a weapon you're very skilled with."

Jonathon gave a slight chuckle, and then shoved the knife back into its holster. "Yeah, I suppose so," he agreed. "I guess you could call it my good luck charm," he added thoughtfully.

"Really?" Silas said, picking up his sandwich again. "So does it work?"

"Does what work?"

"The knife…as a good luck charm?" Silas bit into the sandwich.

"Well, yeah, I suppose so. It gets me out of a jam every now and then."

Silas chewed his food, but waved his hand in an effort to urge Jonathon to continue.

"Okay, I got snake bit once on a dig in the Badlands of Montana. It was the biggest rattler you've ever seen. I never saw it until it latched onto my boot."

"So it got your boot, not you?"

Jonathon nodded. "As soon as I felt the pressure on my boot, I reached for the knife. I took a quick swipe at it and hoped for the best. Fortunately, it all worked out. The snake lost its head, and its fangs never touched me."

"Well, true enough, that is luck. However, I'm a firm believer that some people make their own luck. I believe that it's an ability not everyone has. To me, it's just as amazing as having the power to fly. A man that can make his own luck can find ways to cheat death. I sense that you've got that ability, Jonathon."

He stared at Silas, waiting for some sort of punch line. One never came.

"You're serious about all that?"

"Dead serious," Silas replied, and his stone-faced expression backed up his words.

"I hope you're right." *I got a feeling I may need an ability like that soon,* he thought.

"I know I'm right," he replied and he slapped the table as he got up. "It's my bed time. By the time you get in the cabin, I'll probably be asleep. Do me a favor and don't make too much noise when you come in, alright?"

"I won't be too far behind you, but I promise to tiptoe in," Jonathon said.

Silas retreated down the hallway and Jonathon heard the cabin door open and click shut.

Now alone, he decided to take a trip up on deck and check on Lucy. The boat continued to sway back and forth, but by now he was becoming used to it. Fortunately, he had never experienced sea-sickness. Being on the water in a boat of any size was not something he was accustomed to. In fact, when he thought back, he could only think of a few times throughout his entire life that he'd been in a boat. But for whatever reason, sea-sickness was never an issue for him.

Once on the deck, the first thing that caught his attention was the eerie darkness in all directions. If the flood light over the deck wasn't on, he was pretty sure he wouldn't even be able to see his own hand in front of his face. He looked up at the sky above and was stunned at how incredibly gorgeous the night sky truly was. Being on the ocean with virtually nothing obstructing your view in any direction made the vastness of the sky and stars slightly overwhelming. He could hear water slapping the bow as *Bethany* cut through the Atlantic with ease.

"Goodnight, Jonathon," Lucy said abruptly from somewhere behind him.

He turned and saw her headed down below. "You turning in early too?"

Lucy stopped, and turned back to look at him. "I think I drank a little too much, I feel a little tipsy. I knew better than to do that. We've got a big day tomorrow. You should get some sleep too."

He waved her off. "I assure you I'll be bright-eyed and bushy-tailed in the morning, ready for whatever tomorrow can throw at me. I'm mostly concerned about you, actually. Are you alright?"

"Yes, I'm fine," she said. "Sorry if I snapped at you earlier, I was just mad."

"No problem," he replied. "Have a good night."

She disappeared below deck, and when Jonathon turned around, he was surprised to see Annie standing there. Her back was against the wind and long locks of red hair blew around her face with the breeze. She was only a few feet away from him, and she threw both arms around his neck and drew her face very close to his.

"What are you doing?" she asked.

She sounded more like a young girl than a grown woman talking. He smelled the alcohol on her breath and knew she probably had no idea what she was doing. *If Lucy was tipsy, she must be full-fledged drunk.*

"Getting some fresh air," he replied calmly. "I think I know what you've been doing."

"Really? What have I been doing, smarty pants?" She practically leaned against him now, pressing her body tightly against his.

"Just how many beers did you put down?"

"Oh, I don't know…seven, I think." She then paused a moment and looked up. "Or it could've been eight… I don't know," she giggled.

"It's not safe for you to be up here like this, you need to get to bed," he told her.

"You want to go with me?" she asked, still giggling.

"Go with you? To bed?" The pitch of his voice and his blood pressure went up simultaneously.

"Yes…where else?" she asked, looking around in all directions. Drunk or sober, it didn't matter. She was a knockout and very seductive.

He turned away from her and bit his fist in frustration. He was ashamed as he thought to himself that he actually *did* want to take her up on the offer, but he knew how wrong that would be on several different levels.

He took her by the arm and began to lead her toward her cabin. "Come on, you need to go to bed." She smiled a big smile, and he realized she still believed he was going with her. "Alone. You're going to bed alone," he clarified.

Suddenly, she lunged at him again and planted her soft lips tightly against his. Even though he tasted the alcohol in her mouth, he could not hide the fact that he actually enjoyed it. Before he even realized what he was doing, he kissed her back and held her tightly against him. They stumbled down the steps and into the lounge, and before he knew it, she'd fallen backwards on the table and pulled him down with her. They kissed a few minutes longer. It felt like pure heaven to him, and it was only when she began to pull her top off that reality set in and he came crashing back down to earth. He jerked back from her.

"Oh no…what are we doing? We can't do this," he said, in total disbelief. Jonathon pushed himself off the table and Annie sat up abruptly.

"What's the problem?" she asked, very innocently. She reluctantly pulled her shirt back down over her stomach.

"You're drunk, and I'm kind of attached to Lucy," Jonathon said. He grabbed her arm and gently pulled her up from the table. "You need to get some sleep. We have a big day tomorrow and you're going to need all the rest you can get."

He began to lead her toward the hallway that led to her cabin, and she didn't protest.

"Lucy said you guys were finished," she said quietly. "I'm sorry…I feel so stupid." Jonathon glanced over at her and saw a few tears rolling down her cheek. Her rollercoaster of emotions was beginning to exhaust him.

"It's okay, Annie," he said assuringly. "Everything is fine, you get some sleep, and we'll pretend like none of this ever happened."

He opened the cabin door and was relieved to see that Lucy was already asleep in the top bunk. Annie clumsily sat on the edge of the lower bed and Jonathon kneeled down to snatch off her hiking boots. When he rose again, he discovered Annie's eyes were closed and her relaxed breathing clearly indicated she'd already fallen asleep. He grinned and gently laid her over, then pulled her sock-covered feet up in the bed. He covered her with a blanket then tiptoed back into the hallway.

As he shut the cabin door, a sound caught his attention, and briefly startled him. He stopped and listened closely. With the exception of the subtle hum of the ship's engine, there was nothing but silence. Just when Jonathon had decided his ears were playing tricks on him, he heard the sound again. It sounded like someone crying. His first thought was Annie. He placed an ear against the cabin door, but heard nothing. The muffled crying continued, but it was not originating from Annie and Lucy's cabin. He peeked into his own cabin and found Silas in a deep sleep. The only other cabin occupied was Frank and Travis's, and he felt pretty confident that those two weren't emptying a box of tissue either. The cries continued periodically, and the only place left to look was one of the two doors that remained at the end of the hallway. He did confirm that one of the doors was a bathroom, but he still didn't know what was behind the other one. He studied the door a minute, trying to decide what to do next. He couldn't imagine who it could be. He knew that Angus, Captain Blackstone, and Denny were up on the bridge. There had to be someone else on the ship that he and the others were not aware of. He carefully walked toward the door and reached for the handle. His heart began to race as he twisted it, anticipation welling up in him.

"What are you doing?" Angus called out abruptly from behind him.

Jonathon snatched his hand away from the handle and quickly turned to face him. "What is behind this door?" He did his best to sound calm, but failed miserably.

Angus's expression turned into concern. "Are you alright, Jonathon?"

"Yeah, I'm alright," he snapped. "Just tell me what is behind this door." His voice was rising along with his anger.

Angus held up a finger to his mouth. "Jonathon, please…there are people trying to sleep. Don't be so loud. Why do you want to know what is behind the door?"

Jonathon walked toward Angus and got in his face. "Tell me who is behind that door, right now!" His face was mere inches from Angus's and he stared right into his blue eyes.

Angus stared back and grinned. "You think someone is in there?" he asked, pointing to the door.

Jonathon nodded.

Angus shook his head and smiled widely. "For heaven's sake, go open the door, Jonathon," he responded, amused.

Jonathon spun on his heel to face the door; he grabbed the handle and opened it quickly. The room was dark, and it took a long moment for his eyes to adjust. When they did, he saw nothing but a row of crates and boxes stacked neatly. The back wall was covered with a metal shelf with a wide variety of non-perishable goods. His head swiveled back in forth, desperately searching for someone in distress. He didn't see anyone and the crying had ceased ever since Angus arrived.

"It's a storage room," Angus said softly behind him. He placed a hand on Jonathon's shoulder and gripped it tightly. "You need to get some sleep, you're exhausted."

Jonathon continued to stare into the room, ignoring Angus. "Is anyone in here?" he called out, hoping someone would respond to prove he wasn't crazy. No one did.

"What makes you think someone is hiding in there?" Angus asked.

"Someone was crying," he answered through clenched teeth. Jonathon pulled away from Angus and entered the room. "The sound was coming from inside here," he insisted, pointing both hands to the floor.

Angus stared at him a moment, then chuckled awkwardly. "Jonathon, you haven't been on many boats have you?"

"What? No, I haven't. Why?"

The old man closed his eyes and nodded. He moved in front of Jonathon and placed an arm around him. "This particular ship is very, very old. At night, when it's very quiet, you'll hear lots of creaks and moans. Someone that isn't used to that sort of thing could mistake the sounds for something else."

Jonathon stormed away and out of the room. "No, I'm not crazy...I heard crying."

"Okay," Angus called after him. "Okay, fine. Then where exactly is the person that you heard crying?"

Jonathon stopped walking away and peered back into the room. Angus stood in the center with his arms outstretched. There was no one else in the room and he still didn't hear any more crying. Angus approached him again.

"You're just tired. I know you have a lot on your mind," he said softly.

Jonathon wanted to argue further but thought better of it. The old man was right; there was no one else in there. The explanation he gave certainly made sense. It became more and more obvious his mind and his ears were playing tricks on him.

"I think I just need some fresh air," he said, sounding defeated.

"Good idea," Angus said. "I think I'll join you."

The two men strolled up the stairs and stood near the railing on the bow of the ship. The damp wind blew sharply against them, and it was cool enough that Jonathon wished he'd brought a jacket. He had to remove his hat, for fear of the wind swiping it off his head. The full moon's silver splendor projected a bright column of white light across the surface of the ocean. *Bethany* seemed to be traveling directly into the reflection, as if the moon was showing them the way to the island. Jonathon took a deep breath of the moist Atlantic air and felt rejuvenated.

"Beautiful sight, isn't it?" Angus said, pointing at the moon over the horizon. The stars were scattered across the cloudless sky, completing the perfect scene.

Jonathon nodded. "Yes, it really is. I've never seen a sky like this before."

"This is just the beginning. What you will see tomorrow will top anything you've ever seen in your entire life," Angus said proudly.

"Yeah, we'll see," Jonathon responded, refusing to concede that he was actually beginning to believe the old man. He moved his foot to the side and bumped into a large red gas can. There were several other gas cans beside it and stacked on top of it. He'd noticed them when he boarded the ship, but hadn't thought much about them since. "What's up with all the gas cans?"

Angus glanced down at the stack of cans. "Those will provide our fuel for the ATVs."

Jonathon allowed a slight grin to appear on his face. He hoped Angus was unable to see it in the shadows of the dark. When he was a child, he'd spent a lot of time on a four-wheeler his dad had gotten him for his eleventh birthday. His weekends were usually spent motoring through whatever mud holes he was able to find in the woods behind their house. "You didn't say anything about ATVs," he said calmly.

"Well, to be honest, I'm not sure how much use they will be to us. The jungle may be too dense to pilot the vehicles where we want to. Travis will probably have to spend a great deal of time cutting us a path."

"Actually, I think there's a good possibility there may be plenty of places to drive them," Jonathon replied.

"Really?"

He nodded. "Yes, you have to remember that if dinosaurs live on the island, there are going to be trails and paths the animals frequently travel to get around. Considering that there are possibly a lot of large dinosaurs on the island, many of the paths will probably be quite wide."

Angus stroked his chin, and smiled broadly. "That's great news, Jonathon. Thank you for that."

Jonathon shrugged his shoulders.

"However," Angus continued. "I couldn't help but notice the wording you just used."

"What are you talking about?"

"You said '*if* dinosaurs live on the island' and 'there are possibly a lot of large dinosaurs on the island'," he said, turning to gaze across the ocean.

"You should really give up," Jonathon replied. "I'm not believing anything until I see it with my own eyes."

Angus just gave a friendly smile in response, realizing it was useless to argue about it right now.

Jonathon was about to head for bed when he suddenly thought of one other matter he needed to discuss with the old man. He decided it was a good time to bring up the situation with Travis and Lucy.

"Angus, something is bothering me, and I think you need to know about it," he said.

Angus's expression turned serious. "I'm listening," he answered, anxious to hear what he had to say.

"Your boy Travis is making Lucy very uncomfortable." Jonathon said as he leaned on the railing. "He's making me uncomfortable too."

Angus shuffled his feet nervously. "How so?"

"Let's just say he's taken a liking to Lucy, and he's been very vocal about it."

Angus nodded, his gray eyebrows slanted with disapproval. "I see," he said. "That isn't acceptable for him to behave that way. You two are my guests and you will both be treated with respect. I assure you that I will handle this in the morning."

Jonathon could tell Angus was very serious, and though he appreciated the concern, he didn't want things to escalate either. "Thanks, Angus, but please don't make too big a deal out of it. I don't want the guy ticked off at us the entire time we're out here."

Angus held up a reassuring hand. "Don't worry. I know how to handle him. You both have nothing to worry about."

"Thanks, I really appreciate it," Jonathon replied, and he held out his hand. Angus looked at the gesture, surprised. He took his hand and shook it, a wide smile appearing on his face.

"Don't get too excited," Jonathon quipped. "I still don't trust you."

Angus's smile disappeared. "Of course you don't. Not yet."

Jonathon slapped him on the back and trudged off to retire for the night. "I'm off to bed, see you in the morning."

"Sleep well, Jonathon, and remember if you hear crying—"

"It's just the ocean. Yeah, I know," he cut in without looking back.

Angus stood alone on deck and continued to gaze out across the peaceful ocean. There was an unsettling knot in his stomach, and he felt like he'd just dodged a major setback to his plan. Jonathon heard crying and his ears did not deceive him. It wasn't the ship and it wasn't the sea.

He glanced over his shoulder up at the bridge towering above and gave a wave to Captain Blackstone. He waved back and began talking to Denny. Angus glanced at his watch and estimated it had been about five minutes since Jonathon had retreated to his cabin. He spun around and quietly made his way below deck; there was a situation he needed to address in the storage room. He crept down the hallway and carefully turned the handle, doing his best to remain as quiet as possible. Once the door was shut behind him, he reached for a small flashlight on the shelf next to the door. He clicked the light on and directed the beam to a large wooden crate that was padlocked shut directly in front of him. His free hand reached into his trouser pocket to retrieve a key chain with six keys on it. After flipping through a couple of keys, he found the tiny silver one he needed and opened the lock. The top of the huge crate hinged backward and the flashlight illuminated the inside. Osvaldo and Armando were crouched down on opposite corners of the crate. There were a few empty soda cans and potato chip bags scattered on the bottom between them. They both looked up and squinted at the bright light. The moisture glistening on Armando's cheeks confirmed that he was the one Jonathon had heard crying.

Angus shoved the flashlight an inch from Armando's nose, and if he wasn't so afraid someone would hear, he would've smacked the young man hard for nearly screwing up his plan.

"Boy, I'm only going to say this once…I hear another peep out of you, and you will be swimming back to shore. Do I make myself clear?"

Armando bit his lip and nodded.

Osvaldo suddenly reached up and snatched the light away from Angus. "You threaten him again and he won't be the one you have to worry about making noise," he snarled.

Angus stared down coldly at the two of them, and then jerked the flashlight back. "Go ahead…you know what will happen. You, your grandson, and everyone else on this ship will be shot and thrown overboard. I swear, I don't understand why you're making this so hard. You do what I ask and you and your grandson will be fine. It's pretty simple. I don't, however, have a whole lot of patience. You should know that by now. I don't want to hear another sound out of either of you or Armando will be thrown to the sharks. Don't test me on this," he said sternly.

Armando closed his eyes and bit his lip. The boy wanted to cry, but held it back with all his might. Osvaldo slid over to his grandson's side and put a comforting arm around his back. He looked up at Angus, rage clouded his eyes.

"We will be quiet and I will cooperate. Just leave Armando alone," he said softly.

Angus flashed an evil grin. "Very well. Get plenty of rest. Tomorrow is your big day."

He carefully lowered the lid back into place and locked it back down.

The sound of the door closing was a relief to Osvaldo. He continued to hold his grandson, saying nothing. There was nothing to say. He shook with anger, and he knew what he had to do. Some way, somehow, he had to kill Angus Wedgeworth.

CHAPTER 12

A ringing bell ripped Jonathon out of his slumber and he quickly sat upright on the bed. Unfortunately, the ceiling wasn't very high and his head cracked it hard enough to rattle his teeth. He slapped a hand against his aching head and clenched his teeth in an effort to keep from cursing. Silas rolled out of the bed below him and stood up abruptly.

"What the devil is going on?" he snarled.

The bell continued to ring and it seemed to be originating from the lounge. It sounded like a hand-held bell. Jonathon threw his tired legs off the bed and landed on the floor with a *thud*. He glanced out the small round window and noticed sunlight. Apparently, this was their wake up call.

"I guess it's time to get up," he said, groggily.

"Well, I need a second before I go out," Silas said.

"Why is that?"

"Because if I go out right now, I'm gonna shove that bell right up—"

"Whoa," Jonathon cut in. "Say no more...take all the time you need," he said, chuckling.

They sat in the cabin a few more minutes and listened as Annie and Lucy came out moaning and groaning about having to get up. Jonathon took particular notice to Annie complaining about an awful headache. He wondered how much of last night that she remembered.

Finally, they too trudged outside and were pleasantly surprised when they entered the lounge. The small table in the middle displayed a hearty breakfast that seemed to boost everyone's spirits. Angus stood near the table (annoying bell in hand) and motioned for the four of them to sit down. They all did, and the eggs, sausage, and pancakes tasted as great as they looked.

"This is really nice," Jonathon complimented, pointing his fork at Angus.

"This is the last good meal you'll get until probably late tomorrow. I want you all to enjoy it. And the credit belongs to Denny. He is terrific in the kitchen," Angus replied.

Jonathon nibbled on a chunk of sausage impaled on the end of his fork and he glanced across the table to Lucy and Annie. Lucy flashed him a smile and Annie never even acknowledged him. To be fair, she didn't acknowledge anyone. She didn't seem to eat much either. All she did was sit there and massage her temples, no doubt a consequence of her alcohol abuse the night before. He felt a small amount of pity for her, but he was also somewhat relieved that her thoughts were solely on her aching head, and not the awkward event that happened on the table they were presently eating on.

"You girls sleep well?" he asked.

Lucy had a mouthful of pancakes and nodded. She was clearly well rested and eager to see some dinosaurs. Annie picked her head up and it was the first look he got at her eyes. They were bloodshot and her face was puffy. She wasn't nearly as beautiful as she was the day before.

"Please kill me," she pleaded, and then bowed her head down again.

Jonathon and Silas looked at each other simultaneously. It was all the both of them could do to keep from laughing uncontrollably. Lucy shot them both a disapproving look and shook her head.

When they finished breakfast, Angus stepped forward again with a stack of paper in one of his hands. "There is one more order of business before anyone gets off the ship," he said.

Jonathon crossed his arms. "And what's that?"

"As you all know, your protection is a top priority of mine. Frank and Silas will both be armed with rifles. We will take every precaution imaginable to guarantee your safety on the island."

Jonathon purposely let out a loud sigh.

"I'm waiting for the *but*," he said.

Angus glared at him, and bit his lip to keep from telling Jonathon what he really felt. After a brief, awkward moment, he continued.

"But," he said, giving another piercing stare at Jonathon, "this is an island full of dinosaurs. There is still the slight possibility that someone could become injured."

"Or killed," Jonathon added.

Angus ignored him. "Each of you will need to sign a waiver before you set foot on the island."

Jonathan watched Lucy's eyes, and prayed she would rethink things now that the moment of truth had arrived. Unfortunately, he didn't get the response he so desperately wanted. She was the first to reach out and take the waiver. There was no hesitation whatsoever.

Annie signed hers immediately after. Silas was the only one to actually take the time to read the document, but he too signed it.

Angus held one out to Jonathon.

"We have little time to waste," he said.

Jonathon snatched the waiver from him and scribbled his name out. Everyone in the room could see he was visibly troubled.

After Angus took the waivers up the four of them ascended on deck, and the first thing they heard was a *Journey* ballad blaring out of a small radio on the bridge. Captain Blackstone seemed to be dancing to the music and enjoying himself, completely oblivious to the fact that they were all watching and laughing to themselves. Suddenly, Jonathon felt a firm tap on his shoulder.

"Take a gander at that," Silas whispered.

Jonathon whirled around to face the bow of the ship. Straight ahead, on the horizon, was a massive cloud just hovering on top of the water. It was unlike anything he'd ever seen before. He was just about to comment on the mysterious sight when Angus approached from behind and spoke first.

"There is our destination," he whispered. "Behind that veil of mist is an island unlike anything you've ever seen."

"You didn't say anything about a mist," Jonathon said. "Are you sure there is an island in there?"

"Trust me, it's there. That mist always remains around the island. We've been unable to figure out why. It covers every side, and it covers it from above keeping its secrets hidden from the world."

The cloud of mist on the horizon grew larger as *Bethany* drew closer. Jonathon pulled the brim of his hat down low to shield the sunlight, and he squinted hard to see any evidence of an island beyond the mist. He saw none. He glanced over at Lucy and noticed a hint of concern on her face.

"You're not nervous, are you?"

She looked over at him, a few strands of black hair blowing across the front of her face.

"Not really nervous...more excited I guess," she replied. "We're so close to seeing something we thought we'd never see in our lives. I'm glad we have the chance to experience this together."

Jonathon nodded and smiled.

"Me too," he said as he grabbed her hand.

The ship's bow cut gently through the wall of mist, and before they knew it, everyone on the ship was immersed in a damp, thick shroud of fog. Jonathon had rolled the sleeves up on his dark green shirt. It wasn't long before he noticed moisture collecting on his arms.

"Man, this stuff is thick," he said.

"Yeah, I hope the whole island isn't like this. Exploring it would be hopeless in this stuff," Silas added.

Angus stood behind both of them, placing his hands on each of their shoulders.

"Another minute or two and we will be through it. The island itself is clear of mist and fog. It will not hamper us from exploring anything. The island doesn't get a whole lot of sun though due to the mist overhead, so the temperature is fairly comfortable. The only thing we may encounter is a rain shower or two. We've noticed that those are quite frequent here."

Anxiety built up steadily in Jonathon's gut, and he could sense that Lucy, Annie, and Silas were feeling the same way. Any minute now and they would be on the other side. Silas shuffled around a bit next to him, clearly uncomfortable.

"You all right?" Jonathon asked.

"Yeah...I'm just wondering what would keep an aquatic dinosaur from jumping up in the boat with us and eating us all," he said, very seriously.

Jonathon smiled and patted him on the back.

"First off, there is no such thing as an aquatic dinosaur. Dinosaurs are the terrestrial reptiles. Anything in the ocean is simply referred to as a marine reptile. The only thing I'd be concerned about is a plesiosaur, but I'm really not that worried."

"So far, we haven't found any evidence of ocean dinosa—... I mean *marine reptiles* anywhere around the island," Angus said confidently. "Everything seems to be on the island. There are, however, a few flying dinosaurs," he added.

"Pterosaurs," Jonathon said. "There is no such thing as flying dinosaurs. All of the flying reptiles are called pterosaurs, it means 'winged lizard'."

Angus smiled widely. "And *that* is why I wanted you to come along, Jonathon. I never knew that little factoid you just gave us."

"Are the pterosaurs...dangerous?" Silas asked, leaning against the railing.

"Not really sure, some of them had teeth and some of them did not. Of course, just because some of them had teeth doesn't necessarily mean that they don't eat meat. More than likely, they would be more afraid of us than we are of them. I'm pretty sure we don't have to worry about them too much. I'm more concerned about some of the terrestrial reptiles," Jonathon answered.

Things began to brighten up quite a bit and everyone felt a sense of relief as the bow of the ship broke through the other side of the dense fog. Just as Angus had promised, almost two hundred yards ahead of them was the mysterious island. It looked gloomy from the lack of sunshine and it was overrun with dense vegetation. There was a small sandy beach, but beyond that was a wall of countless varieties of trees and bushes. To the left of the beach was a tall, rocky cliff a few hundred feet tall. Jonathon couldn't see the very top of it because it disappeared into the mist above. The whole island reminded him a lot of Skull Island from *King Kong*.

"Isn't it wonderful?" Lucy said, gawking at the view.

Even Annie had perked up at the realization of what they were about to experience.

"I've got to go get my camera," she said, darting away to retrieve her equipment.

Once he got the ship as close to shore as safely possible, Captain Blackstone dropped *Bethany*'s anchor. Jonathon estimated that they were roughly fifty yards from shore. He watched as Angus walked over to a wooden crate and hopped on top of it very spryly for a man in his seventies.

"May I have everyone's attention," the old man shouted as if he were trying to pull them from their excited trances.

Everyone on deck turned to face him just as Frank and Travis appeared from below deck. But they weren't alone; there were two men with them that Jonathon hadn't seen the entire trip. One appeared to be a teenage boy and one seemed to be in his mid-twenties. They both looked Hispanic.

"Angus, who are they?" Silas asked, pointing at the two men.

"Everyone this is Osvaldo and his younger brother Armando," he replied. "Osvaldo has a lot of experience in this sort of terrain and will serve as a guide. Armando will help with our equipment and camping supplies. Neither of them speaks very much English, but we've made them aware of what this expedition is all about. They are fully aware of what we are all here to explore, and I assure you that they are just as excited about it as all of us."

Jonathon eyed both men closely. They both peered ahead with blank stares. Their hair looked ragged and their clothes were very wrinkled. Osvaldo looked very strong, and almost seemed angry. Armando seemed as if he were trying desperately to keep from looking terrified. Something didn't seem right about either one of them. Jonathon leaned close to Silas.

"If those guys are excited, then I'm suicidal," he whispered.

Silas shrugged and nodded. "I hear ya, they don't seem very cheery to me either."

Annie suddenly climbed back on deck, looking very confused. "Uncle Angus, I can't find my camera," she said.

"Well dear, that's because we've already loaded it into one of the boats that will take us to shore," he answered, still standing atop the crate. "All of your equipment has been loaded into a boat that Denny will pilot to shore. Travis will take us ashore with the other boat. Once Denny unloads our equipment, he will return to the ship with Captain Blackstone where they will await our return. We will keep the other boat on the shore in the unlikely event that an emergency occurs. Somewhere along this side of the island is a large crate that contains four ATVs with a small supply of fuel. I had the crate dropped from one of my planes a week ago. As you can see, we have extra fuel on board the ship in the event that we run out," he said, pointing to the stack of fuel cans. "There is a large valley in the middle of the island that we can safely cross when we acquire the ATVs."

"Whoa…wait a minute," Jonathon interrupted. "Why do we need to cross a valley?"

Angus sighed, and looked disappointed that his instructions were interrupted. "Well, we're here to explore the island, Jonathon. I figured that would be easier to do on an ATV than on foot." The old man's thoughts were obviously on finding the fountain of youth as quickly as possible. He had to be careful with his words. "Why do you ask?"

"Because," Jonathon answered, "before we go joyriding all over the island, I think we should take a minute to make sure it is safe to do so."

Angus tried hard not to roll his eyes. "I'm listening," he grumbled.

"You brought me and Lucy for our knowledge on these animals. Those photos you showed me had a herd of *Triceratops* on it. If they feel threatened by us, they will probably charge. Let us be the judge of how safe it is to go exploring the entire island."

"He's right," Lucy chimed in. "Let's be smart about this. Give us an opportunity to see what's out there first."

Get in my way and you won't get an opportunity to breathe anymore, Angus thought.

"Alright, I will wait for you two to give us a green light before we go too deep," Angus said reluctantly. "Before everyone starts getting too nervous, let me remind you that Silas will be armed. His hunting rifle is on the supply boat. That is one of the reasons I asked him to come along. And as I mentioned earlier, Frank will also be armed. We will be well protected."

Silas noticed Angus glancing at him as if he wanted reassurance.

"Yes," he stammered. "I'll be armed and ready for anything that springs out on us."

Jonathon didn't think his words were very confident, and he wasn't sure if it was because Silas was caught off guard or if he was simply telling them all what they wanted to hear.

"If there aren't any more questions, I think the only thing left to do is head toward the island," Angus said, hopping off the crate. He led the group to port side and turned back to face them. "Travis will get in the boat first, then the ladies. The boat is already in the water, so make sure you put on a life jacket before you climb down the ladder; I don't want anyone drowning out here," he said calmly.

Jonathon waited a moment for Travis to climb down to the boat, and then he peeked over the railing. The water was choppy, but not nearly as rough as he imagined. The main thing he wanted to find out was exactly how far down the boat was from *Bethany*'s deck. He was afraid his fear of heights would cause him to freeze up if it was too far down. He was relieved to find that the boat was approximately fifteen feet below the edge of the deck. His fear of heights never seemed to kick in unless there was a significant chance of death from a fall. Breaking a limb didn't frighten him, but the possibility of dying from a fall is what got to him. Fifteen feet would be no problem.

Annie climbed down the ladder next. Her long red hair whisked around in the cool Atlantic breeze. She seemed to have forgotten all about the apparent hangover she was experiencing earlier in the morning. The only thing on her mind now was taking a Pulitzer Prize winning photograph. She wore blue denim shorts and a teal tank top underneath an unbuttoned orange and red plaid flannel shirt. The tail of the shirt floated about in the breeze like a cape, but she had absolutely no problem handling the rope ladder. Lucy followed, dressed in her usual brown cargo pants and white tank top. She seemed a little aggravated that her backpack was already loaded into the other boat. She would've already been wearing it if she had it. He then watched Osvaldo and Armando climb into the boat, still looking nowhere close to being excited about any part of this trip. Something was terribly wrong with those two and the tension seemed to be growing the more they went along with everything Angus asked them to do. Jonathon was certain that they hadn't been treated very well by someone, probably Travis, but it wouldn't be surprising at all if it was Angus either. Finally, Silas climbed down dressed in his usual safari attire, complete with bush hat. Jonathon handled the ladder with no problem and took a seat next to Silas near the rear of the boat. There were no seats left, so Frank had no choice but to squeeze into the supply boat with Denny.

Seconds later, the two boats glided across the ocean surface. The only sound anyone could hear at the moment was the loud whining of the boat's engines. Jonathon found himself glancing into the ocean, wondering if he would catch a glimpse of a *Plesiosaurus*. He saw a few small fish, but nothing at all that alarmed him. He sensed that the island would be pretty humid, so he relished every second of the boat ride. The cool, damp wind against his face was pleasant, but it also forced him and Silas to remove their hats for fear of losing them. When the boats got within mere feet of the shoreline, Travis and Denny jumped into the water and pulled them closer. Everyone hopped onto the white sand and kept their eyes glued to the dense jungle growth ahead of them.

"Alright," Angus said. "Congratulations to you all. You're now famous." He peered in both directions along the shoreline as if he were looking for something. "Somewhere on this side of the island, there is a large shipping container with the ATV's. We need to find that container."

Jonathon watched as Annie drifted away from the others, her camera in hand, apparently looking for a good photo opportunity.

"Annie," he called after her. "Don't stray too far from us."

She seemed to ignore his words, already enchanted by the mystery and intrigue of the island.

Jonathon felt that familiar firm grip on his shoulder again.

"She'll be fine. She knows what she's doing," Angus said.

"That jungle is pretty dense. We have no idea what's in there watching us right now," Jonathon warned. The others were listening and immediately began squinting hard into the foliage. He also noticed that Osvaldo was sweating profusely, and he looked pale. There was fear in his eyes. "We need to be very, very careful. I can't stress that to you enough."

"And we will be," Angus replied. "We're going to be extremely careful."

Suddenly, a high-pitched scream shattered the discussion. Jonathon spun around and was stunned at what he saw. Annie was perfectly fine, but something standing a few feet in front of her startled her. A small two-legged dinosaur, probably three feet tall, stood before her. The dinosaur had a streak of white that ran down from its neck, across its chest and belly, and all the way to the tip of its tail. Its top half was a dark shade of green. The animal tilted its head to the side as it curiously stared at the screaming woman in front of it.

Almost everyone stood dumbfounded, unsure of what to do. Silas ran to retrieve his gun from the boat.

"Wait," Jonathon shouted. "It's alright…it's an herbivore."

"Wh-What's an herbivore?" Travis stammered.

"Plant eater," Lucy answered, annoyed by his ignorance.

Annie continued to stand still, in complete shock. Her mouth was still wide open and a loud, shrilled scream still poured out of it.

Lucy ran over to her and grabbed her arm.

"It's okay, Annie. It won't hurt you."

Her touch seemed to jar Annie from her state of shock, and she immediately began jogging backwards, away from the dinosaur. She nearly dropped her camera in the process. The dinosaur took an inquisitive step forward.

Jonathon could see the wonder in the animal's dark brown eyes. It had never seen anything like them before. He sensed that the animal was far more intelligent than one would think at first glance.

"I think it's a *Parksosaurus*...completely harmless," he said. "It seems to be just as amazed by us as we are of it."

He approached the dinosaur carefully, and he was very surprised to be able to reach out and touch the animal's head. It jerked away and let out a commanding hiss, signaling its displeasure. Jonathon reacted, pulling his hand back quickly.

"Careful, Jonathon," Lucy cautioned. "I'm sure it has a few tricks to defend itself if it feels threatened."

"Good call." He spun around and let the dinosaur be. It responded by slowly walking backwards into the veil of jungle. Moments later, it disappeared for good.

When what had happened finally soaked in, he let out a joyful laugh and ran straight for Lucy. He hugged her tightly.

"Can you believe this?"

She laughed, and kissed him on the cheek.

"In my wildest dreams, I never thought we'd get a chance to see something like that," she replied.

Jonathon kept an arm around Lucy's neck and he peered over at Silas and Annie. Annie still seemed rattled by the whole experience, but she too recognized the significance of what had just happened. Silas shook his head in disbelief.

"I've seen a lot of interesting animals in my day," he said. "But this one definitely takes the cake. I can't believe what just happened."

Jonathon noticed Angus wasn't anywhere near them and neither were Osvaldo or Armando. He peered around and caught sight of them a good distance behind Annie and Silas. Angus was speaking at both of them and Travis and Frank flanked him as he spoke. They didn't seem to have any interest in what had just happened. If anything, they were using it as a diversion so they could have a little meeting.

"What are they doing?" Silas asked, quietly.

"I don't know, but I'm going to find out. There is something strange going on with those two," Jonathon said, referring to Osvaldo and Armando. He marched through the sand, and when he got close, Angus spun around to meet him.

"Are you a believer yet?" the old man asked, as if nothing had been going on.

"For someone so eager to explore an island and discover dinosaurs, you sure didn't seem too interested in the one we just encountered," Jonathon spat.

Angus shrugged his shoulders. "There are plenty of dinosaurs to see, Jonathon. We were just discussing a few things."

Jonathon adjusted his hat and put his hands on his sides.

"Like what?"

"We were trying to decide how to find the ATVs. It's very important that we find them."

Osvaldo stood silently and watched them talk. He could tell that Jonathon wasn't very fond of Angus. He considered the man to be his ally, and at some point, he may have to rely on him to get Armando off the island alive. Moments before Jonathon approached them, Angus was continuing with his threats and already asking him to point them in the general direction of the fountain of youth. The shoreline they were on looked vaguely familiar, but he didn't really see anything to indicate to him which way they needed to go. He tried to explain that to Angus, but the old man wasn't hearing any of it. He was in the middle of another one of his threats when Jonathon approached. Somehow, he had to get a moment alone with him so he could tell him what was really going on. For now, he continued to watch their conversation with interest.

"I told you that Lucy and I will decide when and if we venture deeper inland. Stop with the secret conversations," Jonathon demanded.

Angus held up his hands defensively, and Travis popped his knuckles loudly as if he were trying to give Jonathon a subtle hint to back off.

"You're right, Jonathon," Angus said. "It was very rude of me to keep you out of the loop. You're the expert and I assure you it will not happen again."

"Thank you," Jonathon answered through gritted teeth.

"We believe that it is possible the crate was dropped somewhere nearby in the jungle. After all, doing an air drop on a small narrow beach is a tricky task. Throw in a misty sky and it's almost impossible to drop it exactly where you want it. I think we should search the nearby jungle. That is, if you see it safe to do so," Angus said.

Jonathon kept his hands on his hips and he turned his head toward the wall of trees.

"Give me an opportunity to have a quick look first, then you can come in," he said.

Angus nodded his head.

"Very well," he answered. "Would you like for Travis to go with you?"

Jonathon looked over his shoulder at Travis. He was staring at him with icy eyes, a crooked grin across his face.

"Uh...no that's okay," he said. "I'll manage."

CHAPTER 13

Jonathon took the large hunting knife from its sheath and stepped softly toward the dense vegetation in front of him. If there was something in there waiting for him, it could lunge at him faster than he would be able to react. But as long as he had his knife, he had a chance. One quick stab into an animal's head, it would fall limp, and he would be able to escape. That was the plan anyway. As he entered the shadows of the jungle, he tried desperately to keep from breaking and snapping too many twigs. As silent as the jungle was, the ordinarily small noises echoed loudly for anything in the vicinity to hear. As it was, he was doing a miserable job of keeping his footsteps quiet. There was just simply too much crunchy debris on the ground for his large boots to avoid. He kept his head swiveling both directions, watching for any signs of movement. With no sun, the jungle was much darker than it would ordinarily be and the environment was spooky and uncomfortable. He carefully parted bushes and shrubs out of his path and suddenly a flock of birds sprang into flight in front of him. The abrupt noise startled him and he felt his heart skip a couple of beats. He stood still a moment panting and trying to recompose himself when he heard another sound. Something was walking nearby him and it sounded like it had a little more mass than the *Parksosaurus*. He crouched down, trying to find an opening of some kind through the dense undergrowth to get a look at what was walking nearby. He finally found a hole and was amazed to see a *Protoceratops* lumbering casually through the jungle. It occasionally stopped and nibbled on some of the large leafy bushes as it walked. Jonathon stood back up and worked his way through the brush in an effort to get closer to the animal. He didn't fear the animal that much; it was a herbivore and it wasn't much bigger than a sheep. It had a large neck frill and a beaked mouth. In fact, it looked a lot like a miniature *Triceratops*, but without the horns.

This was a dinosaur Jonathon knew well. Their fossils were very plentiful throughout Mongolia, and although he'd never actually had the opportunity to unearth any, he'd examined many specimens throughout his career. Several years ago, he'd seen photos of a fossilized *Protoceratops* and *Velociraptor* in combat. The extraordinary find was reconstructed exactly the way it had been discovered in the rocky earth. Another thing that fascinated Jonathon was that the Greeks actually discovered *Protoceratops* and mistaken it for a mythical creature, the griffin. It was surreal now that he found himself looking at a real live breathing one. The animal finally noticed him approaching, and it let out a moan that sounded similar to a cow. Jonathon continued to creep closer to the animal. It responded by scuffing a paw through the soft soil and moaning again.

"Easy, fella. I'm not going to hurt you," he whispered.

The *Protoceratops* sniffed the air and took a step toward Jonathon, then immediately stepped back. It was clear that it wanted to investigate the strange new life form further, but it was being very cautious about it at the same time. Jonathon continued to take slow, careful strides toward it, and after several minutes, he finally got within arm's reach of the animal. He held out his hand in a fist and the *Protoceratops* stretched its neck out so that it could sniff the hand.

"That's it...I'm harmless," he said softly, trying not to get too excited. "You're just like a big old dog."

Suddenly, *Protoceratops* jerked its large head back and took another sniff of air. It turned its entire body around and began looking in all directions as if it heard something.

"Something got you spooked, boy?"

Jonathon squinted and did his best to peer into the jungle. He saw nothing, but suddenly an uneasy feeling overcame him. Then the most terrifying sound he ever heard erupted somewhere deep within the jungle ahead. It sounded like ten lions roaring in unison. It was a thunderous blast of sound and almost impossible to detect exactly how far away it was. The *Protoceratops* wailed and frantically tore away through the bushes, clearly familiar with and terrified of the roaring beast. Jonathon felt his heart rate pick up as a realization began to overcome him. Deep down, he knew what made that sound without even seeing the animal. He had wondered to himself all along if there would be *Tyrannosaurs* on the island and now he was certain that there were.

This definitely changes things, he thought.

He turned back, knife still clutched tightly in hand, and began running furiously in the direction he had come. Thoughts of tripping and falling on the knife crossed his mind, but he felt much safer with it in his hand than not. As he ran, it became apparent he'd wandered a lot further into the jungle that he had realized. Time seemed to escape him as he too had become enchanted with the majesty of the mysterious island. The roar had done wonders to break that enchantment, and the only thing he wanted to do now was get back on the boat. There was definitely research to be done here and he no doubt wanted to come back, but as things were now, they were way unprepared for exploring the island. They needed more men and weapons than they had now. More exploring needed to be done from the air; it was simply too dangerous to blindly venture further inland the way that they were. He knew Angus wouldn't like his recommendation that they get off the island at once, but at this point, he also didn't care. If the old man wanted to get himself killed that was fine, and if he could convince Travis and Frank to follow him, so be it. The rest of them, however, would head back to *Bethany* immediately.

***

Angus looked down at his watch and released a sigh of disgust. He stood at the edge of the ocean as the others unloaded the supply boat further down the beach. He needed a moment alone to think. His plans were already going into disarray and they hadn't even left the beach yet. Playing along and acting like he wanted to listen to Jonathon's advice was frustrating and demeaning. He was the one in charge and he knew he had to start acting like it. The only thing he wanted to do was locate the fountain of youth and take a drink. He needed the others to accomplish this and he wanted nothing less but for all of them to receive the gift of immortality also. Part of him wondered if he should just spill the beans and tell them everything. After all, they had just come to realize he was telling the truth about the dinosaurs, getting them to believe there was a fountain of youth on the island should now be easy.

On the other hand, he also knew that telling the truth may result in more chaos. If he told them the truth, they would quickly realize he lied to get them all to the island. It could be argued that he was asking them to risk their lives for his own selfish reasons. They may all turn on him at once and that could be disastrous. The unfortunate truth was that he needed them all to accomplish his goal. The risk of telling them the truth was just not worth it. His thoughts turned to Jonathon and he wondered what was taking him so long. It suddenly occurred to him that maybe he wasn't coming back. He grinned and knew it was unlikely he would get that lucky. Nevertheless, he had to be ready to adapt to the possibility. *Good thing I brought two paleontologists*, he thought.

"We've finished unloading the supply boat," Travis said as he approached, sweat beading up all over his forehead.

"Very good. Tell Frank to keep a close watch on Osvaldo and Armando. I'm afraid they're getting a little restless, and I don't need them complicating things any more than they already are," he replied. Travis nodded and began to walk away in the direction of Frank.

"Travis," Angus called out.

He stopped and glanced back. "Sir?"

"Make sure your gun is loaded and ready. Tell Frank to do the same. I'm going to give Jonathon five more minutes, and if he hasn't shown back up, we may have to go on without him," he said coldly.

Travis snorted. "But how in the world are we gonna convince the others to go on without him?"

"Leave that to me, we will be able to persuade them," he answered, pulling his jacket back to reveal a sleek, silver revolver in a shoulder holster. "But don't worry, I feel confident Jonathon will be back. Better to be safe than sorry though."

"I understand," Travis replied, his smile revealing a few crooked teeth.

Lucy had just plopped down on a fallen tree trunk when she heard a rustle behind the trees. She squinted, trying to see into the darkness of the jungle.

"Jonathon, is that you?"

"Yeah, it's me," he answered, stepping out onto the open beach. He was out of breath from all the running.

Lucy could see a look of excitement and fear all over his face.

"What's wrong? What happened?"

She helped him sit down on the log, and Silas, Annie, and Angus came running over.

"We can't do this. We've got to call the expedition off," he said, panting heavily.

Annie sat down beside him.

"What do you mean? What happened?" she asked.

Jonathon took off his hat and fanned himself as he spoke.

"I took a long walk into the jungle. I went much deeper than I meant to go. I heard something…something really, really big."

"Did you see what it was?" Silas asked.

He shook his head. "No…I didn't go looking either. It was the most terrifying sound I've ever heard. There is only one thing it could be."

"Tyrannosaur," Lucy said, her voice quaking just a bit. "You think it's a tyrannosaur."

He nodded, saying nothing.

Angus kneeled down in front of him and put one knee in the sand.

"Jonathon, do you need some water?"

"Yeah…that would be great," he replied.

Angus looked over his shoulder and shouted for Travis to bring over some water, then turned his attention back to Jonathon.

"You say you didn't see what made the sound?"

"No, but like I said, I didn't go looking for it either. It was unlike any roar I've ever heard before. We're not prepared to travel deeper into this island with tyrannosaurs back there." He paused a moment as Travis tossed him a bottle of water. He took a gulp and wiped his mouth with his arm.

"I'm sorry, Angus, it's just not safe. We'll have to come back with more help."

Angus nodded, and then stood back up, his knee popping as he did.

"If you didn't see the animal that made the sound, then how can you be sure it was a tyrannosaur?"

Jonathon put his hat back on and stood up.

"Look, Angus," he said, slightly annoyed by the question. "I believe with all my heart that it was a tyrannosaur. But if it wasn't, it was still something I don't want to be anywhere near. It was loud and it sounded extremely dangerous. I realize how badly you wanted to explore this island, but I'm telling you, it's not safe. You wanted my expert opinion and I'm giving it to you. We need to leave right now."

Angus stared at Jonathon for a few seconds then turned to look across the ocean all the way to where it met the mist. The others remained quiet, unsure how to react. Angus looked to Silas and smiled.

"What do you think, old friend?"

Silas adjusted his hat and rubbed the back of his neck.

"I don't know, Angus, Jonathon seems pretty shook up by whatever it was that he heard. Maybe he's right. Maybe we need some more help."

Angus shook his head and chuckled. "I would've never expected an answer like that from you of all people." He shot Lucy a look. "I guess you agree with them?"

She looked down and shook her head.

"Yes, we'll have to come back," she said softly.

Angus rolled his eyes and threw his head back, frustration beginning to appear in his movements.

"What about you, Annie? Don't you want that prize winning photograph?"

Annie walked over to him and gently grabbed his arm.

"Uncle Angus, they're right. Jonathon and Lucy are the ones we need to be listening to. If they say it's too dangerous, then it is. A prize-winning photograph won't do me any good if I'm dead."

Angus jerked his arm away and stomped off.

"I can't believe how easily you are all persuaded by an animal that Jonathon didn't even see," he muttered. He stood for a long moment thinking. He was so close to finding the fountain of youth. There was no way he was going to turn back now. Travis drew near him and patiently awaited an order. Angus could sense that he was practically begging him to allow him and Frank to pull their guns and force them forward into the jungle. The truth was, he desperately wanted to oblige him, and he knew that all he had to do was say the words and Travis would gladly spring into action. They were armed and the others were completely at their mercy. He glanced over at Jonathon. He and the others hadn't moved, they just watched and waited for him to say something. Angus noticed Travis inching closer to him.

"Just say the words, boss," he whispered.

Angus held up a dismissive hand. He'd made up his mind. As bad as he needed the others help, he decided kidnapping them all would be an unwise decision. He still had Osvaldo to point him in the right direction. He and Travis had handguns. Frank was equipped with a high-powered hunting rifle. Armando was expendable. If they found themselves in a desperate situation with a hungry tyrannosaur, one bullet in the young man's leg would allow them to escape with their lives. He spun around and smiled widely.

"Jonathon," he began. "I wanted you and Lucy to give me your honest opinions about the dinosaurs on this island. You both have done so and I truly appreciate it."

Jonathon stood and nodded.

"Angus, I'm sorry, I know you were looking forward to this," he said, displeasure in his voice. He truly felt bad for having to spoil the old man's plans.

"And for the record, I'm sorry I didn't believe you. I believe you now," he said with an awkward chuckle.

"You only did what I asked you to do, don't apologize," Angus replied. "I do, however, wonder if you could do me a favor?"

"Yes, of course. What do you need?"

"Please take one of the boats and return to the ship with Silas, Annie, and Lucy. The four of you will be safe there, and as soon as we get back tomorrow, we will return to the states," he said, a hint of arrogance in his voice.

Jonathon blinked and shook his head.

"What? I don't understand?"

Angus let out a deep breath. "Jonathon, I don't know how else to say it. Take those three back to the ship with you. We'll see you tomorrow," he quipped, then turned away to gather Osvaldo and Armando, still being guarded closely by Frank.

"He's lost his mind," Silas whispered.

He jogged over to Angus and grabbed him tightly by the arm.

"Have you lost your mind?"

Angus stopped walking and gave Silas an icy stare, and ordered him to let go of his arm.

Silas released his grip and Angus immediately began walking again without saying another word.

"Let him go," Lucy said.

Annie started to speak, but she knew better. Angus had always done what he wanted and when he set his mind on something there was no talking him out of it.

"She's right, let him go. There's no way to get through to him now."

Jonathon began walking toward the boat and motioned for the others to follow.

"Come on, let's get out of here. If he wants to get himself killed, who are we to stop him?"

The others half-heartedly padded across the sandy beach and began to board the boat. Jonathon was about to step on board when he suddenly heard angry shouting began between Osvaldo and Angus. He stepped back onto the beach and the others looked on curiously to see what was happening. Angus pushed the much younger and stronger Osvaldo. The younger man was just about to retaliate when Travis threw an arm around his neck and restrained him. Frank immediately did the same to Armando.

"What in the world is going on over there?" Lucy asked.

Silas stood in the boat and looked ready to intervene.

Jonathon looked over at him and held up a calming hand.

"Easy, Silas," he said. "I'm gonna go over there and see what is going on."

"Well, you're not going alone," Silas answered. He jumped out of the boat and began stomping along the beach.

Jonathon began jogging behind him, but took a brief moment to look back at Annie and Lucy. "You girls wait here...we'll be right back," he said.

"Hurry up," Lucy replied. "If Osvaldo and Armando want to come with us, there is plenty of room for them too."

Jonathon nodded and then caught up to Silas. He wondered to himself if that was the cause for the confrontation. Ever since he'd laid eyes on Osvaldo and Armando, neither of them looked very happy about being there. He wondered if they resisted when Angus told them they were going on without the others.

"I don't know what's gotten into Angus," Silas said gruffly. "He's always been a bit of a jerk, but he sure is taking it to the extreme today. I've just about had enough of it."

As they approached, Angus turned to face them and a sly grin appeared on his face.

"You two have a change of heart?" His words dripped with sarcasm.

Jonathon was about to speak, but Silas beat him to it. He marched right up to Angus, a foot away from his face.

"What are you doing to these two?"

He pointed at Osvaldo and Armando, still being held by Angus's henchmen.

"They work for me, and they're trying to back out of our deal," Angus replied calmly. "This matter doesn't concern either of you, get back to the ship and we'll see you tomorrow."

"No," Silas snapped. "Not without those two. They clearly don't want to go with you and you're not going to make them."

Jonathon looked over at Osvaldo. He didn't look afraid, but more like angry. Armando, on the other hand, was a shivering mass of pure fear. As Angus and Silas continued to argue, Jonathon calmly walked over to Osvaldo. Travis watched him with curious eyes.

"Osvaldo, would you like to return to the ship with us?" Jonathon asked softly.

Osvaldo didn't say a word; he just nodded in response. Armando seemed relieved that he'd been asked.

"Let him go, Travis," Jonathon ordered.

"Go back to the ship and stay out of this," Travis responded coldly.

Angus noticed Jonathon speaking to Osvaldo and rushed over to them.

"Jonathon, this doesn't concern you, I'm going to have to insist that you and Silas return to the boat and let us handle Osvaldo and Armando."

Jonathon marched over to Angus and poked a finger in his chest.

"Well, I'm going to have to insist that you let Osvaldo and Armando come with us. They don't want to go with you on your suicide mission. They're coming with us."

Angus slapped his hand away and stood silent a moment, fuming.

"I cannot go further without them," the old man said, desperation in his voice. "I'm taking them with me and you're going to go back to the ship."

Jonathon took a deep breath and spat out a curse word.

"Fine, do this the hard way then," he replied, stomping through the sand back over to Osvaldo. He grabbed Travis's arm and tugged. "Get your hands off of him; he's not going with you."

Travis smiled and tightened his grip around Osvaldo's throat. Osvaldo grabbed at the massive arm and gagged. Jonathon felt a surge of fury build up inside him that he hadn't felt since he faced the school bully when he was a teenager. Before he knew what was happening, he made a fist and thrust a firm punch into Travis's ribs. The large man let out a loud groan as the air was forced out of his lungs. He fell to his knees and involuntarily released Osvaldo. He darted away and stood near the edge of the water.

"What are you doing?" Angus yelled. "Have you lost your mind?"

"Probably, but at least I'm not alone," Jonathon yelled back. He stormed over to Frank and shot him an icy stare. "Let him go," he said firmly.

Frank let out an arrogant chuckle.

"You must want to do this the hard way too," Jonathon replied angrily. As he took another step toward Frank, he heard Silas call out to him from behind.

"Look out!"

Jonathon spun around just in time to catch a glimpse at Travis charging at him. He didn't have time to dodge the attack and took a bone-jarring collision with Travis's shoulder into his gut. He fell hard on his back in the sand and Travis took a backhanded swipe across his right cheek. He felt his teeth cut into the inside of his mouth and the copper taste of blood followed. Travis stood up and began making his way back to Osvaldo who began running across the beach to where Lucy and Annie were standing. After seeing the attack on Jonathon, they both came running over. Lucy was cursing at Travis as she went.

Jonathon rolled over and shook the cobwebs out of his head. He spit out a mouth full of blood and stood back up, leaving his hat lying in the sand. He pulled his shirt tail out of his pants and marched back toward Travis.

Lucy had done a wonderful job of distracting him with her screaming and he never saw the right hook Jonathon firmly planted on his jaw. He tumbled to the ground and caught himself on his hands and knees. He shook his head a moment then returned to his feet, charging again at Jonathon. Jonathon dodged him this time, but Travis stopped abruptly and took another swing at him. Jonathon ducked and returned a punch of his own. Travis avoided it and countered with a sharp, stinging blow to Jonathon's jaw, much harder than the back-handed swipe he'd given before. Jonathon fell to the sand, blood now gushing through his teeth. He reached down and grabbed a handful of the blood-soaked sand and threw it hard into Travis's eyes. Travis instinctively rubbed at his face and Jonathon got back up swinging furiously at him. Seconds later, he felt another sharp pain on the back of his head and his entire body went limp. He fell backward onto the beach, his ears ringing loudly and his vision blurred. Frank now stood over him, rubbing the pain out of his fist from the sucker punch he'd just delivered. Jonathon blinked his eyes, trying desperately to regain his focus. He wasn't about to stop fighting now. Just as his vision was straightening out, he saw Frank lunge forward as someone apparently grabbed him from behind.

"If you're not gonna fight fair, neither will I," Silas growled as he grabbed Frank tightly in much the same way he'd gotten Armando minutes earlier. Frank clawed and tore at the much older man's large arms, but was unable to peel them loose. Travis had finally gotten the sand out of his eyes and he prepared to come to Frank's aid. Jonathon stood up and ran at him to ensure that it didn't happen.

As the four men continued to struggle, Annie screamed and pleaded with them to stop. Lucy grabbed Angus and begged him to do something. The old man watched them struggle for a few moments more, and then pulled the large revolver from under his coat. Lucy's eyes widened and she gasped.

"He's got a gun!" she screamed.

A second later, Angus pulled the trigger and a loud boom thundered across the beach. Jonathon and Travis instantly stopped fighting and Silas loosened his grip off of Frank. Frank pushed Silas back and just as he was about to deliver a punch, Travis grabbed his arm.

"It's alright...let him go," he said. He then bent down and pulled his pant leg up revealing his own handgun strapped to his calf. He grabbed the gun and immediately aimed it at Jonathon.

"You said it very well..." Angus said calmly, his robin egg blue eyes piercing sharply at Jonathon. "...when you said we'll do this the hard way. I tried to let you all go, but you just couldn't get on the boat and leave, could you?"

He casually walked over to Jonathon and poked the gun into his chest.

"You have no idea who you're dealing with. How dare you come over here and interfere with something that doesn't concern you? How dare you run over here and poke your finger into my chest and make demands? You're in no position to bully me," the old man growled, pulling the gun back and scratching at the back of his neck with it.

If it wasn't for Travis still pointing one at him, Jonathon would've taken the opportunity to knock the old man's teeth out.

"Uncle Angus...what are you doing?" Annie asked innocently, in total disbelief that her uncle could be so cold.

Angus glanced over at his niece and a brief expression of shame crossed his face.

"My dear, I'm sorry you've been put into this most unfortunate situation. I'm afraid Mr. Williams here ruined it for all of you," he said, and without warning, he punched Jonathon hard in his stomach.

He fell over on his knees and Travis hit him hard on the back of his head with the grip of his gun.

"No!" Lucy screamed as she dropped down on her knees next to him. "What is wrong with you?" she asked, looking up at Travis, tears now welling up in her eyes.

"You don't need him, honey. I think you'd be much happier with me."

She quickly sprang back on her feet and drew back to slap him, but before she could, he grabbed her by a handful of hair and jerked her close to him.

"That's not nice, sweetheart."

Silas ignored the fact that Frank's gun was pointed at him and rushed to Lucy's aid.

Angus slid in front of Travis and pointed his gun at Silas.

"Calm down, old friend," he hissed.

"Any friendship we may have had before is history," Silas replied through clenched teeth. "Make your baboon let Lucy go," he demanded.

Angus nodded.

"Let her go, Travis…that is not a way to treat a lady," he snapped.

"Aww, I was just having a little fun, boss."

"Don't let it happen again, Travis. I mean it. Do not harm women in that way," he said, sounding very serious.

Travis nodded and instantly released Lucy's hair. She kicked him hard in the shin and ran over to where Annie, Osvaldo, and Armando were standing. Travis cringed, clearly feeling pain from the kick, but did his best to hide it.

Angus walked to Lucy and left Silas and Jonathon under the watchful eyes of Travis and Frank.

"Lucy, I apologize for the way Travis just treated you. That was out of line."

She crossed her arms and her face reddened with anger, the cool breeze in her face did nothing to calm her down. "You're damn right it was out of line! When we get back to the states, you and your little buddies are in big trouble!"

Angus nodded and closed his eyes. "It would be best for all of us if that didn't happen, my dear," he replied. "I'm afraid since the circumstances here have suddenly changed dramatically, I'm going to need to call for your assistance again. I assure you it will be worth your time, and you probably will feel differently once you see what this is all about."

She uncrossed her arms and put her hands on her hips.

"What is this all about? What are you talking about? I thought this was all about the dinosaurs. You're nuts if you think I'm going anywhere with you."

"I'll explain everything when the time comes."

He looked down at Jonathon and watched him rub the back of his head.

"I'm afraid since Jonathon is so combative, you're going to have to come along and be our dinosaur expert."

Lucy felt a chill rush across her body. She took a step back and contemplated running. Angus read her eyes and pointed his gun at her.

"Lucy, please don't make this difficult," he said.

Osvaldo watched everything unfold and suddenly begin to feel a wave of relentless guilt wash across him. These people whom he'd just met were now in extreme danger because of his resistance minutes earlier. He knew he had to do something and he had to do it fast. Without thinking about it anymore, he stepped forward and quickly got everyone's attention.

"Angus, leave these people out of this," he said, drawing a gasp from Annie.

"He speaks English," she said, pointing at him as if he had two heads.

He smiled at her. "Yes, I speak English. Angus, I'll do whatever you ask, just let these people go and let Armando go. They don't deserve this treatment," he pleaded.

Angus let out a chuckle. "Oh, it's too late for that, Osvaldo. Believe it or not, I was actually going to let them all go back to the ship and wait until we returned. Unfortunately, you ruined all that for everyone. Things have changed...we've crossed a line where there is no turning back now. Lucy will accompany us through the jungle. Armando will join us also. As for the others, I have no intentions of bringing them along," he said coldly, and Lucy immediately sensed murder was on his mind.

"No! You can't do that," she screamed. She stomped her feet and as her face reddened tears began to stream down her cheeks. "Please don't kill them!"

Annie began sobbing also, fearing the same fate. "Uncle Angus, please don't kill us," she begged, her voice shaking.

The old man threw his head back and let out a hearty laugh. "Kill you? Oh heavens, do I look like a murderer? I'm not going to kill anyone," he said through laughter.

Silas stepped forward, but was sure to keep his hands up as he eyed the gun Frank pointed at his chest. "So you're going to let us go," he said hopefully.

Angus's laughter died off and he shook his head solemnly. "You know I can't just let you all walk away either," he replied. "I'll have to tie you three up until tomorrow."

The ringing in Jonathon's ears finally ceased and he struggled to get to his feet. He stumbled a bit as if he was drunk and Travis no longer felt threatened by him. He'd listened to the conversation and finally regained enough composure to speak. "Wedgeworth, if you tie us up on this beach, you might as well call it murder. There are meat-eating dinosaurs on this island, and if they find us, we're dead," he said, rubbing the back of his head.

Angus seemed to ignore him. He walked over to where they'd unloaded the boats and picked up a bundle of rope. He tossed it to Frank and led Silas over near Travis so he could watch him. Then he looked up and down the edge of the jungle as if he were looking for something. "I think that one will do, Frank," he said, pointing to a large palm tree. "Tie them to that one."

Jonathon stared at Angus, amazed at just how cold the man could be. "Did you hear what I said?" he asked. "You leave us tied to a tree, we're dead."

"I heard you, Jonathon. If something happens to you while we're gone, it's hardly my fault. I asked you very nicely to return to the ship and you obviously didn't listen. Now get against the tree," he growled.

He pointed the revolver at Jonathon and pulled back the hammer to reassure him he wasn't kidding around. Jonathon reluctantly walked over to the palm tree and put his back against it. Travis forced Silas to do the same. Then he turned to find Annie. She was slowly backing away toward the boat at the edge of the water, roughly thirty yards away. "Annie, would you mind taking a spot against the tree?" he asked, no hint of regret existed in his voice.

Annie began crying uncontrollably and turned to run. She ran as fast as she could, and as she reached the boat, she frantically tried to push it into the water. Travis ran after her and easily caught her before she could make her escape. As he carried her back, she kicked and slapped at him the entire way. He pushed her against the tree and held her in place as Frank began wrapping the rope around the three of them.

"Please, Uncle Angus," she screamed. "Don't do this to me…don't leave me here! I'm your niece, for God's sake!"

As Frank tightened the rope to the point where she could no longer move her arms, Angus approached and placed a hand on her forehead, brushing her shiny red hair aside. "Sweetie, I've never been much of a family man. Let's be honest, I hardly know you and you barely know me. All the family I've ever known has only wanted one thing out of me: money. I'm sorry things have turned out the way they have. I want you to know I truly hope that you will still be alive when I return. I sincerely mean that." He leaned over to kiss her forehead then began to walk away. Annie dropped her head and sobbed, no longer able to speak.

As Frank finished tying the knot, Silas struggled for a minute, and then fell still and silent also. Jonathon watched as Angus and Travis gathered up a few supplies (including a couple of high-powered hunting rifles). They made Armando and Osvaldo carry the heavy packs containing tents, sleeping bags and other supplies. Then they began to walk toward the jungle. Lucy glanced over at Jonathon and mouthed out the words *I love you* without speaking. He winked at her, hoping she'd read the response as an indication that he had every intention of getting loose and coming after her. Angus too glared over at him as he walked by and Jonathon couldn't resist spitting out a threat to him.

"Angus, you better hope I don't get loose. You'll be begging the dinosaurs to come and eat you if I get a hold of you," he growled.

Angus chuckled. "I have to admit, I admire your spirit," he said.

Jonathon shook with rage and pulled hard against the rope, wishing desperately it would break. He heard Annie whine and realized he was actually making it cut deeper into her skin.

Travis couldn't resist one last verbal assault on Jonathon either. He walked over, leaned forward, and began to whisper just loud enough for only Jonathon to hear. "I can't wait to see the buzzards plucking your eyeballs out tomorrow afternoon…that is if you have any eyeballs left," he said coldly. He laughed loudly and cracked one more punch against his jaw as he walked away.

"You alright?" Silas asked, panic beginning to appear in his voice.

Jonathon spit out a tooth. "I'm going to kill him," he mumbled through swollen lips. "And I won't be alright until he is dead."

CHAPTER 14

Jonathon had never been very good at tying knots. He'd been a boy scout as a child, but he must have missed the lesson on tying knots because every knot he ever tied was pretty much done the same way he tied his shoes. Frank apparently hadn't been very good at tying knots either because as he struggled to break free, the rope began to loosen. Silas swelled his body up and desperately tried to break free and Annie repeatedly told them both that as they struggled, the rope burned and cut her fragile skin.

Jonathon estimated that they'd been deserted on the beach around twenty minutes. He'd spent most of that time doing his absolute best to convince Annie that they were going to find a way to break free. At first, he only said it to make her feel better, but as he felt the knot in the rope slowly loosen, he began to genuinely believe it. Silas struggled almost the entire time, and at one point, he lost his cool and yelled out some profane words that made Annie blush. The words were all directed to Angus and he did his best to make sure the old man heard them. Jonathon knew that more than likely he didn't hear them, but it made Silas feel better so he let the big man vent.

"Believe it or not, I think the rope is loosening," Jonathon said through clenched teeth.

Annie perked up. "Really? How do you know?"

Jonathon wiggled his shoulders side to side and tried to slide up and down on the jagged palm tree bark. "Because, I can feel it," he mumbled.

Annie immediately began struggling frantically, trying hard to mock the motions Jonathon was doing.

"No...don't," he said. "You two stay as still as you can and let me wiggle around. If I can just get enough slack to move my arm, I can grab my knife and cut us free. We just got to be patient, but I know I can get it."

Silas breathed a sigh of relief. "Let me know if I can do anything to help," he said. "I'll try to suck my stomach in as much as I can to give you some room to work."

"Thanks, that'll hel—"

Jonathon words were cut off by a rustling in the bushes about fifty yards away where the jungle met the beach.

"What was that?" Annie asked, her eyes wide.

Jonathon stared into the bushes for a long moment, watching and listening intently. "It didn't sound like anything big," he muttered, then went back to working on the rope.

Annie was unconvinced and she did her best to not blink. She kept her eyes focused on the bushes. Silas sensed her concern. "Sweetheart, it's alright. Everything is going to be alright. We'll be out of here in a few more minutes."

"Give me about fifteen," Jonathon corrected.

Annie frowned, but finally allowed herself to blink. She dropped her head down, her red hair dangling in front of her face. She wanted to believe that they would be alright. But somewhere deep down, she didn't.

The bushes rustled again and this time another *Parksosaurus* hopped out onto the beach. It began to make short little clicking sounds that sounded similar to a dolphin. It paid them no attention; it was as if they weren't even there.

"What is it doing?" Annie whispered, her eyes widening again.

Jonathon stopped moving for a second and studied the animal and the strange clicking noises.

"It's almost like it's calling a buddy or something," he said.

"Uh, you did say those are plant eaters," Silas stammered. "They eat plants...right?"

Jonathon began to work on the rope again and chuckled. "It won't bother us," he assured them. The rope was loosening more, and he was almost mobile enough to retrieve the knife.

Silas and Annie continued to watch the dinosaur when suddenly another one popped out of the trees. They both made more clicking sounds, this time much more frantic. Then just as quickly as the first one had popped out, four more appeared simultaneously.

"Jonathon, something is wrong," Silas said softly.

At that moment, all of the *Parksosauruses* took off in a furious sprint across the beach. The small dinosaurs had very muscular legs that propelled them across the sand quickly and with ease. Suddenly, dozens more of them began leaping out of the jungle, all of them clicking loudly.

Jonathon never ceased working on the rope; he was extremely close to getting them free. He gave the animals a glance and had a feeling he knew what was going on. *Something big is after them*, he thought.

Annie began crying and shook her head from side to side. She wasn't speaking, probably because she couldn't. She whimpered loudly and made no effort to disguise how terrified she was. The animals kept coming, and they all suddenly heard the sound of tree limbs snapping and popping within the jungle. Out of nowhere, a large tyrannosaur crashed through the trees and made its frightening presence known on the beach. The *Parksosauruses* continued to scramble away, but the tyrannosaur plucked one up off the beach with almost no effort. The animal squealed in pain as the larger dinosaur clamped its massive jaws down, instantly breaking the dinosaur's back. The tyrannosaur opened its jaws, allowing the crippled animal to drop on the beach, and then it wasted no time tearing the flesh from its body. The white sand under the *Parksosaurus* quickly turned red, and it actually surprised Jonathon to see just how much blood poured from the animal's body in such a short amount of time.

Annie glanced at the gore in the sand, then back up to the terrifying jaws that were responsible for it. She shook violently for a second, and then let out a blood-curdling scream.

"No! Don't scream," Jonathon pleaded.

The tyrannosaur stopped feasting for a moment and whipped its big head in Annie's direction. As it studied her, it looked at her the way a curious dog would, tilting its head sideways.

"Don't make another sound," Jonathon whispered. "And be still!"

Silas said nothing, probably too stunned to speak, although Jonathon could hear him breathing heavily. Finally, he had enough slack to move his arm, and he quickly slid the large knife from its sheath.

"I'm about to cut the rope, but when the rope drops, no one move until I tell you," he commanded. He waited for some sort of response, a nod, a shrug, a grunt...something. "This is very serious, did you two hear me? I need to know. I can't cut this rope and have one of you panicking and taking off across the beach. If you do that, you are dead meat. Do you two understand me?"

"Y-Yes, I d-do," Annie stuttered, barely in a whisper.

Silas glanced over at him, his face pale and ghostly. He didn't say a word, only nodded.

"Okay," Jonathon responded. "Here goes nothing." He placed the blade against the rope and gently slid it upward. The knife was extremely sharp and that was all it took. The rope fell on the sand, barely making a sound. Jonathon eyed the tyrannosaur carefully and breathed a sigh of relief as it apparently had lost interest in them and dropped its massive head back down into its meal. The whole animal was massive, much larger in real life than he could've ever imagined. He'd seen his share of reconstructed tyrannosaur skeletons in many museums, but seeing a real live one complete with muscle and skin made it much more intimidating. Its skin was a deep dark green; the hide along the animal's spine was so dark it was almost black. The belly was green also, but a lighter shade.

He studied the animal's eyes and took note at just how much it resembled a bird's eyes. Many paleontologists believed that dinosaurs evolved into birds; he was one of them. Seeing the tyrannosaur's eyes cemented his belief.

"Okay, we're going to move very slowly toward the trees," he said calmly. "No sudden movements and be as quiet as possible."

They both nodded at him and waited patiently for him to make the first move. Jonathon waited and watched the tyrannosaur tear more flesh from the *Parksosaurus*. He could literally hear a tearing sound as the dinosaur's teeth pulled meat loose from the bone. When he was certain that the animal was completely oblivious to their presence, he gingerly began to back away from the palm tree and into the more secure shadows the jungle provided. Silas still had enough presence of mind to allow his chivalrous side and he waited for Annie to move next. He held his breath and kept his eyes locked onto the tyrannosaur until it was his turn. Jonathon put a steady hand on Annie's shoulder and helped her into the dense foliage; the tension in his body was literally beginning to make his muscles ache. Annie kneeled down, and Jonathon put a finger over his mouth to remind her to be quiet. Silas looked over his shoulder to make sure that the other two were still there, then quickly swiveled his head back toward the tyrannosaur. He planted his feet on the ground very softly, doing his best not to snap any sticks or twigs as he walked backwards. He felt sweat rolling down his cheek and dripping off of his chin, but he still managed to keep his concentration on the dinosaur.

"Almost there," Jonathon whispered.

Silas took another step back and his heel caught a tree root hidden under a thin layer of sand. He wind-milled his arms around, desperately trying to keep his balance. It was no use, and he cringed as he fell backward to the earth. The harsh reality stung him immediately as he realized that when he hit the ground, the tyrannosaur would come charging. *How could I have been so careless?* he thought. He wanted to curse out loud, but refrained from doing so. Suddenly, he felt someone catch him under his arms, stopping him from striking the ground. He glanced over his shoulder and was relieved to see Jonathon struggling to hold him up.

"Nice catch, bud."

Jonathon gave a weak smile, and then gently allowed Silas to make contact with the ground.

"Gather yourself back up. We gotta get away from here fast," he said, still whispering.

The three of them stealthily made their way through the jungle until Jonathon was certain it was safe to stop and catch their collected breaths.

Annie fell to her hands and knees and began sobbing again, a great deal of hopelessness rained down with her tears.

Silas and Jonathon both kneeled down beside her and did their best to comfort her.

"It's alright, Annie. We're going to get out of here, but you've got to stay calm for me," Jonathon pleaded. He looked around making sure there weren't any more dinosaurs nearby. "We're safe now, please calm down."

She listened to him and nodded in agreement, but she couldn't help herself. She cried a few minutes longer until it seemed there weren't any more tears left for her to cry. Silas put an arm under her and took care in helping her up.

"It's gonna be alright, dear. We need to keep moving. Everything will be alright, you'll see," he said soothingly.

Jonathon shook his head. "Actually, I think we should wait here a moment," he said.

Silas frowned. "For what?"

"I just need a few more minutes to think. We've got to find a way to get you two back to the ship, but we can't exactly go back that way," he said, pointing in the direction of the tyrannosaur. He crossed his arms and stared at the ground, deep in thought. "Maybe we should just wait here for a while and give the tyrannosaur time to leave. I'll take you two back to the beach and see that you both get on the ship."

Silas grinned and pulled his shirt tail out of his shorts in an effort to find some comfort in the uncomfortable environment. "And just what do *you* plan on doing? You think you're gonna leave us on the ship and take off?"

Jonathon stared into his eyes. Silas read them and got the answer he needed. "Jonathon, you can't go after them. When we get on the ship, we'll radio for help."

"You're assuming Captain Blackstone and Denny aren't in on this," he shot back. "They both work for Angus Wedgeworth, don't forget that. Besides, we have no idea how long it'll take to get some help here. I've got to go after her. It's not a choice. There aren't any other options right now."

Silas took a breath. "Lucy will be fine. She's a tough girl. She knows these animals better than Angus does. He'll listen to what she says. He talks big, but he loves himself too much to do something that'll get himself killed."

Jonathon clenched his jaw and shook his head. "Okay, let's say you're right and he does listen to her. It doesn't matter. If a dinosaur wants to eat them, it is going to. The rifles they are carrying are nowhere near big enough to stop an animal the size of the one we just saw on the beach. They are very vulnerable out there. If anything happens to Lucy, I'll never forgive myself. The whole reason I came on this suicide trip was to look out for her and that is what I intend to do."

Silas stared at him and didn't have any idea what to say to convince him he was wrong. The unfortunate truth was that he was right. "Alright, I see there's no talking you out of this. If I were in your position, no one would be able to talk me out of it either," Silas said, conceding. "You're the boss; we'll wait around until you lead us out of here."

Jonathon smiled and was relieved that Silas understood. "Thanks." He walked over to Annie; she looked back at him, but there didn't seem to be much going on behind her tired green eyes. "Annie, I promise you I'll get you out of here."

She licked her lips and nodded slowly. "I need another beer," she said, her voice hoarse.

Jonathon smiled and put an arm around her, squeezing her shoulder tightly. "There is still plenty of that on the ship for you to drink when we get there," he responded with a chuckle.

CHAPTER 15

Travis slashed through the dense vegetation with a machete and led the others single file through the path he cleared. Osvaldo and Lucy were immediately behind him with Angus closely following. Armando walked ahead of Frank, visibly shaken by the fact that Frank kept a rifle pointed at him the entire time. They'd been travelling for about half an hour and none of them had said a word since they'd left the others at the beach. The only sound was the occasional bird chirping, or some squeaks and groans from some of the smaller dinosaurs scurrying nearby.

Lucy didn't know whether to feel fear or anger at her current predicament. Perhaps anger was the better option and who better to direct it to than herself? Jonathon had practically begged her not to go on this trip. He told her that Angus was a man that couldn't be trusted. She didn't listen to him and now she found herself in an extremely dangerous situation. And if that wasn't bad enough, she also felt tremendous guilt and responsibility for Jonathon's life. It should've been her tied to a tree and left for dead. It was her reckless decision that led to the both of them being there. Deep down, she told herself that he would find a way to get loose, but there was still a nagging feeling that reminded her she may never seem him again. That terrified her more than meat-eating dinosaurs. She wanted to do something to make things right. But how could she? As they walked through the jungle, Angus held a gun firmly against the small of her back. She noticed that Osvaldo seemed to be leading them. He occasionally stopped, looked around, and pointed in a direction that they should go. No one ever questioned him and it was almost as if they were heading somewhere specific. She was beginning to think that there was something else on the island driving Angus besides dinosaurs. She couldn't help but notice how little the *Parksosaurus* excited him when they all saw it. For a man suddenly so obsessed with dinosaurs, he sure seemed unimpressed. Ever since they set foot on the island, very little that happened made any sense.

"You think I'm an evil man, don't you?" Angus suddenly asked from behind her, seemingly reading her thoughts.

"Yes I do," she snapped. "Maybe if you'd get that gun out of my back I'd reconsider."

The old man let out a chuckle. "If I remove the gun, you may try and run. I wouldn't want anything to happen to you. I'd feel responsible."

She rolled her eyes. "You can't be serious. You're keeping a gun on me to keep me safe? That makes perfect sense," she said sarcastically. To her surprise, Angus pulled the gun away from her. She stopped and looked back at him.

"You're right, it doesn't make a lot of sense, does it?" he said.

She arched an eyebrow at him, unsure about what to say. Travis took the opportunity to stop a moment and rest. He slumped over and put both hands on his knees, sweat dripping off his head.

Angus reached out and put a hand on Lucy's shoulder. "My dear, I didn't mean for things to happen this way. Really, I didn't. Things got out of control quickly and I had to make some difficult decisions."

Lucy slapped his hand off of her shoulder. "You're crazy," she hissed. "Listen to yourself! You sound completely ridiculous. You're kidnapping us, Angus!" she screamed.

The old man smiled at her nervously. "Lucy, I'm quite sure that Jonathon will be fine. From what we've observed, most of the larger, more dangerous dinosaurs forage throughout the heart of the island. The smaller plant-eaters are more numerous along the borders."

She crossed her arms and shook her head. "Gee, that makes me feel so much better, thanks," she replied, her words once again dripping sarcasm. She eyed Angus's right arm, extended downward along his side, the gun still gripped tightly in his hand. *If I can just get him to relax a little bit more...* she thought.

"Boss, Osvaldo seems a bit confused about where to go next," Travis said from up ahead.

Angus looked past Lucy. "What? We've just started," he mumbled as he walked past her. He shook his head. "We don't have time for this," he growled, as he approached Osvaldo.

Lucy remained still and immediately looked over to see where Frank was. He watched with interest as Angus began yelling at Osvaldo. Lucy didn't even know what Angus was yelling about, but she didn't care. All she knew was that if she was going to make a run for it, now was the time. She looked to her right and surveyed the landscape ahead, searching for any difficult obstacles that may prevent her from escaping. Although the foliage was thick, outside of a few vines there was very little she could see that would present a problem. She glanced back at Frank, then up at Angus and Travis. All three were paying her no attention. *Now or never*, she thought and suddenly she was off. She ran into the shroud of leafy plants and tore through anything and everything in her path. She felt a thin vine tear into her leg, but it did little to slow her down. Angus called after her and soon she heard someone pursuing her. She assumed it was Travis, but it really didn't matter. She'd ran as fast as her body could manage and had very quickly put some distance between herself and whoever was chasing her. She noticed that the plants and trees thinned out a bit ahead. Quickly, she decided it would be better to duck and hide than to take a chance and run into the open where she could be seen. She dove to the ground and held her breath. A few seconds later, she heard her pursuer huffing and puffing his way to where she was. She remained deadly still and glanced up at Travis as he jogged by completely oblivious to the fact that she was a mere six feet from him. He ran right by and didn't stop. She waited until she heard his footsteps fade away into the distance; only then she felt comfortable enough to move again. When she did she moved in a completely different direction from where Travis had gone and from where Angus and Frank were. She decided she'd move back in the direction of the beach, basically parallel to the path Travis had cut through the jungle earlier. Although she was out of breath and her side ached, she knew stopping at this point simply wasn't an option. She estimated that if they'd walked for half an hour from the beach, then surely if she ran she could cover the distance in at least fifteen minutes. She hadn't gone far before she realized that it would be impossible to get there as quickly as she wanted. The jungle seemed to be working against her as the plants became more and more abrasive and prickly. She carefully maneuvered her way through a patch of briars and was pleasantly surprised to find a clearing on the other side. A large, oddly shaped tree trunk rested in the center and as much as her heart told her to keep going, the old tree was just too inviting to pass up. It was a perfect place for a short rest. She stumbled toward the log, and when she got within twenty feet of it, the tree suddenly stood up on four stubby legs. She gasped, clearly startled, then the realization set in that the log wasn't actually a log at all.

"*Ankylosaurus*," she gawked, in awe at the massive, twenty-foot-long armored dinosaur with the clubbed tail. *Ankylosaurus* looked just as most paleontologists had imagined. Its back was knobby and rough, very similar to that of a crocodile, but on a much larger scale. Lucy doubted if a bullet would even be able to penetrate it. The dinosaur was five feet wide and dark brown in color, its head, small and triangular. The tail was long, with a bony club at the end of it used as a defensive weapon. As she caught sight of the tail, she felt a chill hit her when she suddenly realized how close she was to the massive animal. She held her breath and began to ease her way back. The *Ankylosaurus* turned its small head toward her and let out a deep groan that made her guts vibrate. She tried her best not to look afraid, but it was quickly becoming harder to hide as the dinosaur suddenly turned to face her and dug its claws into the ground, kicking up dirt in the air behind it. It looked as it if it was going to charge at her.

"Easy, boy," she stammered. "I'm leaving. Sorry I bothered you." She wasn't afraid the *Ankylosaurus* would eat her because it was a herbivore but, that didn't mean it couldn't kill her. She eyed the bony, clubbed tail and imagined it slamming into her, breaking every rib in her body. The broken ribs would be bad enough, but it would probably also turn all of her internal organs to gelatin. She closed her eyes and tried her best to shake the unpleasant thoughts out of her head. She took another step back, but it seemed every time she took a step, the animal became more agitated. It eyed her for a moment more and pawed at the ground, as if it were daring her to try and run. When it decided she wasn't going to move, it charged at her moaning like a bull all the way. She screamed and turned to flee, knowing that would be her only shot at survival. The *Ankylosaurus* was surprisingly fast and it ran ahead of her, cutting off her escape. She flinched as the dinosaur drew its massive clubbed tail back, and suddenly it swung low at her. She dove just beyond the tail's reach, feeling a gust of wind as it flew by her. Lucy scrambled back on her feet and immediately began running again, screaming all the way. To her horror, the last thing she expected to see tore through the trees ahead of her, another *Ankylosaurus*, and this one just as large and just as aggressive. She looked over her shoulder and knew running back the other direction would be useless as the other one quickly closed in behind her. She came to an abrupt stop and knew she'd have to run a different way, but she wasn't sure she wanted to. A tear rolled down her cheek as she knew running would only delay the inevitable. *There was no way she could outrun both of them.* She put her hands over her face and screamed loudly, the two dinosaurs began wailing at her, and if she didn't know any better, they seemed to be taunting her.

As she stood, eyes closed and hands over her face, she waited for the crushing blow to end her life. The blow never came. Instead, a thunderous boom echoed loudly behind her and the two dinosaurs fled, wailing like a couple of large scolded dogs as they ran. Lucy peeled her hands away from her face and opened her eyes, relief overcoming her body like a cool drink of water. She looked over her shoulder and spotted Frank standing in the shadows of an oak tree, the barrel of the rifle smoking in his hands. He said nothing, but he motioned for her to come to him with the barrel of the gun. She reluctantly did, knowing that unfortunately she would be much safer with the armed bad guys than she would be alone with the dinosaurs.

CHAPTER 16

"That was a gunshot," Jonathon said softly. He was unable to hide the worry in his voice after the crack of a gunshot echoed loudly somewhere deep in the jungle.

Silas took a step in the direction of the sound. He too was worried, but there was no way he was going to let Jonathon know it. "I know what you're thinking, Jonathon, so do yourself a favor and stop thinking that way right this instant," he said, desperately trying to keep his new friend calm.

Annie stood nearby, still silent as she had been for quite a while. She kept her arms cross and stared at the ground. Silas wondered if she was beginning to be overtaken with shock.

Jonathon adjusted his hat and rubbed some tension out of the back of his neck. "Silas, there isn't one good thing that could've come out of having to fire a weapon," he said somberly. "Either those thugs shot someone, or a dinosaur attacked them and they had to shoot at it. I'm certainly hoping it's the latter so at least Lucy, Osvaldo, and Armando have a chance."

"It was only one shot," Silas said.

"Yeah, that's what worries me. It would only take one shot to kill a person, but it would take several to kill most of these dinosaurs." Jonathon felt a knot tighten in his stomach as he imagined Lucy being shot in the head. He closed his eyes and bit his lip. It was a weak moment for him, probably the weakest one he'd experienced since arriving on the wretched island. He was concerned for a moment that he might cry and that was the last thing he wanted to do. Annie was already upset enough; he had to keep a strong face to keep her calm. Desperately, he searched inside himself for answers. He didn't know what to do. He flinched as a soft hand gripped him firmly on the shoulder. He turned and found that it was Annie; her gorgeous face suddenly looked older and tired. She still managed to supply a fake smile, and he knew it was solely to keep his hopes up.

"Don't give up," she whispered. "I need you to hang in there."

He grabbed her and hugged her tightly in an effort to reassure her she would be alright. "Silas, I'm sorry, but the plans have changed. You're going to lead her out of here, but I'm not going with you," he said, his voice suddenly strong again.

Silas nodded. "When I get her to the ship, I'm coming back to find you," he replied.

"I'd rather you didn't."

"I really don't care how you feel about it," Silas answered sternly.

Jonathon smiled. "Alright, suit yourself. You two be careful."

Silas grabbed Annie around the shoulder and the two began to walk back in the direction of the beach. Jonathon turned and began walking deeper into the jungle. He had taken no more than ten steps when the deafening roar of the tyrannosaur rang out again from the direction of the beach. He spun around on his heel. Silas and Annie were already rushing toward him.

"Jonathon, I'm sorry, but the plans have changed again," Silas muttered. "It's not safe to go back to the beach yet."

Jonathon stood silent a moment, thinking.

"We're going with you," Annie said abruptly.

Jonathon and Silas looked at her simultaneously. Annie suddenly seemed alert and awake again.

"I've never been so scared in my life," she said. "But I'm going to put my big girl pants on and be tough for you guys." She wiped tears away from her eyes and took a deep breath. Suddenly, she seemed much more composed than she had moments earlier. Perhaps it was because she had accepted the fact she wasn't getting out of there as soon as she wanted. Maybe it was because she felt that she was being selfish. Whatever the reason, Jonathon was grateful for her new attitude.

"We're going to find another way to get to the beach," he told her. "We'll get you out of here as soon as possible."

"I know you will," she said. "You lead and I'll be right behind you."

Silas threw his large arm around her neck and squeezed gently. "That's the spirit, honey," he said. "We'll all get out of here, you wait and see."

Jonathon motioned for them to follow, and he once again began marching forward through the foliage. He longed for a machete, but he hacked and sliced his way with his knife the best he could. Occasionally, a small cat-sized dinosaur would scurry away from them and it wasn't long before they hardly noticed them anymore. It seemed the further they went, the darker the jungle became. All of the plants were damp and the humidity made the trek miserable. Countless insects, some they'd never seen, buzzed around them. Some of the strange insects bit them. Silas asked Jonathon if they were dangerous. He lied and said that they weren't. The truth was that he simply didn't know. There were probably countless insects from the Cretaceous Period that no one knew anything about. And the ones they did know about, it was next to impossible to be able to tell if they were dangerous.

"What do you think Angus is up to?" Jonathon asked Silas.

"Well, I don't know about you, but I'm starting to wonder if the old man has done gone senile on us," he muttered in response.

Jonathon shook his head as he hacked the knife at a stubborn vine. "I don't think he's gone senile. But I do think there is something else going on. He sure is taking some extreme measures to get some pictures of some dinosaurs."

"Yeah, but think of the money he's gonna get for the pictures," Silas said.

"But that's just it. The man has millions of dollars. He doesn't have any reason to kidnap people and put their lives in danger to make some money. He already has plenty of money," he replied. "And if it was all about taking pictures, then why didn't he take her along?" he said, pointing at Annie. "She's the professional photographer."

Annie frowned. "And I'm his niece. I just don't understand how he could be so coldhearted and leave me for dead," she said.

"He's a jerk, Annie," Silas said gruffly. "I thought he was a friend, but apparently I was wrong too. You don't need that guy and neither do I. We'll have the last laugh, you'll see."

Annie was about to respond when she and Silas suddenly noticed Jonathon stop abruptly. Then they looked around either side of him and realized why. They'd reached the end of the jungle and a wide valley stretched out across the earth ahead of them. The view resembled something you'd see on the plains of Africa. The tall grass whispered as a cool and steady breeze blew across it. But it wasn't the valley that made the three of them awestruck. It was the numerous herds of dinosaurs roaming and feeding on the plain that grabbed their undivided attention.

"Wow," Silas said, his jaw dropped. "This is amazing."

"Angus showed me some pictures of this area they'd taken from an airplane," Jonathon said. "The pictures don't do this place justice at all. I've studied dinosaur bones my entire life and always wondered how close many of the theories in the paleontology community would be to the way these animals actually lived. I never dreamed that we'd ever know for sure, yet here I am. I'm seeing it with my own two eyes."

There was a large group of *Triceratops* marching like a herd of elephants on the south end of the valley. Jonathon estimated that some of them were thirty feet in length and ten feet tall. Their scaly skin was gray with dark spots speckled across their backs. The frills on top of their heads resembled crowns and added to their majestic presence. The horns were fiercely intimidating and he couldn't imagine many dinosaurs picking a fight with the heavily armored, yet peaceful herbivores. He smiled as he watched the young ones cling closely alongside their mothers, who were no doubt scanning the landscape closely for predators.

Jonathon then directed his attention toward the center of the valley where a great lake glistened in the grey light that filtered through the thick mist across the sky. A large group of *Gallimimus*, perhaps more than a hundred, gathered near the water's edge to drink. They stood on two legs, the adults roughly six feet tall. Their skin also was gray. He couldn't be sure due to the distance, but they also appeared to have light tufts of feathers along the center of their backs covering the spine. In a lot of ways they resembled ostriches, further fueling the increasingly popular belief that many dinosaurs evolved into birds. At one end of the lake, a small stream branched out and led into the jungle a few hundred yards from where they were standing. Jonathon suspected that if they could make it to that stream, it would provide an easy path back to the beach.

"They look like big cows," Annie said softly, pointing toward the grazing herd of *Triceratops*.

Jonathon kneeled down and chuckled. "Yeah, I guess they kind of do," he agreed.

"Will they hurt us?" she asked.

"They *can* hurt us, but they won't if we don't bother them," he answered. "Let's head over to that stream and make our way back to the beach. We'll come out south of where we saw the tyrannosaur. We should be able to sneak up on it and turn back if it's still out there."

"Good idea," Annie said. "You ready, Silas?"

Silas didn't answer and Jonathon stopped and turned to look at him. He was staring intently toward the wood line at the northeast corner of the valley. "Do you see that?" he asked, pointing a chubby finger.

Jonathon squinted and soon saw what he was looking at. He could barely make out six people walking in a single-file line. Although the distance made them look tiny, Jonathon managed to make out Lucy and he breathed a sigh of relief. Angus was close behind her and he suspected the old man had a gun against the small of her back. Nevertheless, she was alive, and at this point, that was all that mattered.

"They're all alive," Jonathon whispered. "Thank God, they're all alive."

"I told you," Silas said, smiling. "That girl can take care of herself. Angus needs her and he'd be putting himself in jeopardy by killing her."

"Yeah, there's no doubt that she talked them into staying along the wood line instead of venturing out across the open valley where a carnivore could easily get them. Thank God they're listening to her. I'm still not going to be comfortable until I get her back though," he replied. "And don't forget about Osvaldo and Armando. They shouldn't be out there either."

"None of us should be out here," Annie said softly.

Jonathon peered back at her and remembered the task at hand. He had to get her back to *Bethany*. Captain Blackstone and Denny would be able to protect her there. He would still try to persuade Silas to stay there also, but he knew it would be useless. Part of him was grateful for that.

"Okay, let's get going. The sooner we get Annie back to the ship, the sooner I can go back after Lucy," Jonathon said, and he began marching along the wood line toward the stream.

As they went along, suddenly Annie became very chatty and began giving them her life story. Both of them pretended to be interested, but Jonathon spent most of his time scanning the jungle for carnivorous dinosaurs. He tolerated her talking for a little while because he knew that it was her way of coping with her fear. As they drew nearer to the stream, he began to feel uneasy and asked her politely to be quiet. She abruptly snapped her mouth shut and jumped behind Silas, expecting something to jump out of the jungle. Jonathon crept closer and closer to the stream, and suddenly, he heard a very large splash. It was definitely larger than a fish. He quickly reached for his knife.

"Stay back," he whispered to them, and they promptly obeyed.

He crouched down and slowly made his way behind a large oak tree near the stream. He peeked around the corner and was astonished at what he saw. There was a pair of eight-foot-tall, two-legged dinosaurs drinking from the stream. He estimated from nose to tail they were about twenty or twenty-two feet long. He bit his lip and thought hard as he tried to identify them. He caught a glimpse of a tiny horn protruding from the very top of the dinosaur's skull, and suddenly, he knew what they were. *Majungasaurus*, he thought. *Carnivore*. At the moment, it appeared that they had no idea that he was nearby. He decided not to push his luck. As he turned to head back, his boot inadvertently stepped on a stick. It snapped loudly in the silent jungle and both dinosaurs stood straight up and peered in his direction. Jonathon began to slowly back away, doing his best to remain calm. But when the dinosaurs began to approach, he knew the only thing left to do was run. He ran as fast as he could toward Silas and Annie. Annie saw him coming, and when she saw the first *Majungasaurus* tear out of the bushes, she opened her mouth to scream. Silas abruptly slapped his hand over her mouth and threw his other arm around her waist. He quickly dragged her to the ground behind a nearby fallen tree. He wanted to help Jonathon, but didn't know how he could.

Jonathon saw Silas drag Annie with him behind the log, but didn't even give them a glance as he ran past. He could hear both *Majungasauruses* behind him, and for the first time, he felt panic. There was no way he would be able to outrun them and he knew it. Stopping was not an option either so he kept running. He scanned the environment for something to protect him. He found nothing. Suddenly, his foot caught a rock and he tumbled painfully to the ground. He scrambled to get to his feet, but stumbled again. He rolled over on his back to face the dinosaurs as his inevitable death loomed extremely near. Both dinosaurs were already at him, but to his shock and surprise, they ran past him, paying him no attention at all. He looked on in disbelief as both dinosaurs ran into the nearby herd of *Gallimimuses* drinking at the pool at the end of the stream. They found a sickly one and ripped it apart as the rest of the herd fled.

Jonathon watched the carnage and breathed a sigh of relief as he realized and accepted that he wasn't going to die just yet.

"Buddy, you alright?" he heard Silas's panicked voice ask.

He stood up and dusted the sand off his pants. "I'm alright," he said. "They clearly lost interest in me. Guess I didn't look very appetizing."

The three of them stood silently and watched the two dinosaurs quickly devour the *Gallimimus*. When they began to polish off a few bones, Annie turned and threw up in the nearby brush.

"That's disgusting," she said, heaving. "Can we please leave?"

Jonathon patted her on the back as she continued to kneel over the bushes, coughing and gagging. "Let's go," he said smiling.

CHAPTER 17

Jonathon led Silas and Annie along the bank of the stream with care. Each step he took made soft contact with the ground and the others followed his example. The soft dirt along the edges of the stream made the task easy. Jonathon did what he learned very quickly was vital to survival on the island. He listened. Fortunately, the only sounds he heard was the frequent cascades in the stream, and the pleasant soft sounds of the ocean breeze flowing effortlessly through the trees and bushes nearby. A lot of insects buzzed about the stream, more than they'd encountered anywhere else on the island thus far. He suspected they were some form of mosquito, but he couldn't be sure. They were tiny and very annoying, but he paid them little attention. *It's not the bugs that can kill you*, he thought.

He glanced back at Annie and expected to see her in a miserable state. He was pleasantly surprised to see that she was in much better spirits than she was earlier. Apparently, her behavior hours earlier was, at least in part, a direct result of the stress they'd all endured. It's not every day that a person wakes up with a hangover, sees real live dinosaurs, is taken hostage at gun point, then tied to a tree and left for the dinosaurs to eat. Those were all the things Annie had experienced, and mentally, she was overloaded. That was the nice way to put it. Most people would just say she went nutty for a little while.

"It can't be much farther," Jonathon said in almost a whisper, trying to keep their spirits up.

Annie smiled in response; Silas remained serious and just as focused as Jonathon. They approached a slight bend in the stream, and as they rounded the corner, another surprising sight laid across the stream.

"What in the world is that thing?" Silas asked, scratching his head.

Jonathon cautiously approached the large tan-colored dinosaur. It appeared to be dead.

"It's a sauropod, not totally sure which kind though," he whispered. "I can't believe there are sauropods here too."

Silas could hear the wonder in the paleontologist's voice and then he visibly saw it when he noticed a smile crack Jonathon's face. "This thing's got to be thirty-five or forty feet long," he said. "What do sauropods eat?"

Jonathon's smile widened. It was becoming quite amusing that the common first question when they encountered new dinosaurs was: "What do they eat?"

"If I had to guess, I'd say this is a *Saltasaurus*. All of the dinosaurs here seem to be from the Cretaceous Period." He paused a moment and turned to look at Silas and Annie. "But to answer your question, it's an herbivore. Furthermore, it's dead so we don't have to worry." Suddenly, a look of panic and fear simultaneously spread over Annie and Silas's faces. They weren't looking at him anymore, they were looking past him. Behind him.

"Do we have to worry about that one?" Annie asked, pointing.

Jonathon spun around on his heel and once again jerked the knife out of its sheath. He immediately recognized the new dinosaur standing atop the belly of the *Saltasaurus*. *Dromaeosaurus*. He had been on a dig in Montana once and had personally helped extract a large chunk of rock containing a nearly complete fossilized skeleton of *Dromaeosaurus*. The animal was relatively small, about the size of a wolf. It had a lot of blue-and-red feathers on it; its arms almost looked like wings except for the claws on the end of each arm. There were more feathers on the *Dromaeosaurus* than any other dinosaur he'd seen on the island. The legs looked powerful, and he quickly remembered that this was an animal known for its quickness. It was about six feet long, and as the animal hissed at him, he caught sight of a mouthful of dagger-like teeth. Hunks of flesh, dripping with blood hung from the animal's lower jaw.

"Yeah, we gotta worry about this one," Jonathon said. He felt his pulse quicken. "I think we interrupted his lunch."

"Well, what do we do?" Silas asked, as Annie darted behind him.

"We're going to slowly walk backward," Jonathon said, doing his best to sound calm. He immediately began taking steps back, and Silas and Annie did the same.

The animal hissed loudly again and began thrashing its tail back and forth like an angry cat.

"Are you sure we should keep moving?" Silas asked.

Jonathon felt sweat trickle into his eye and burn, but he resisted the urge to raise an arm and wipe it away. "We don't have a choice, Silas," he answered through clenched teeth. "I mean, if you'd rather s—"

Jonathon's words were cut off abruptly as the dinosaur unexpectedly lunged off the dead *Saltasaurus* and crashed into him. He fell on his back and let out a yelp as the animal dug its claws into his stomach. *Dromaeosaurus* possessed a sharp 'sickle' claw on each foot similar to the ones found on a *Velociraptor*. He felt the sickle claw dig deeper into his flesh and cringed as he thought of his insides spilling out of his belly and onto the ground. Fortunately, he still clutched the large hunting knife and he drove it hard in between the dinosaur's ribs. *Dromaeosaurus* let out a shrill sound of utter pain and instantly released its grip. As it retreated away from him, he pulled the knife out and hot, sticky blood poured out over his arm. The animal ran away and disappeared into the jungle wailing the whole way.

Silas and Annie rushed over to Jonathon and knelt over him. Annie began sobbing again, expecting the worst.

"Are you alright?" Her already swollen and reddened eyes barely produced tears.

The truth was he wasn't sure if he was alright or not. He sat up and tore open his top shirt, buttons flying everywhere. The white undershirt was all red around the bottom. He frantically pulled the shirt up and examined his wounds.

"Hold still," Silas said calmly as he retrieved a white handkerchief from a cargo pocket on his shorts. He took the cloth and slowly wiped away blood from one of the wounds. "It's only punctures," he said. "Can't tell how deep though."

"I don't think it's too deep," Jonathon grunted. He took the shirt he ripped off and applied direct pressure to the wound on his right side. Annie quickly took off her over shirt and did the same on his left side.

"It stings a little, but I'm fine."

"If you didn't have that knife, you'd be in big trouble right now," Silas said. He threw the now red hanky aside and began washing his bloody hands off in the stream.

Jonathon breathed a sigh of relief as it became more and more apparent he was going to be alright. "Thanks for the concern, guys," he said thoughtfully.

"You're our ticket out of here. Of course we're concerned for your safety," Silas answered with a wink.

Jonathon used the blood-soaked shirts as a temporary bandage to keep the dirt and insects out of his wounds. Annie helped him back on his feet, and they continued along the stream without further incident. When they finally arrived at the beach, Jonathon took a deep breath of fresh Atlantic air. It was refreshing and seemed to give him a much-needed boost of energy. The wall of mist was still present several hundred yards into the water.

"Where is the ship? I don't see the ship," Annie said, cupping a hand over her eyes.

There wasn't a lot of sunlight, but it was still much brighter on the beach than it had been under the canopy of the jungle.

"The ship is up the beach, not as far as you probably think," Jonathon said assuringly. "Right now, I'm more interested in that," he said, pointing in the direction of a large black shipping container planted solidly in the sand.

"That's gotta be the container Angus was looking for," Silas said.

Jonathon nodded. "The ATVs have got to be in there."

The three of them rushed over to the container. Jonathon arrived first and frowned when he saw a large shiny padlock on the door. Frustrated, he grabbed the lock and slammed it against the door.

"A four-wheeler would be extremely useful out here. We could get Annie to the ship quickly and I'd be able to find Lucy much faster than I could on foot."

"Well, just hold on a minute," Silas replied. He padded back across the beach searching the ground, and then he knelt down and dug up a large rock. "Maybe we can break it off," he said as he returned.

Jonathon gave him a skeptical glance, but said nothing.

Silas raised the rock high above his head. "Stand back!" He drove the rock forcefully against the lock and the metal container clanged loudly with the impact. The sound literally echoed across the beach. The lock received a minor scuff, but still remained very much intact. Silas gave it another blow and then another. The lock held. Again, he struck the lock and again the sound of clanging metal echoed loudly across the beach and into the jungle.

"This isn't working," Jonathon said. He scanned the area to see if any curious dinosaurs were coming to investigate the noise.

Silas seemed to ignore him and he hit the lock again, determined to break it loose.

"It's not working," he repeated. "Stop before all the racket leads that tyrannosaur back over to us."

Silas frowned. "Sorry, I tried," he said, panting.

Jonathon gave him a pat on the back. "I know; you gave it a good try. Now let's get out of here, I suddenly don't feel very safe here anymore. The sooner we find the ship, the better."

Jonathon led them back near the tree line so they could at least remain partially hidden in the shadows as they walked. He felt some concern about walking so closely to the tree line. A dinosaur could easily sneak up on them within the shroud of the jungle, but he felt much safer there than he would out on the open beach for the tyrannosaur to easily spot them. After about ten minutes of walking, they finally spotted the silhouette of *Bethany*, the mist serving as an eerie backdrop behind her. Thankfully, the small boat still rested where they'd last seen it on the edge of the beach. Annie jumped in the boat while Silas and Jonathon hurriedly shoved off from the beach. Then they too jumped into the boat. Jonathon fell awkwardly into the boat and the wounds on his belly quickly reminded him of they were still there. He winced as the sharp pain tore across him and he placed a firm hand on his right side desperately trying to ease the pain. Silas started the engine and steered the boat toward the ship and the ladder that hung over her hull. As they drew close, Annie began to shout at the captain out of pure jubilation. Jonathon felt some weight off of his shoulders when he realized he'd gotten her back in one piece. But no sooner had a small sense of relief set in, it was quickly replaced with a very uneasy feeling. As he peered up at the ship looming ahead of them, something felt wrong.

"Where are they?" Annie asked. "Can't they hear me?"

"Maybe they're busy," Silas said.

Annie crossed her arms nervously. "Doing what? The ship hasn't moved since we left it this morning."

As the boat drifted to the ladder, Jonathon clenched his teeth and forced himself to get up. The pain in his belly was getting worse, but he had to ignore it.

"You two wait here a minute," he said. "I'm going to climb aboard and make sure it's safe first." He turned to grab a rung on the ladder when Silas tugged his arm away.

"You're a stubborn man, has anyone ever told you that?" he asked. "You're already hurt. Sit back down, I'll climb up and check it out."

Jonathon shook his head. "No, Silas. I appreciate it, but I'll take care of it."

Silas stared at him without blinking. A stern disapproving look spread across his wrinkled face.

Jonathon smiled, trying to lighten the tension. "More than likely they're just asleep or something. I'm sure it's no big deal. But just to be on the safe side, I'm going to go have a look first. You need to stay here with Annie. If something was to happen down here, I probably wouldn't be much good busted up the way that I am. She'll be safer with you."

Silas took the bush hat off of his head and raked his fingers through his blond hair. "I still think I should go," he snorted. "Just hurry up!"

"I will," Jonathon answered back, and then quickly ascended up the ladder.

When he reached the deck, he immediately began shouting out for Captain Blackstone and Denny. Neither one of them responded and a sick feeling began to overcome him. He decided to check the bridge, and on the way there, he noticed a dark, almost black, streak of some sort of liquid across the steel surface of the deck. He took his right foot and rubbed the toe of his shoe near the edge of the thick liquid. The spot he disturbed thinned out and suddenly displayed a reddish tint. Jonathon gasped and took a step back as his initial suspicion was confirmed. It was blood. He forced himself to follow the thick trail of blood along the deck until he found himself behind a large wooden crate. What he found there made him grimace and that response was followed by gagging. There was very little left of Denny's midsection. His rib cage remained, bits of purple and pink strips of meat hung from the bone. There was practically nothing beyond that. In fact, his midsection was so hollowed out it was easy to see the bones in Denny's back including his spinal column. Jonathon noticed injuries to the young man's arms and especially his fingers. He winced as he realized the poor guy was alive when he was being eaten. *He literally fought for his life and lost.* Perhaps the most horrifying part of the grisly scene was the part of Denny's body that had seemingly remained untouched: his head. The expression on his face gave Jonathon a very unsettling vision of his last moment of life. His mouth was gaped open, a scream of pain and terror no doubt spilled from it. His eyes were wide, so wide in fact that they almost didn't look real. His last moment was one of sheer agony. Jonathon grabbed his stomach and fell to his knees. The urge to throw up was overwhelming, but somehow he fought it off. *Get on your feet,* he thought as a sudden revelation occurred to him. *Whatever did this to Denny may still be on board.*

He sprang to his feet and whipped his head around to look behind him. Fortunately, nothing was there. He called out to Captain Blackstone again. There was still no response.

"You alright up there?" Silas's muffled voice shouted from down below, port side.

"Yes," he answered, trying his best to sound calm. "Don't come up here."

He closed his eyes for a second trying to figure out what to do. As he thought, a loud shrill pierced through the sky above him. He glanced up and saw the silhouette of a large flying reptile swooping toward him. The massive pterosaur had a wingspan of nearly thirty feet. He stumbled backwards, surprised and terrified at the same time. He landed on his bottom and scrambled to regain his footing. The pterosaur released another bone-chilling shrill and glided at him with lightning speed. He felt a gust of wind as the large animal thrust its wings back and forth just before it touched down. Jonathon failed to get on his feet and decided to roll out of the way instead. The move was successful, but there was no time to breathe a sigh of relief. The huge reptile suddenly drew its head backward, and then thrust its long, slender beak forward like a spear straight at him. He jumped back again, barely missing the attack. The pterosaur locked its beady eyes on him and wasted no time going after him again. The animal opened its beak and clamped down on his leg, tugging him backward. Jonathon reached down and scrambled to get his knife. The pterosaur had no teeth, but the edges of the beak were still razor sharp. He felt his calf muscle slice open; fortunately, he was too frightened to feel the pain. The beak tugged at him again, forcing him to fall onto his back. He watched, terrified, as the reptile loomed over him, drawing its head back yet again. He imagined Silas finding his body in much the same way he discovered Denny's. He knew the pterosaur was about to thrust its hungry beak into his belly if he didn't react quickly. The animal's head fell forward and Jonathon met it swiftly with his knife straight through the bottom of the reptile's skull. He closed his eyes and held the knife firmly in place a long moment to make sure the job was done. The animal shook for a brief moment, and then fell limp. Blood flowed heavily over his hand and down his arm, soaking his shirt sleeve along the way. The blade had penetrated all the way through and the tip of the blade protruded out of the top of the skull. It was a brief struggle to work the knife back out of the animal's head, and as soon as he did, he returned to his feet and looked to the sky yet again. His jaw dropped as he saw three more pterosaurs circling above. He instantly crouched down and placed his back against the crate where he'd found Denny. Suddenly, he thought of Silas and Annie.

"Silas, get that boat back to shore," he shouted.

"Not without you, get down here," he yelled back.

"If I go down there, those birds may chase me and kill us all. It's not worth the chance. Get back to the island, I'll figure something out."

There was a moment of silence. Silas was apparently mulling it over. Finally, he responded, making no attempt to hide his displeasure. "Okay, I'll take Annie to shore. I'm gonna give you ten minutes and I'm coming back for you."

Jonathon rolled his eyes and knew it was useless to try and argue. "Okay, get going. I'll be there in ten minutes," he reluctantly agreed.

He waited until he heard the boat buzzing loudly back to shore. He took a breath and glanced upward again, the pterosaurs still swarmed above. *What are they waiting on?* He took a breath and decided his best bet was to run toward the bridge for protection. He prayed the door would be open, and when he found the courage to run for the bridge, he was relieved to find that it was. He slammed the door shut and put his back against it, sliding slowly to the floor. As the ship rocked gently in eerie silence, another terrifying sight caught his eye. Straight ahead of him, about twenty feet away, another body was facedown and lifeless on the floor. Captain Blackstone's remains were in much better condition that his first mate. He'd apparently been attacked but managed to escape into the bridge, dying of his mortal wounds shortly after. A dark, crimson pool of blood circled his body and the thick liquid gleamed in the light from the large windows at the front of the bridge. Jonathon grimaced at the realization that already two lives had been taken due to the negligence of Angus Wedgeworth.

Suddenly, a loud *thud* echoed above his head. A second later, a loud screech rang out and Jonathon felt his heart begin pounding again. He remained deadly silent; however, he couldn't help but wonder how much that actually mattered. *That thing knows I'm in here. It'll wait as long as necessary for me to come out.* He weighed his options and realized there were very few to be weighed. In fact, the more he thought about it, the more he liked the idea of just sitting there and seeing just how long the pterosaur would be willing to wait. He peered around at his surroundings. He highly doubted the animal could get in there with him. The windows at the front of the bridge could be broken out, but as large as the pterosaur was, he felt certain there would be no way it could get in. He'd all but made up his mind when another horrifying realization hit him like cruel slap in the face. He glanced at his watch. *Silas is going to come back for me any moment!* Waiting it out simply wasn't an option anymore. He crawled over to the nearest window and quietly raised his head just enough to peek out. There was a slight shroud of mist between the boat and the beach but it wasn't enough to blot out his view. He breathed a sigh of relief as he caught sight of the boat still at the edge of the beach and then of Silas and Annie watching intensely. Unfortunately, he knew it wouldn't last long. Silas would keep his word and he would no doubt attempt to come after him. Jonathon hoped that Silas could see the large pterosaur on the roof of the bridge, but he couldn't be sure. The mist seemed to get thicker the higher up you got and the top of the bridge had to be at least fifty or maybe even sixty feet off the ground. Jonathon heard the pinging, clicking sound of claws scurrying across the roof. He instinctively crouched back down and banged the back of his head against the wall. He caught a glimpse of his bleeding leg and almost immediately felt a surge of pain. With all the excitement, he'd forgotten all about his injury. The wound burned, but it wasn't bad. After all, a banged-up leg wouldn't matter much if the rest of him became bird food. *Think! There's got to be something in here that can help you out of this!*

He skimmed over the area again and a brightly colored object immediately jumped out into view. His answer was in a cabinet under the large table in the center of the room. A single-shot flare gun lay innocently on a metal shelf, it's brightly orange color shone like a beacon of hope. He crawled over to it and held the pistol grip tightly. He remembered the jugs on the deck the night before, Angus had told him they were fuel reserves. A crazy plan began to form in his head. The only thing he needed now was bait.

The sound of a boat engine starting made him jump. *Not yet, Silas!* Time had suddenly run out and he continued to search desperately for something to use as bait. A bag of chips or maybe even a piece of chicken. *Anything!* There was no food of any kind to be found. Jonathon chewed his lip as he heard the motor boat drawing near. Finally, an idea popped into his head. It wasn't a good one, but it was all he had on such short notice. He scurried over to Captain Blackstone and pulled off his Atlanta Braves baseball cap. He then took the cap and dragged it through the thick layer of blood all over the floor. He made a disgusted face, but continued to sop up as much blood as he could. His eye caught a glimpse of a large ring of keys lying close to Captain Blackstone; they reminded him of a ring of keys a jailor would use. Jonathon thought of the locked shipping container on the beach. *Worth a try, I guess.* He snatched up the keys and wiped the blood off of them the best he could on Captain Blackstone's shirt. After placing the keys in his pocket, he grabbed the blood-drenched cap and scrambled back on his feet (his leg reminded him painfully that it was injured) and he ran for the door. When he swung it open, the flying reptile above his head screamed with nightmarish glee. Then he heard another scream and realized there were two of them on the roof! He peered out toward the bow and spotted the jugs of gasoline. Jonathon retrieved his knife from its sheath one last time and looked down at it with remorse. He'd had that knife since he was a teenager and it had practically become a part of him. Now, if things worked out right, it would save his life. He pinched the blade between his index finger and thumb, allowing the handle to rest on his wrist. He'd been throwing knives his entire life so hitting a wide stack of gasoline jugs would be a piece of cake. He took aim and whirled the knife effortlessly. The blade penetrated the center jug he aimed for. Immediately gasoline began chugging out, spilling all over the deck. *Couldn't have worked out any better,* he thought. *Now the bait.* He grabbed the cap by the bill and threw it like a Frisbee. It landed almost perfectly next to the jugs. The pterosaurs leapt off the roof, clumsily tripping over each other as they hastily chased after the smell of fresh blood. As soon as they reached the cap, Jonathon raised the flare gun and squeezed the trigger. A bright ball of fire ejected with a bit more kick that he'd anticipated. Jonathon had never fired a flare gun; he'd never had a reason to. The shot wasn't pretty, and it wasn't spot on, but it was close enough. He didn't stick around to see what happened next, he just ran. He ran as fast as his injured leg would allow, and as he approached the end of the deck, he didn't even take time to look over the side and make sure Silas wasn't directly below him. There wasn't time for that. The gasoline ignited, and he heard the roar of the giant fireball erupting mere feet away from him. A wave of heat seemed to push him outward and further away from the boat. He opened his eyes briefly to see that Silas indeed had been directly below where he jumped off. However, it didn't matter now; he would clear him with ease. He splashed down hard in the cool Atlantic, plunging deep below the surface. The icy sensation felt great and he was just happy to be feeling anything. It meant he was alive.

As soon as his head broke the surface, he heard Silas calling out to him. His new friend and the boat were only a few feet away, and he casually swam over to him. Suddenly, a blood-curdling scream pierced through the sky and Jonathon jerked his head around in time to see one of the large pterosaurs tumbling off the deck, its body engulfed in bright orange and yellow ribbons as it too plunged into the ocean. For a moment, he felt pity for the animal. It was a horrible way for any creature to die. He shook the thoughts out of his head as he remembered Denny and Captain Blackstone. *That wasn't any way for a human to die.* Jonathon reached out and grabbed one of Silas's massive forearms, the older man pulling him aboard with relative ease.

He looked over at Silas. His face was pale, a mixture of shock and disbelief. "You alright?" Jonathon asked.

Silas nodded, a partial smile cracked his face. "Yeah, the better question is are *you* alright?"

Jonathon nodded.

The two men sat in silence for a moment, staring at the flames wisping over the bow of the boat. "The deck's metal. When the gas burns off, the fire will go out," Jonathon said. "We'll still be able to use the ship to get out of here."

Silas nodded. "I'm assuming you found the captain and Denny?"

Jonathon rubbed seawater from his eyes and nodded somberly. "What was left of them."

Silas's face grew paler, and for a moment, Jonathon thought he may pass out. Suddenly, he shook his head, seemingly forcing himself to remain calm. "Okay," he said finally. "Let's get back to shore, get your girlfriend, and get the hell off this island."

"I agree," Jonathon answered.

CHAPTER 18

Lucy's feet ached, her skin itched from insect bites, and her throat was parched from thirst. As if she weren't bad enough off physically, she was also emotionally drained. Life had been a rollercoaster ever since she'd set foot on this wretched island, but she'd gritted her teeth and held on for all she was worth. That is until an extraordinarily painful thought began bothering her like a bad toothache. It had been a few hours since she'd been forced to leave Jonathon and the others tied to a tree. They were left for dead. There were two possibilities: either they managed to escape or they'd already been eaten. Obviously, the first scenario was the one that she preferred, but the more time that passed, the more she began to feel doubt. She knew Jonathon and she knew him quite well. One thing she knew was that if he *had* managed to escape, he would come for her. *It's been hours...plenty of time*, she thought. She began to tell herself that there was a real possibility that she may never see him again. Suddenly, she felt dizzy. She needed to sit down.

"We need to stop," she said sternly.

She stopped unexpectedly and Angus inadvertently jabbed the barrel of his handgun into her back rather sharply.

She jerked away from him and glared back at him, her eyes burning with anger. "I'm tired. Osvaldo and Armando are tired. We're thirsty and we need to rest for a few minutes," she demanded.

The last thing that Angus wanted to do was stop. The fountain of youth was getting close; he could feel it in his gut. There would be plenty of time to rest at nightfall; every ounce of daylight should be spent walking. However, as he stared into Lucy's brown eyes, he knew trying to force the others forward without listening to any of their complaints would cause more conflict. He glanced at his watch. It was three o'clock. Nightfall was roughly three hours away. When he looked up, he noticed that Osvaldo was eyeing him sharply, eagerly awaiting his response. Deep down, Angus believed that Osvaldo probably wanted him to push them onward. He wanted more conflict to arise so that he could plot an escape. Angus clenched his jaw. *Not today, buddy.*

"Very well," he said finally. "We'll take five minutes then continue on."

Lucy said nothing; she just turned away from him and took a seat on a nearby boulder covered in moss.

Angus walked to Osvaldo and leaned over to speak, doing his best to keep their conversation as private as possible. "How much farther?"

Osvaldo stared into the old man's eyes a minute, and then he scanned the landscape around him.

"How much farther?" Angus asked again, this time a little louder.

Osvaldo shrugged. "I do not know. I told you, it's been a long time."

Angus exhaled deeply through his nose. "Think!"

Osvaldo put his hands on his hips and surveyed the area again. "I'm sorry; I'm just having trouble remembering." He shot Angus a quick, arrogant smile.

The old man's blood pressure picked up immediately. He was somewhat surprised that Osvaldo was still showing signs of defiance after everything that had happened. It enraged him. *How dare he?* Without saying a word, he quickly lifted his gun and planted it against Armando's temple. Osvaldo jumped to his feet, but stopped short of attacking. He didn't want to do anything to cause Angus to pull the trigger. Armando's eyes widened and he began to pull away. Angus grabbed the boy's thick hair and held him against the gun. "Be still, boy," he growled.

Lucy jumped to her feet. "What in the hell are you doing?" She began to approach, but Travis grabbed her from behind and squeezed her tightly against him.

"Stay right here with me, honey. You'll be safe with me," he whispered in her ear.

She rolled her eyes and gritted her teeth. Travis smelled of sweat and dirt. She wanted to struggle, but knew it was useless.

"It seems that Osvaldo is having trouble with his memory," Angus replied to Lucy. "I'm trying to help get it in gear again."

"You're out of your mind!" Lucy yelled. "He's just a kid, get that gun off of him!"

Angus completely ignored her. "Osvaldo, do you remember anything now?" he asked coldly.

Osvaldo remained silent, but Lucy could see him trembling with fear. *Or was it rage?*

Angus stared at him, there seemed to be no soul behind his eyes. "Fine, have it your way," he said. He pulled the trigger and a deafening boom followed.

"No!" Lucy screamed. She tried to jerk loose, but Travis tightened his arms around her.

Osvaldo let out a howl of sheer agony and charged at the old man. Frank darted between them and firmly planted the butt of his rifle into

Osvaldo's jaw. He tumbled to the ground and crawled to his grandson. When he reached him, he expected to find blood, flesh, and bone. He was pleasantly surprised to find none of that. Armando was face first on the ground. He was sobbing uncontrollably. Angus hadn't shot the boy, but firing the weapon next to his head had done plenty to get his point across. Lucy breathed a sigh of relief, and then turned her attention back to Angus. The obscenities that spewed from her mouth would make a sailor blush. If Angus heard her, he did a good job of hiding it. He glanced down at Osvaldo again and repeated his question. "Do you remember anything *now*?"

Osvaldo raised his head, tears flowing down his cheek. He didn't say a word, only nodded.

Angus allowed an arrogant smile of his own. "That's better," he said. He glanced at his watch. "Okay, break time is over. Let's get moving."

They all resumed their places in line. Lucy was more than happy to get out of Travis's grasp.

Angus never wanted things to unfold the way that they did. He didn't want conflict because he knew that was exactly what Osvaldo wanted. As it turned out, Osvaldo got his conflict anyway. *So*

much for conflict, he thought. *There's no question about who is in charge now.*

***

Annie was distraught when Jonathon and Silas returned to shore. She was so close to escaping the dreadful island and the realization that it wasn't going to happen was beginning to hit her. Of course, there was concern for Jonathon. She'd seen the explosion on the ship and feared the worst. Jonathon could clearly see relief on her face when she saw him, but her relief turned back into despair just as fast. He told her about Captain Blackstone and Denny, purposely leaving the gruesome parts out. After some time, he managed to calm her down, once again promising her that they would get her off the island alive and as soon as possible. Unfortunately, it was going to be a while longer. Jonathon squinted as he peered up the beach. "We've got to make our way back to that shipping container. I got these off of the captain," he said, dangling the ring of keys in the air. "Surely one of them will fit the lock."

Silas quickly led the trio back toward the shipping container. Jonathon's leg throbbed with pain and his gut didn't feel much better either, but he limped along behind Annie, doing his absolute best to keep pace. Silas sensed his struggling.

"You gonna be alright, champ?" he asked, not looking back.

"Yeah," he grunted in response. "Don't slow down for me, I'll keep up."

He did, but when they finally arrived at the shipping container, he collapsed on his hands and knees in the sand.

"Oh my gosh," Annie said, obvious concern in her voice. "Are you sure you're okay?"

Jonathon didn't answer at first; he was too exhausted to. Silas had just begun to reach for the lock, but jerked away when he saw Jonathon on the ground. He knelt down beside him, placing a hand on his back.

"You don't look so good, pal. I don't think you're up for this."

"No, I'm fine," he snapped back. "I just need to catch my breath." He regained his footing and snatched the lock from Silas. "Don't worry about me, I'll be fine."

Silas didn't believe him, but he didn't argue either. Jonathon grabbed the lock and began trying different keys. He went through eight of them before he found one that released the shackle. He took the lock off and dropped it in the sand beside him. Silas grabbed the bolt and worked it loose. He swung the large metal door open and gawked at what was inside. It was four all-terrain vehicles, all of them top of the line with plenty of power. They were large enough to easily seat two people and could carry a third if necessary. Each one wore camouflage skin and knobby tires that could probably tear through asphalt. The keys were in all of the ignitions.

Silas whistled. "Ole Angus went all the way with the four-wheelers, didn't he?"

"I'd say so," Jonathon agreed, walking toward the impressive machines.

"We should be able to catch up to them in no time with these," Silas said.

Jonathon shook his head. "Yeah, but we have got to be careful. These things will make a lot of noise which means they'll draw a lot of curious dinosaurs."

Annie moved closer, her arms crossed. "But they won't be able to catch us, right?"

Jonathon looked at her, hearing the constant fear in her voice. "We should be able to outrun anything," he lied.

Her wide, worried eyes narrowed; the answer seemed to fight off some of the fear.

Jonathon opened the fuel cap and stuck a finger inside the tank.

"Anything?" Silas asked.

"It's full," he replied. He wasn't sure how far a tank of gas would take them, but as he thought of the fuel cans that exploded on the ship, he knew they would have to last. He took a seat on the ATV closest to him and gripped the handlebars. "Okay, here's the plan," he said calmly. "We're going to take the four-wheelers back up the stream where we came down earlier, then—"

A familiar roar rang out nearby, cutting off his words. Silas whipped around in time to see the tyrannosaur walloping toward them from the wood line. Annie screamed.

"You two, get a four-wheeler and go!" Jonathon stood on the foot pegs and frantically motioned for them to hop on the ATV next to him. They did and Silas had the vehicle moving in mere seconds. The four-wheeler kicked up a plume of sand as he piloted it across the beach. The tyrannosaur immediately turned its massive head in the direction of the fleeing ATV and gave chase. Jonathon started his, squealing the tires as he exited the shipping container. Once he hit the sand, he slammed on the brakes and yelled as loud as he could.

"Hey! Over here!" He waved his arms wildly in a desperate attempt to try and coax the vicious animal to come after him instead. The tyrannosaur slowed its massive legs and turned toward him, cocking its head sideways in a curious manner.

"That's right, ugly. I'm right here!"

The tyrannosaur responded by opening its large mouth and releasing a thunderous roar. The awesome display made Jonathon shiver; he had to get away quickly. He gunned the throttle, briefly raising the front tires off the sand as he took off. The tyrannosaur came at him from the left in more of a fast walk than a run. Jonathon zipped by with ease and he allowed a smile to form on his face. One glance over his shoulder and the smile vanished. The tyrannosaur was now running after him with blistering speed. He'd always believed the animals were fast, but what he was now seeing behind him was beyond his imagination. Jonathon kept the throttle wide open, but the tyrannosaur was closing in on him fast. Suddenly, he spotted a small group of *Parksosauruses* foraging on the beach ahead. An idea popped into Jonathon's head, and he steered the ATV toward the tiny dinosaurs. A few of them stopped what they were doing long enough to look toward him, clearly puzzled by the strange, noisy object approaching rapidly.

Stay right there, boys. Just a few more seconds.

The dinosaurs continued to stare with wonder, when something else finally catches their attention. The tyrannosaur released another deafening roar and the terrified *Parksosauruses* scattered in all directions. Jonathon bit his bottom lip and prayed that the tyrannosaur would forget about him and chase after the easier targets. The four-wheeler zipped by the spot where the *Parksosauruses* were foraging moments before. Jonathon looked over his shoulder, desperately hoping that the tyrannosaur would no longer be there. A large, gaping mouth with jaws full of teeth larger than his hand was all that he saw. He felt his heart skip a beat, and it felt as if all the blood in his head rushed away. He felt woozy and felt as if he were going to pass out. Death was close if he didn't think of something very fast. He could literally feel the tyrannosaur's hot breath on his neck. He skimmed over the landscape ahead of him and spotted a small trail leading up a hill at the edge of the jungle. He guessed it was probably a trail used by the *Parksosauruses* he'd seen so many of on the beach. Jonathon turned the ATV up the rocky trail and the vehicle began the climb with ease. He found himself thanking Angus for not going cheap on the four-wheelers. The jungle formed a low canopy over the trail. This suddenly gave Jonathon hope as he realized the tyrannosaur was far too tall to get through the trail. He looked back again and his jaw fell open as he witnessed the relentless animal tearing and crashing through limbs and vines. The jungle did cause enough of a hindrance to slow the massive animal, but it wasn't nearly enough to stop it. All Jonathon could do was keep the ATV moving as fast as possible. He still had the throttle gunned wide open, and he was pretty sure it hadn't been released at all since he'd left the shipping container. The trail continued to climb the hill and it became steeper and steeper. Much like it had been everywhere else within in the jungle, it was much darker than it had been on the beach, but Jonathon noticed a bright light straight ahead at the top of the hill. It seemed that the trail came to an abrupt end and then a frightening realization overcame him. *It's a cliff. I'm driving straight toward a cliff.* He looked back over his shoulder yet again, and the tyrannosaur was still chasing him. It seemed it was never going to stop until it got the opportunity to taste Jonathon's blood. He looked back toward the bright light ahead and knew there was only one way out of this. His timing would have to be perfect or he would surely die. He felt his heart rate increase as he considered what he was about to undertake. He wanted to think of another way out, but it was useless.

Jonathon clenched his jaw and held the throttle wide open. The tyrannosaur never slowed either, tearing limbs away and thrashing its tail wildly in its wake. The moment of truth had arrived as Jonathon reached the light; he spotted the edge of the cliff and quickly leapt from the ATV. He crashed hard against the rocky trail and allowed his body to roll as many times necessary to prevent as much injury as possible. The ATV continued onward and rocketed off the cliff. It arched a great distance through the air. Jonathon felt his body continue to slide along the hard ground until it seemed to drop out from under him. *Oh my God, I've gone over the edge!* His legs went over first and he clawed at the ground, trying with all of his might to hold on. He saw the tyrannosaur still lumbering toward him like a steam locomotive, seemingly unaware of the cliff ahead. Jonathon wondered if the dinosaur would even be able to see it with its head in the trees. He finally found a sapling to hold on to and prayed it would hold his weight. It did, and as he dangled over the edge of the cliff, he could hear the ATV clang and break into pieces against the jagged rocks below.

The tyrannosaur finally *did* catch sight of the cliff, but it was too late. The large animal gave its best effort to stop. It tried to dig its large black claws into the trail, but the ground was too rocky. The animal's legs slid out from under it and inertia carried it right over the edge. Jonathon narrowly avoided being dragged down with the beast. He watched, wide-eyed as the most fearsome predator to ever walk on planet earth gazed up at him as it fell. There was fear in those eyes and it just felt wrong for Jonathon to see it. He looked away before the animal hit bottom; he didn't want to see the animal die. Unfortunately, he still heard quite a bit. He heard bones break, he heard the air forced out of the *T-rex*'s massive lungs. He heard a pitiful grunt as the animal died in a painful and terrible way. Jonathon carefully pulled himself back onto the edge of the cliff and let out a sigh of utter relief. It was good to be alive.

CHAPTER 19

Silas slammed on the brakes and the ATV came to a sliding stop in the muddy soil. Annie lurched forward, but clung to his waist tightly to keep from falling off. He killed the engine and they sat quietly for a moment, looking back, desperation and fear was etched all over their faces.

"I can't believe this is happening," Silas said. "I can't believe the crazy fool did that."

"He did that to save us," Annie replied, tears streaming down her face. "Do you think he's...okay?" Her words came out softly, as if she were afraid to speak them.

Silas felt his eyes water up and a knot forming in his stomach. "No, I don't think so."

"How are you so sure?"

"Listen," he said, and paused a second. "I don't hear the ATV. It's loud enough we should be able to hear it."

Annie wiped the moisture from her eyes, trying to convince herself it wasn't true. "Well, maybe he stopped. Maybe he's hiding. We've got to check."

Silas glanced over at her. He felt sorry for her. He wanted desperately for Jonathon to be alright, and he wanted to tell Annie that. But he just didn't see how it was possible. He wished Annie would allow herself to accept it also. "Sweetheart, we can't go back there. That *T-rex* is back there." He turned away from her before he spoke his next words. "Jonathon's dead honey. You've got to accept that."

Annie closed her eyes tightly. The helpless feeling overcoming her at the moment was horrible. She felt that it must be the next worse thing to actually dying. She sobbed for a few long minutes. Silas turned and held her close, doing anything he could to comfort her. "We have to go look," she said, barely clear enough to understand through the sobbing.

Silas said nothing.

"Did you hear me? We have to go look for him," she said a little louder, still hard to understand though. "Just to be sure."

Silas looked over Annie's shoulder up the stream where they'd come from. He listened for any signs of the ATV again, or the roar of the tyrannosaur. He heard nothing. It seemed as if all of the animals in the jungle were aware of the hopeless, bitter moment because they were silent too.

"He would go back if it were us," Annie said, her voice firm and clear now.

Silas took a deep breath and let it out slowly. "Okay, we'll go check."

"Thank you," she replied softly. "We just have to be sure."

Silas turned the key and the ATV roared to life once more. He turned the vehicle back toward the beach, kicking up mud as he went.

***

It had taken a great deal of effort for Jonathon to get on his feet. He figured his body had been beaten and abused more in one day than it had ever been in his entire life. His leg was literally sliced open at the calf, and he knew it would only be a matter of time before an infection began to fester. His torso ached where the *Dromaeosaurus* had made a failed attempt to gut him alive. The puncture wounds weren't deep, but he feared that they too would become infected. The jump from the ATV to the rocky ground felt like the equivalent of someone taking a Louisville Slugger and hitting him as hard as they could with it. Now a headache began to throb mercilessly between his ears, probably more from the stress of the day than the actual physical punishment he'd been taking. The only good news, he decided, was that to his knowledge he didn't have any broken bones.

His thoughts turned to Silas and Annie. He was thankful that they'd managed to escape, and he hoped that they hadn't encountered any other dangerous dinosaurs when they'd headed into the jungle. As he walked down the steep trail, he wondered where they were and how they would probably alter their plans. If he could guess right, maybe he would be able to find them. The first thing he needed to do was get another ATV. It would take him forever to try and catch up with them on foot when he knew they had an ATV of their own. Suddenly, a faint sound somewhere far away (probably on the beach) got his attention. He shook his head with disgust as he wondered what species of dinosaur was ready to fight him next. The humming sound began to get closer, and he couldn't help but laugh out loud when he realized what it was. He knew there was no reason to keep walking. Where he was at was as good a place as any to wait for Silas and Annie to arrive.

They did eventually arrive and Annie leapt off the four-wheeler and hugged him tightly.

"Thank God you're okay!"

"You guys shouldn't have come back here looking for me," he answered. "But thank you, I'm so glad you did."

Silas approached and held out a hand. Jonathon took it and pulled the big man to him, hugging him also.

"You made it easy for us to find you," Silas said. "Your tire tracks showed up real good in the sand, led us right to the trail." He stopped talking as something dawned on him. "Jonathon, where is your four-wheeler?"

Jonathon gave a sly grin and glanced back up the trail. "Silas, this trail ends at the edge of a steep cliff. My four-wheeler took off that cliff without me and our friendly tyrannosaur chased after it."

Silas's jaw dropped and he let out a hearty laugh. "You're joking," he said.

"No, sir, our tyrannosaur is dead and so is the four-wheeler."

"You've got more lives than a cat," Annie said.

"Let's hope I don't have to use any more of them for a while," Jonathon replied. "I got a feeling I may have to use a few more when we catch up with Angus."

"Let's head back to the beach and get you another ATV," Silas said. "And try not to break this one."

CHAPTER 20

Angus felt his feet aching and though he desperately wanted to stop and take a break, he made no mention of it. *Soon,* he thought, *I'll be young again. My feet will be able to walk all day and I won't even break a sweat. Soon.*

Unfortunately, he knew the others were physically fading also. Maybe they weren't fading as fast as he was, but fading nevertheless. Lucy hadn't said a word since the altercation a couple of hours earlier. He knew she was fuming mad, but that was okay as long as she did what she was told. Osvaldo seemed more confused than ever. This continued to frustrate Angus, but he did his best to hide his displeasure. *Patience,* he told himself. Suddenly, Osvaldo stopped walking and began wheeling his head around in both directions.

"What's the problem now?" Angus grumbled.

Osvaldo said nothing at first; he just kept looking left to right. Finally, he slowly turned back toward Angus.

"I'm lost. I'm tired and disoriented. I need to rest, please." His words were genuine; exhaustion was all over his face.

Angus was about to respond, but Travis spoke first. "We don't have time to rest, now turn around and get—" Suddenly, a rustle in the foliage ahead cut off his words.

Osvaldo backed away quickly, and then made it abundantly clear he wasn't leading them any further.

"What are you waiting for? Move forward," Angus barked.

Osvaldo looked back at him, eyes filled with fear. "Something is out there."

Angus rolled his eyes. "Whatever that was couldn't be much larger than a deer. Now get going or I'll have to ask Travis get rough with you."

"Something the size of a deer is plenty big enough to rip us apart," Lucy interrupted. "Depending on what sort of animal it is, of course."

"That is why we have guns, dear," Angus snapped. "Now move!"

Osvaldo didn't budge and the display was more than Angus could handle. He marched away from Lucy and had every intention of reminding Osvaldo who was in charge.

Lucy had finally had enough.

"No! No! We're not walking another step, Angus!"

Angus stopped abruptly and gave Lucy a stare.

"You've pushed us all day. And I'm not going another step until you tell me what this is all about! If you want to shoot me, then you go ahead and shoot me. I really don't care anymore." She did care, but she was running out of ideas. This madness had to stop.

Angus looked surprised and she was glad that she'd at least rattled him.

"Lucy, I have no intentions of shooting you," he said, trying to sound calm.

"Then what is this all about?" Her hair fell across her face, further enhancing her anger. "This doesn't have anything to do with dinosaurs, does it?"

Travis moved toward her; he was going to enjoy shutting her up.

"Travis, no! Leave her be," the old man said, finally sounding worn down. He noticed a large boulder nearby, coated in wet moss. He was too tired to care if his pants got wet, he just sat down. "I suppose I do owe you an explanation," he said.

"Boss, you don't have to tell her anything," Travis assured him.

"Travis, sit down. I suppose we do need to take a break. But keep your eyes on him," he replied, pointing at Osvaldo. "Don't let him out of your sight."

Travis nodded and pushed Osvaldo down on the ground. "Break time," he said coldly.

Angus motioned for Lucy to take a seat near him and after a brief moment, she did. However, there was no doubt in his mind that she didn't want to be anywhere near him.

"My dear, first let me assure you that I didn't mean for things to get this out of control," he began.

"Well, things started getting out of control right around the time you left Jonathon and the others to die," she snapped at him.

Angus reached in his pocket to retrieve a handkerchief, he then wiped perspiration from his brow. "Lucy, Jonathon is very resourceful. I'm quite confident that he is fine."

She stared at him without blinking. Rage oozed from her gaze. "You better hope and pray you're right," she said. "Because if you're not, I won't give you any choice but to kill me to save your own hide."

Angus didn't respond; the truth was, her words had little effect on him. He was in control. Instead, he decided it was best to tell her what this was all about. It was worth a shot. "You are correct. There is something else on this island that I want. Something that I've kept from you and the others."

"What is it?" she asked firmly.

"I will tell you, but I must warn you, it may be hard for you to believe."

"Try me."

"There is something very powerful on this island. Some people would probably call it magical. It's something you've heard of your entire life and up until now you probably have always felt the same way I have. You've believed that it was a legend, a bedtime story of sorts."

Lucy rolled her eyes and she was unable to hold in her rage. "Get to the point!"

"The fountain of youth," he snapped, and he didn't even have the courage to look in her eyes when he said it.

Lucy pursed her lips together and raised an eyebrow. "The fountain of youth? Are you joking?"

"It is real, my dear. I assure you. Please believe me. I wouldn't have put any of us through all of this if it was not real."

"You brought us all here and you've risked all of our lives to find something that doesn't even exist?" She stood and shook her head, shock and disbelief overcame her. *This man is insane,* she thought.

Angus stood as well, trying desperately to plead his case. "Look around you, for heaven's sake! Up until this morning, did you think any of this was real? Do you honestly think it was easy for me to believe that the fountain of youth is real?"

Lucy drew near him and poked a finger in his chest. "I've seen dinosaurs today, so I've accepted that they are real. Have you seen this fountain?"

"No, not yet," he answered.

She laughed, in a psychotic sort of way. "Then how in the world do you know it is real?"

"Because there is someone among us that has seen it," the old man shot back.

Osvaldo stood up. Travis pointed the barrel of his gun at him. "It's true," he said. "The fountain does exist. I am the one who was seen it."

Lucy's mood softened a bit. She hardly knew Osvaldo, but she was more interested in hearing him speak than to listen to anymore of Angus's dribbling. "Tell me more," she said.

"The one and only time I found the fountain was almost five-hundred years ago. I drank from it and I have lived ever since. I don't age, I don't get sick, and I'm always full of energy. You might say it was a blessing, and some would call it a gift." He paused a moment and let out a deep breath. "I call it a curse. I've seen generation after generation of my family die. After a while, you get tired of burying your family members. You get tired of burying your friends."

There was no mistaking the pain in Osvaldo's eyes. Lucy could see it, and she was actually beginning to believe him. "You're telling me that you are unable to die?"

He shook his head quickly. "Oh, I can certainly die. I am able to be mortally wounded."

"You can kill yourself?" Lucy didn't mean for the words to come out so blunt, she spoke them as soon as they popped into her head. Osvaldo seemed unaffected by the coldness of it.

"Yes, and do not think I haven't considered it," he answered. "It simply is not an option for me at this time."

"Suicide is never an option for you, Osvaldo," she replied.

There was a moment where no one said anything. Lucy used the precious time to attempt to process what she had heard. Osvaldo was either an Academy Award winning actor, or he was telling the truth. She chose to believe the latter. Actually, the more she thought about it, the more a lot of it made sense. The island, seemingly undiscovered (except for Osvaldo of course), had been inhabited by dinosaurs for millions of years. Somehow, they had managed to avoid extinction. It was possible, she supposed, that if the fountain of youth did indeed exist on the island, it could've had something to do with that fact.

Osvaldo began to speak again, shattering her thoughts. "I know this is all hard for you to believe, but I am telling you the truth. I've been forced against my will to find the fountain again."

"I am not done living," Angus said abruptly. "Lucy, I need to find the fountain. I just turned seventy-four years old. I don't have nearly as many years left as I would like. You must understand why this is so important to me."

"Oh, I understand," she snapped. "I understand that you want to play God and you don't care who gets hurt along the way." She sighed and pointed toward Osvaldo. "Did you just hear everything he said? Living forever sounds great, but it isn't. Osvaldo just did a pretty darn good job explaining why."

Angus shot her an icy gaze. "I'm not Osvaldo. I'm Angus Wedgeworth and I *will* live forever."

The statement chilled Lucy, but she did her best to hide it. The old man was clearly obsessed and that one statement cemented the fact that there was nothing she could do to persuade him to abort the search.

Angus sensed the wheels turning in her head and tried to throw a different angle at her. "My dear, I'm not just doing this for me. I want us all to experience it."

Lucy smiled, and shook her head in amazement. "You're crazy. You've completely lost it." She allowed another hint of that psychotic laugh to escape her. "I do not want to live forever, Angus!"

"I do, boss," Travis said, awkwardly interrupting the conversation.

"Drinking from the fountain won't be forced on any of you," Angus replied. "On the other hand, helping me find it will be."

Lucy sat back down and held her head in her hands, her black hair cascading down around her face as she let out another sigh. "Fine," she said finally. "But we've got to stop for the night."

"We can't stop, we still have another hour of daylight," Angus said firmly.

"We need that hour to find a place to camp. We need to build a fire. There are lots of meat-eating dinosaurs out there that will be very active at night. If we try to make camp after nightfall, we won't have a chance."

Angus turned away from her and stroked his chin, obviously mulling it over.

Lucy stood and approached him. "Angus, we'll help you find the fountain of youth. You haven't given us a choice on that matter. However, it won't do you much good if you die before you find it."

Angus looked over his shoulder back at her. He took his hat off and fanned a buzzing insect out of his face. "Alright. Frank, take Armando and start gathering firewood. Travis, take Osvaldo and gather some large rocks to make a fire pit. We better make a large fire to keep the hungry dinos away."

The four men trotted off and began gathering. Lucy and Angus sat back down on the damp, moss-covered boulder.

"You think I'm mad, don't you?" he asked her.

"I think you're insane," she replied.

"I will do what I can to make sure you're protected above everyone else, please believe that. Jonathon made me aware of your concerns about Travis. I will keep my eye on him."

"I can take care of myself," she snapped back, but secretly she hoped he was telling the truth.

***

Nightfall was fast approaching. As soon as Silas stopped the ATV next to the shipping container, an idea occurred to him.

"It won't be long before it'll be pitch black darkness out here. We've got to camp somewhere for the night, and I don't think the *Bethany* is an ideal place to spend the night," he said.

Annie clutched Jonathon's arm. "I'm not going anywhere near that ship tonight," she said.

"Well, what do you suggest?" Jonathon asked.

143

Silas slapped the metal side on the shipping container. "This thing should provide more than enough protection to get us through the night. We'll shut the door and spend the night right here."

Jonathon peered back in the direction of the woods. He wanted to continue searching for Lucy, but he forced himself to accept the fact that the search would have to wait until morning. It would be far too dangerous to venture into the jungle after dark. Silas was right when he pointed out that the island would soon fall under a veil of pitch black darkness. Even if the moon was out tonight, it was pretty unlikely that the silver beams would be able to penetrate the thick mist in the sky above.

"Alright, we'll spend the night here," he agreed. "I think we better get your four-wheeler in as well."

Silas pushed it inside and the trio spent a few more minutes out on the beach. Annie stared out across the rolling ocean and secretly hoped that she had just dreamed this entire day. She hoped that when she woke up in the morning, she would be back at home in her own bed, safe and sound. She knew, of course, that it was all just wishful thinking. The night would allow her a few hours to dream; to escape. She knew that in the morning death would be breathing down her neck once again. The thought made her tremble. She couldn't shake the horrible feeling she'd had since things began to spiral out of control. She had a sick feeling that she was going to die.

CHAPTER 21

Travis and Frank took shifts during the night. It took a long time for Lucy to finally feel comfortable enough to drift off to sleep. Even then, she tossed and turned on the hard earth, unable to fall into a deep sleep. The ground, she knew, had little to do with it. The dinosaurs, which were quite noisy during the night with odd chirps, growls, and moaning, had little to do with it either. It was the two men taking shifts all through the night that made it nearly impossible for Lucy to get a good night's sleep. She believed that Angus would keep an eye on Travis, and she was now grateful that Jonathon had said something to him about the unwelcome advances. However, Angus was now sound asleep. The night seemed to drag on endlessly. She opened her eyes and glanced down at her digital watch. One-thirty-five glowed orange on the screen, illuminated by the nearby campfire. She was pleasantly surprised at this as she realized the last time she'd glanced at the watch it read eight-thirty. She'd gotten around five hours of sleep so far, although none of it had been constant.

She turned over on her side to see who was standing guard at the present time. She closed her eyes, and then opened one slightly to take a peek. It was Travis. He was seated straight across from her on the ground, his back against a tree. He was staring straight at her. It frightened her to see him looking at her and she shut her eye tightly, doing her best not to tremble as her heart rate sped up. *Just go back to sleep,* she thought.

"Honey, you okay?" he asked in a slight whisper.

She kept quiet and closed her eyes even tighter. *Act like you're asleep, he'll leave you alone.*

"What's the matter, honey, you don't want to talk to me?"

She remained silent.

Travis crossed his arms and let out a deep breath. His displeasure was evident, although he said nothing. Lucy kept her eyes closed and tried to relax her breathing. It became an even harder task when she heard him get up and walk toward her. She heard his knees pop when he knelt down beside her, and moments later, she felt his hot breath on her neck.

"I know you're awake," he whispered. "Open your eyes."

She didn't.

"Honey, you really shouldn't fight this. I want you, and I always get what I want. Now let me see those beautiful brown eyes."

Lucy tried desperately to remain calm, but it was a losing battle. *Don't give up...keep your eyes closed. He'll give up any minute now.*

For a moment, she thought that he was going to leave her alone. He quit whispering to her, and he no longer felt his breath on her cheek. Just as she was beginning to feel relief, something much more horrifying happened. She felt a tug at her shirt. *Oh my God, is he unbuttoning my shirt?*

Travis looked around to make sure the others were asleep. They were, and once he was satisfied that Lucy was asleep too, he decided to take a peek under her shirt. It would be tricky, but he had a couple of hours before his shift was up. He'd use all the time he needed to delicately open her shirt.

Lucy now held her breath, she wanted to scream, but wasn't sure if it was the best course of action. She had almost decided to open her eyes and slap him when Angus's ragged voice spoke from nearby.

"Travis, what do you think you're doing?"

Travis immediately jerked his hand away and scrambled to get on his feet. "Nothing, I thought I heard her talking in her sleep. Just checking to see—"

"Do you take me for a fool?" Angus was clearly angry. He was doing his best to whisper, but it was difficult. "Go back to where you were and do your job!"

Travis wanted to argue. He wanted to tell the old man not to speak to him in that tone. But he knew Angus better than anyone. He knew Angus would kill him if he felt it necessary. He bit his tongue. "Yes, boss." He plopped back down where he had been and crossed his arms as if he were pouting. Angus stayed awake the rest of the night.

***

Jonathon rubbed the sleep from his eyes as he awoke from the most uncomfortable night of sleep in his entire life. As he sat up on the hard metal floor, his back popped loud enough to wake Silas and Annie.

"Geez, you should get that looked at," Annie said, then immediately released a long yawn.

"Yeah, that isn't all I need looked at," he grumbled, clutching his sore leg.

Silas stood without speaking, obviously sleep deprived. He just marched straight to the door and opened it just enough to peek his head out.

"Is the coast clear?" Jonathon asked.

"Affirmative," he replied, swinging the door open the rest of the way. There still was no sunshine, but the piercing white light still forced them to squint.

Jonathon limped out onto the sandy beach, his leg throbbing more than ever. The breeze was cool, but it wasn't until he splashed icy saltwater against his face that he became fully awake. Annie clumsily strolled out of the shipping container; she looked as if she'd aged no less than ten years in one day. Her makeup had all but disappeared, her eyes were bloodshot, and there were signs of the tremendous amount of stress she'd been under etched all over her face.

As he examined her, it suddenly occurred to Jonathon that the three of them had eaten very little since they'd arrived to the island. The day would most certainly bring about new dangers and challenges. A few hours of sleep had helped tremendously, but eating was absolutely essential if they were going to venture back into the jungle.

He stumbled back to the shipping container and looked around for a crate or box that they hadn't noticed before. When he found none, it became obvious that if they were going to eat something, the island would have to provide it.

"Any ideas on what we could eat for breakfast?"

"I don't care what we eat," Annie replied; she was just happy someone brought up breakfast. "I'm hungry enough to eat sand if that's all we've got."

Jonathon smiled at her nervously. He truly hoped it wouldn't come to that.

"There wasn't anything in the container?" Silas asked.

Jonathon shook his head.

"Maybe we could catch some fish," Annie said, gazing across the rolling surf.

"With what?" Silas asked.

Jonathon scanned the environment and just as he was beginning to ponder what *Parksosaurus* meat would taste like, something else caught his eye.

"Coconuts."

Annie's face lit up. "Oh, of course! I love coconuts."

Coconuts were plentiful near the edge of the jungle and they were a safe distance from the shipping container. Jonathon and Silas collected more than enough for them to get their fill. Cracking the coconuts open was no easy task, and Jonathon found himself missing his trusty knife for the first time since he'd lost it. It did not take them long to find a solution. When slammed hard enough, the heavy shipping container door cracked them nicely.

"Okay, we're burning daylight," Jonathon said as he wheeled out another four-wheeler. He walked over to Annie and put an arm around her. "Annie, I'm going to have to insist that you stay here and wait for us."

Her eyes widened, she clearly didn't like the idea. "Stay here? Alone?"

"I can't think of any place on this island that would be safer than right here." He rasped his knuckles against the metal side and it clanged loudly in response. "Do you hear that? That's strong metal. A tyrannosaur can't chew through that."

She looked into the empty container, then back into his eyes. "How long will you be gone?"

"At least all day. If we haven't caught up to them on four-wheelers by the end of the day, then we probably won't ever find them." He paused a moment and looked down as the words he'd spoken registered.

Annie put a hand under his chin and lifted his head back up to meet her eyes. "You'll find her. Don't worry," she said confidently.

He nodded. "Go on and get in. One inside, I would prefer you not to come back out, but I know that would be asking too much."

"Uh, yeah…you think I'm going to go to the bathroom in there?"

"You will if it's necessary," he replied. "Annie, promise me you won't take any chances. If and I do mean *if* you have to go outside, you don't go any more than ten feet from the container."

She rolled her eyes and let out a little chuckle.

Jonathon grabbed her shoulders and shook her. "Promise me! This is serious!"

Her expression immediately turned somber, his words obviously working the way he intended. "I promise," she said finally.

"Alright then, wish us luck."

She did just that and gave them both hugs before they went on their way. She closed the door on the container and listened until the hum of the four-wheeler engines were swallowed up by the jungle. She prayed a silent prayer that they would return for her.

***

The panicked screaming of a man echoed loudly throughout the vast jungle. The alarming sound startled Lucy out of her sleep and she was on her feet in seconds. The screaming man turned out to be Frank, and it seemed surreal that the first sound she'd ever heard pass the man's lips was screaming. Loud, terrified, blood-curdling screaming. At first, she thought that surely he was being attacked by something nasty with plenty of sharp teeth. She was relieved (and a dark part of her was disappointed) to find that Frank wasn't being eaten after all, but he must have thought he was about to be.

A large duck-billed dinosaur was munching on some attractive greenery near the spot Frank had been sleeping. Lucy figured that it probably *was* a horrible thing to wake up to, but yet it was still quite amusing to her all the same. It had scared him so bad, that apparently he was too shocked to reach for his nearby rifle. The dinosaur seemed unaffected by the noisy man and continued feeding as if nothing had happened.

"What is it?" Angus asked, a little worry in his tone. "For God's sake, what is that thing?"

"It's a hadrosaur, and don't worry, it's an herbivore," she replied quickly. "Judging by the front limbs, I'm guessing it's an anatotitan."

"A what?" Travis asked, wide-eyed like the others.

"Don't make me repeat it," she answered. She really didn't want to say anything to Travis, but she didn't want him to know she knew about his unwelcome advances during the night either. It was best for her to act as normal as possible.

"It looks like a big duck," Travis said.

"Yeah, its name literally means 'giant duck'."

"You sure it don't eat meat?" Travis asked, still gawking at the creature.

She rolled her eyes. "Yes, I'm sure."

"Good," he replied, and he took off running and waving his arms at the dinosaur like a madman. The anatotitan immediately darted away, and they could all hear it crashing through the dense foliage for quite a while before it was gone.

Lucy wanted to make a snide comment about the childish act, but bit her tongue. She was just happy they didn't shoot the poor animal. Instead, she began to pack her sleeping bag to prepare for the inevitable merciless walk that lie ahead. Angus unexpectedly knelt beside her.

"Yet again, you prove your worth to me," he said.

"Don't sweat it; let's just get this over with so we can leave."

"Lucy, as bad as it seems, I assure you I'll protect you from the dinosaurs while we're here," he said reassuringly.

"I'm not referring to the dinosaurs," she answered back. "I want to leave to so I can get away from you and those two apes that work for you. I seem to be more afraid of what you idiots will do than what the dinosaurs will do."

The disrespectful words spewing from Lucy's mouth made Angus's heart rate accelerate just a bit. He took a deep breath and kept calm. In a way, he admired her courage; after all, he did put her in a stressful situation. But above all, he still needed her. As much as he hated it, he had to try to be nice to her.

"Lucy, I hope you give more thought to what I said yesterday."

"About?"

"The fountain of youth. I hope you reconsider taking a drink."

She scratched behind her ear and ran her fingers through her dirty hair. "I will not take a sip of that water, Angus. And if there was a way I could stop you from drinking it, I would. That's just what this world needs, an immortal madman like yourself," she said.

Angus said nothing, he just glared at her. Finally, he snorted and stomped away.

"Let's go everyone! I want to find the fountain before the sun goes down today," he shouted. "Let's make it happen!"

CHAPTER 22

Jonathon steered the four-wheeler along the banks of the familiar stream they'd travelled the day before. Their first destination would be the large clearing in the center of the island. Once there, it was pretty much going to be a guessing game about which way to go first. If he didn't see anything to persuade him to go in another direction, he figured the logical place to drive would be where he'd last seen them walking. Once he got over there, things would get really difficult. He hoped he still had a little luck on his side. There was no doubt that today he would need as much of it as he could get.

The muddy banks were barely noticeable on the four-wheelers, and once again, Jonathon was grateful for the special attention Angus had placed on the transportation for the "expedition." It was surprising to him that the old man gave up so easily on the search for them. There was something else on the island driving him onward besides dinosaurs. He'd thought about it for hours and simply could not come up with any ideas about what it could be. Whatever it was, it was important enough to warrant kidnapping, and it had led the man to leaving Annie (his own family) for dead.

His thoughts evaporated suddenly as they approached a familiar-looking skeleton lying in the stream. Jonathon eased the vehicle to a stop and Silas did the same beside him. The ATVs idled quietly as they examined the remains.

"Is this that dinosaur we saw yesterday?" Silas asked.

"Yeah, this was the *Saltasaurus* we saw," he replied. "If you recall, the dinosaur that was eating this gave me something to remember it by." Jonathon lifted his shirt to show the puncture wound he'd received from the *Dromaeosaurus*.

Silas grimaced at the sight of the injury. It was a much darker red and was in dire need of a good cleaning with antiseptic. "That's getting infected."

"Yeah, I know, I know," he answered. "There's nothing I can do about it right now. Time's wasting, we better get going."

"Are you sure these four-wheelers won't do more harm than good. They're noisy."

"I think the majority of the dinosaurs on this island are small plant-eaters. For the most part, I think they're too afraid of these machines to come anywhere near us." He paused a moment and sighed. "However, I

151

must admit I'm worried about the larger ones. The sound may just make them curious."

"The *T-rex*," Silas added.

Jonathon nodded. "Yes, the one that went after me yesterday didn't care that I was on a noisy four-wheeler."

"That's what I was afraid of."

"So, having said that, I think the best offense is a good defense."

"Meaning?"

"Meaning we keep moving," Jonathon said. "Especially when we get to the clearing. In fact, if I sense we're getting close to catching up, we will probably need to ditch these things anyway. I think our odds will be much better if we surprise Angus. We won't be able to do that if he hears us coming."

Silas nodded and smiled, seemingly enjoying what he was hearing. "I'm not worried about that old man. I'm more worried about these giant lizards. I don't want to end up like him," he said, pointing at the ivory skeleton of the *Saltasaurus*.

"You won't," Jonathon said firmly. "At least I hope not."

He didn't wait to see Silas's response; he gunned the throttle and zipped away allowing a sly smile to crack his face. Silas shook his head and took off after him, clearly unamused.

Jonathon enjoyed the few uneventful moments they had driving along the bank of the stream. For the time being, there wasn't any sight of dinosaurs anywhere. He was beginning to feel comfortable that the four-wheeler was doing exactly what he hoped it would do: scare the dinosaurs away. The comfort he felt ceased abruptly when they emerged from the canopy of trees and into the edge of the large valley at the center of the island. Jonathon locked his brakes up and slid to a stop. Silas arrived moments later.

"Whoa, you sure this is a good idea?" he asked.

Jonathon cupped a hand over his brow and gazed upon the numerous herds of herbivores grazing across the valley. It seemed that there were more today than there were the day before. The *Triceratopses* were still there, but that wasn't the first thing that caught his eye. Now there was a sizable herd of *Saltasauruses* enjoying the lush green vegetation there as well.

"I think we'll be alright," Jonathon replied. "We've just have got to jet across there as fast as we can. No slowing down for anything."

"Will they chase us?" Silas asked, eyeing the *Saltasauruses*.

The truth was, Jonathon wasn't sure. In fact, he was more concerned about the *Triceratops* feeling threatened and charging after them. The harsh reality was that he was just as ignorant at predicting how they would react as Silas was. Of course, he couldn't say that out loud. So he lied.

"It'll be fine."

Silas spat and stared at him closely. "You're sure?"

"Yeah, just don't get close to any of them and we'll be alright," he answered. "Look across the clearing to the wood line. Do you see any signs of Lucy and the others?"

Silas squinted and shook his head. "No."

Jonathon pointed to a large tree to the northwest; it appeared to be some sort of relative to a modern cypress tree. "That's the last place I saw them, near that tree."

Silas looked toward the tree and stared for a long moment. Once he was satisfied he wasn't going to see anything, he scanned the wood line both directions opposite of the tree. Something caught his eye. "I don't see them, but I see where they've been."

"What? Where?"

Silas pointed a few clicks to the left of where the large tree stood. At first, Jonathon saw nothing, but after his eyes relaxed a moment, he locked on to what Silas was pointing at.

"Is that smoke?"

"I'd say that's a safe assumption," Silas replied. "Probably had to build a heck of a fire last night to keep the dinosaurs away."

Jonathon didn't respond. Before Silas knew it, he was already driving away across the valley. He immediately followed suit, and seconds later, they were both buzzing across the plain.

The various groups of dinosaurs, large and small, simultaneously ceased what they were doing and watched them with a mixture of curiousness and caution. Jonathon hardly noticed; his attention was totally on getting to the source of the smoke ahead. Silas, on the other hand, began to feel the butterflies in his stomach when he realized the dinosaurs were watching them. The herd closest to them, the *Saltasauruses*, seemed startled. Their quickness surprised him and reminded him of a herd of elephants. They looked extremely slow, but looks were often deceiving. Elephants were much faster than most people thought. It was amazing to watch so much mass move so swiftly.

Fortunately, none of the animals gave chase. As Jonathon neared the wood line, for the first time he glanced over his shoulder to make sure nothing was chasing them. He was pleasantly surprised to find that they'd been allowed to pass through without incident. What he did see was Silas's pale, worried face looking back at him. He gave him a reassuring smile and turned his attention back in front of him. At first, there didn't seem to be anywhere in the dense jungle that would allow the bulky ATVs to pass through. Just as he'd about decided they were going to have to walk a while to find the campsite, he found a narrow muddy trail leading into a thicket. There were countless three-toed tracks in the mud that indicated it was probably a path cut by the high traffic of dinosaurs. Although he only caught one good glimpse of the tracks as they entered the path, a frightening thought occurred to him that he immediately tried to discard from his mind. The three-toed tracks reminded him of a *Velociraptor* foot. Up until now, he'd seen no evidence of the existence of *Velociraptors* on the island. The possibility of the carnivores inhabiting the island had crossed his mind, but he'd kept quiet about it. If they didn't exist, there was no sense in frightening everyone about it. Now, he wasn't so sure.

They continued deeper into the jungle until there was simply no more room for the four-wheelers to maneuver down the path. Jonathon reluctantly brought the vehicle to a stop and dismounted. Silas did the same and retrieved a machete from a sheath mounted on the side of his ATV.

"Yes, definitely bring the machete," Jonathon said, then knelt down. "Although, I don't think we're going to need it yet, though."

Silas looked at him curiously. "Why is that?"

"Someone's already cut us a trail over here." He pulled a vine into view. It had been cut recently, probably with a machete just like the one Silas was holding.

"They're making this too easy," he replied.

They carefully made their way through the trail that had been cut, stopping periodically to look for more evidence of freshly cut vines. The strong aroma of smoke began to creep into their nostrils, and minutes later, they arrived at a large fire pit. A few embers continued to smolder, but there is almost no other evidence that anyone had been there.

Silas let out a whistle. "That was quite a fire they had here."

"Probably the smartest thing they did since we got on this stupid island," Jonathon replied. "Look around for any shoe prints, or another path they've cut."

The two men split up in opposite directions, desperately looking for any clue to point them in the right direction. The search goes on for nearly twenty minutes, when at last Silas spots something.

"Over here!"

Jonathon raced over to him, and when he arrived, he spotted a boot print in the soft soil beside Silas.

"Travis had on boots," Jonathon said.

Silas nodded.

They continued forward, Silas leading, and the foliage became dense and cumbersome again. Silas pressed forward, and soon after, they began to notice an abundance of freshly cut leaves and vines littering the ground.

"You're like an old bloodhound," Jonathon said.

"Watch it," Silas replied, and he began to hack away at some of the vines Travis had missed. In a way, slicing his way through the jungle was therapeutic. There was a lot of frustration and anger built up in him, and it did him good to find an avenue to release it. A few times, he began to daydream, and he couldn't help but imagine himself taking a few swipes at Angus with the machete when he finally caught up to him. Suddenly, Jonathon grabbed his arm and brought him back to reality.

"Shh," he said, a finger to his mouth.

Silas remained silent, holding his breath as he listened for whatever it was that had gotten Jonathon's attention. For a few seconds, he heard nothing, but then:

Click...Clack...Click-Click

Silas stared at Jonathon awaiting some sort of explanation. He just shrugged as if to say, *I have no idea, but be quiet and let me listen.*

Jonathon thought long and hard as he tried to figure out what was making the strange noise.

Clack-Click...Clack...Click

"I have got to get closer to figure this one out," he whispered. He began to creep as quietly as possible in the direction of the mysterious sounds. Silas followed closely behind, the machete clutched tightly in his hand and ready for action.

When Jonathon was satisfied with how close he was, he used one arm to push back the curtain of greenery blocking their view to expose a small meadow with tall, yellowed grass. In the middle of the meadow, there was a pair of horned dinosaurs fiercely rutting with each other. Jonathon immediately recognized the two-legged dinosaur to be *Stygimoloch*. The animal was a deep, dark brown, almost black with a pair of light brown stripes running vertical down its back like stripes on a sports car. The domed head and majestic array of horns near the back of the *Stygimoloch*'s head was what made the dinosaur so recognizable. It had long been speculated that the animals used the horns similar to the way present-day deer do. Apparently, the theories had been correct. Actually, deer wasn't the best thing to compare them too. Jonathon had seen rams behave exactly the same way on television. *Probably on Wild World,* he thought.

"That's amazing," Silas whispered, and he wished he'd gotten hold of Annie's camera. It disheartened him greatly that he would be unable to share such an incredible display with the rest of the world. "Do you think we're in danger being this close?"

Jonathon bit his lip. "Let's just say I think we're definitely close enough. Let's not push our luck."

Silas nodded, but was disappointed with the answer. Jonathon was just about to turn back to resume their search for Lucy when something totally unexpected happened. It wasn't just unexpected, it was utterly terrifying. It confirmed what he had feared minutes earlier.

Like a bolt of lightning, a three-foot-tall, two-legged dinosaur shot out of the woods on the opposite side of the meadow. It leapt onto the back of the nearest *Stygimoloch* and pressed its claws deep into its ribs. *It* was a *Velociraptor*. The animal immediately forgot all about its counterpart and bellowed in pain. It began to thrash wildly in a desperate attempt to dislodge the animal from its back. Just as the other *Stygimoloch* decided to run, another *Velociraptor* attacked from a different direction. Moments later, no less than eight more of the small predators emerged with great speed from the veil of the jungle to join in the slaughter.

Silas slapped a hand over his mouth and Jonathon's jaw dropped open. A lot of paleontologists agreed that the *Velociraptor* was probably a pack hunter, but Jonathon was pretty certain none of them had imagined they were as brutal as what he was now witnessing.

There was blood everywhere. The yellow grass had turned crimson. The *Velociraptors* feasted on the *Stygimoloch* corpses as if they hadn't eaten in days. Silas had watched animals for years, and he'd never seen any animal on the planet as vicious as these were. Wolves seemed like puppies compared to the pack of *Velociraptors*.

"Time to go," Jonathon whispered.

Silas glanced over at him and was surprised to see Jonathon's face so pale. That was enough to convince him they had to move at once. They did, and they did so quickly. Neither of the men spoke again until they were comfortable they were at a safe distance.

"What on God's earth was that?" Silas asked, now panting.

"*Velociraptor*," Jonathon replied. "I don't have to tell you how dangerous they are. I think you just saw that for yourself."

Silas took his hat off and fanned his face. "There had to be at least ten of them," he said.

"Yeah, we've always thought that they were pack hunters. I guess now we know for sure. They sneaked up on the *Stygimolochs* and planned their attack well." He paused a moment as another terrifying thought crept into his mind.

Silas noticed the look of concern. "What is it?"

Jonathon shook his head and smiled. "Aww, it's nothing. I don't want to scare you."

"Tell me."

Jonathon turned to walk away, seemingly ignoring him, and then he stopped abruptly as he had a change of heart. "Alright, I guess I shouldn't keep this from you."

"Under these circumstances, you shouldn't keep anything from me," Silas snapped back.

Jonathon held his hands up, palms out. "You're right, I shouldn't do that and I won't. I just got to thinking that it is entirely possible that the *Velociraptors* have been watching us closely as well, but chose a better meal instead. I saw their tracks when we came in. They probably inhabit this half of the island pretty heavily. By dinosaur standards, they're very intelligent. They hunt in packs, and we just saw a well-coordinated attack first hand. They could be following us, waiting for the right moment to attack, and we may never even know it until it is too late." Jonathon stopped speaking when he noticed Silas's face turned pale. "Are you okay?"

Silas swallowed and forced a smile. "Yes, I'm fine." He paused a moment as he imagined being eaten alive. "As fine as can be expected, I guess." He looked around in all directions. "We better keep moving."

"I agree, keep your eyes open and more importantly, listen carefully for any sounds."

CHAPTER 23

Travis sweated profusely as he continued to hack and slash his way through the unforgiving jungle. Osvaldo trailed him and periodically advised when they needed to change course. Frank followed behind him with the barrel of the rifle planted firmly in his back. For a while, this gesture made Osvaldo nervous, and that made it nearly impossible for him to think. However, after a day and a half, he'd grown used to it.

As it was now, he was able to think quite clearly and was even beginning to believe that they were getting close. He couldn't explain why, he just sort of felt it in his gut. Then, seemingly out of nowhere, a large stone formation ahead of them confirmed it. He smiled widely and suddenly began to feel a sense of hope. Maybe, just maybe, the nightmare was nearing its end.

"We're getting close," he said, pointing at the rock formation. "I think I remember these rocks."

Angus, who had been close behind Lucy, could hardly contain his glee.

"Are you sure?" he asked, his eyes beaming.

Osvaldo nodded. "Yes, we are near the cave."

"Well, what are you waiting on?" Angus asked. "Keep going!"

Osvaldo raked a hand through his damp, black hair as he looked left, then right. "Give me just a moment."

Angus rolled his eyes, and felt his frustration returning. "A moment for what?"

Osvaldo glared back at him with an annoyed expression. "I know that I am close, but please allow me a moment to examine the area a little more. I have to be sure we continue in the right direction."

"Oh for crying out loud," Angus grumbled, throwing his hands in the air.

"Angus?" Lucy called out unexpectedly.

The old man spun on his heel to face her. "Yes, Mrs. Baker?"

She smiled innocently and drew closer to him. "I have to pee," she whispered.

Angus rolled his eyes again. "Well, can you hold it just a little longer dear?"

She shook her head. "I *reeeally* need to go now."

Angus glanced over his shoulder at Osvaldo. "Do you remember anything yet?"

"No, please let me think," he answered, waving him off.

Angus turned back to Lucy and looked at his watch. "Mrs. Baker, you have two minutes. Please hurry. If you are not back here in two minutes, I will shoot Armando," he said very nonchalantly.

Lucy looked at Armando as a feeling of terror overcame him. She'd seen that look in his eyes far too many times since she'd met him.

"I'll be here," she replied, and gave Armando a reassuring wink.

She scurried off into the woods until she found a large leafy bush to squat behind. She looked back toward the others to make certain none of them could see her. They couldn't, and she began to unbutton her pants. Suddenly, a stick on the ground snapped behind her. She whipped around and looming just behind her stood Travis.

She opened her mouth to scream, but he quickly slapped a hand over her mouth. Panic began to rip through her and she allowed her survival instinct to take control. She thrashed wildly and made multiple attempts to slap him. Travis responded by grabbing a handful of her hair, yanking her head violently back. She reluctantly ceased fighting.

"Sweetheart, the best thing for you to do is be quiet," he whispered. "I'm going to take my hand off of your mouth, but if you scream, I'll shoot you. I'll make it look like you were trying to run away."

She looked into his eyes and could easily see that he was serious. He briefly looked away from her to make sure they were out of view. He could hear Angus yelling at Osvaldo, clearly unaware that he and Lucy were still gone. He reached down for her pants and Lucy closed her eyes tightly, preparing for the worst. Ironically, the first thing that popped in her head was Armando. *Was Angus serious about shooting him after two minutes?* If two minutes hadn't passed yet, it had to be extremely close. She felt the waistband on her pants loosen and she knew he'd managed to work the button loose.

***

"I'm beginning to think that you're stalling!"

"No, I'm trying to be sure," Osvaldo replied. He wasn't lying and he wished the old man would believe him. He was so close to finding the fountain, but he didn't want to screw up and go the wrong way. His gut was telling him to go right.

"My patience is wearing thin, Osvaldo!"

"Okay! I think the cave is this way," he growled back, pointing. "But don't blame me if I'm wrong. You rushed me."

"I hope for your sake you're not wrong," Angus replied, and then he glanced at his watch. "Mrs. Baker should've been back by now."

Armando heard him and immediately fell to the ground and began to sob.

"Shut up, boy!" Angus spat. "I'm not going to kill you. Travis go look for Mrs. Baker, but be quick about it. If she ran off, then let her go. I don't think we need her anymore."

He turned around when he did not receive a response from Travis. "Travis? Frank, where is Travis?"

Frank looked around and shrugged.

A second later, they heard Travis scream in horror.

***

Travis pushed Lucy onto her back and knelt down over her. He was surprised at how calm she was about it all. But then again, he hadn't done anything yet. He grabbed her pants at the hips and began to jerk them down when suddenly a look of fear and panic appeared on her face.

"Honey, don't worry. I won't hurt you," he whispered, he looked into her eyes, but she wasn't looking into his. She appeared to be looking past him, over his shoulder.

Travis whipped his head around, and suddenly, he was the one feeling panic and terror. Just behind him, standing almost twenty feet high and eerily quiet, a female tyrannosaur was curiously staring at him.

Travis felt his heart rate race so hard it felt like it would burst out of his chest. He was just about to reach for a handgun he'd laid on the ground beside him when then tyrannosaur dipped at him. He had just enough time to let out a blood-curdling scream.

The last thing Lucy saw was the entire top half of Travis's body disappearing deep into the jaws of the huge dinosaur. She closed her eyes tightly, but unfortunately, she heard everything. When the tyrannosaur compressed its massive jaws, a multitude of bones cracked and popped all at once. She felt something warm spray across her cheek and knew the liquid was blood. She wanted to open her mouth and scream, but knew doing so would only bring attention to herself. So instead, she stayed put and choked back her fear the best she could.

***

Frank couldn't believe his eyes when he arrived at the grisly scene. Travis was now in two pieces. Half his body (the waist down) lay about ten yards away from the top half. The tyrannosaur leaned over the top half of the body and nibbled on the dead man's internal organs. For a moment, Frank thought he would lose his lunch, but then something else caught his eye. Lucy was on the ground nearby, her eyes shut tightly. He could clearly see her trembling; it was a definite sign that she was alive. There was nothing he could do for Travis now, but there was still time to save Lucy. Frank raised the barrel of the rifle and fired two shots into the tyrannosaur's chest. The animal immediately stood up straight and opened its large jaws, releasing a deafening roar. The only thing the bullets seemed to do was draw attention to him. Frank was in full-fledge panic mode and he clumsily took steps backward. The tyrannosaur began charging toward him, roaring with rage all the way. Frank turned to run, but before he could ever get into a stride, he too felt the massive power of the tyrannosaur's jaws. The top half of his body disappeared into a veil of darkness, and as he drifted unconscious, he was fully aware that he was in the tyrannosaur's mouth.

Lucy immediately opened her eyes when she heard the gun shots. She knew that was an incredibly bad idea, but it was too late now. She watched in horror as the tyrannosaur charged at Frank and effortlessly plucked him off the ground. Again, she heard the nauseating sound of bones breaking, but this time, she saw the carnage too. She saw the bright red liquid rain down from the tyrannosaur's jaws. She had seen enough. She turned to run, but Angus, Osvaldo, and Armando were there. All of them seemed to be nearly overcome with shock.

"Run!" she yelled at them, and she didn't wait to see if they listened.

***

"Oh my God," Silas said. "Was that a—?"

"Tyrannosaur," Jonathon interrupted. "It's a tyrannosaur, and it sounds really angry."

"It doesn't sound that far away," Silas replied.

Jonathon took a couple of steps in the direction he thought the sound came from. "God, I hope that Lucy wasn't..."

"We don't know if they are anywhere near that thing," Silas said, trying to comfort him.

Jonathon didn't seem to hear him. He just took off running.

CHAPTER 24

Lucy ran with all her might and never bothered to look back. The tyrannosaur let out another shrill bellow, and it made her legs pump harder. She ran until her side hurt and her clothes were literally drenching with perspiration. When she finally felt she'd gone far enough, Lucy collapsed to the ground on her hands in knees. It was then that she could finally let her emotions catch up with her. She let out a scream and the tears began to flow heavily. She sobbed uncontrollably for what seemed like several minutes. Finally, she felt a hand grip her shoulder.

"It's alright, dear," Angus said. He'd clearly had trouble keeping up as he panted heavily.

Lucy looked past him and was pleased to see that Osvaldo and Armando had escaped too. They both fell to the ground, too exhausted to run any further. Once she knew Osvaldo and Armando were safe, her mood quickly turned into anger. She glared up at Angus, her blood now boiling.

"No, you stupid old man. Things are not alright at all," she growled. "It's because of you that your men are both dead. Travis deserved it, but Frank actually tried to save me!"

Angus released her shoulder and took a step back. He looked ten years older, and for a moment, Lucy believed she'd gotten to him. For a moment, she actually believed that he was feeling some regret.

"It's unfortunate what happened to them, my dear." He paused, and then sighed. "However, they'd want us to push forward. We're so close now," he said nonchalantly.

Lucy felt her jaw drop in disbelief and she was seconds away from physically assaulting the man when Osvaldo called out to them.

"This is it! We found it," he shouted excitedly.

Lucy looked around and finally spotted what Osvaldo had grown so excited about. A couple hundred feet away from them the large mouth of a cave opened behind a curtain of vines and leafy greenery.

"I don't believe it," Angus whispered. "Finally, I've found it!"

The cave entrance stood about twenty feet tall and was nearly thirty feet wide. It was impossible to see anything within the cave. The shroud of darkness inside momentarily spoiled the joyous moment for Angus. With the thoughts of the tyrannosaur still fresh in his mind, visions of all sorts of dinosaurs waiting for them within the cave gave him a shiver.

Osvaldo seemed unnerved and began to approach the entrance with a flashlight in his hand. Lucy wondered why he would act so carelessly, but then it occurred to her that he'd probably reached the point where he didn't care if he lived or died. If he could just get his grandson off the island, he would probably be happy. He believed he was moments away from reaching that goal. She wanted to call out to him and tell him to stop, but she stopped short of it. It may have been for her own selfish reasons. Someone had to go in and check it out, and there was no way it was going to be her. She watched helplessly as he disappeared into the darkness, but prayed silently that he would return.

"Do you see anything?" Angus called out.

For a long moment, there was no response, but finally Osvaldo returned into the daylight. "Come on, the fountain is still here," he said, a wide smile on his face.

Angus took long strides to quickly make his way along the rocky path that led into the darkness of the cave. Lucy and Armando followed closely behind, because for now it seemed they would be safer with them in the cave, than they would be outside with a tyrannosaur nearby.

***

Silas struggled to keep up with Jonathon, and momentarily lost sight of him as he ran carelessly through the dense vegetation. Every few minutes, Jonathon would have to stop and slash through the dense foliage, thus allowing Silas to catch up. He finally caught up to him again, but this time, Jonathon hadn't stopped to cut down any vines or bushes. He just stopped abruptly and seemed to be staring at something. He heard Silas coming, and he turned toward him and motioned for him to be quiet. Silas slowed his pace and crept up next to him. What he saw scared him to death.

"I think it's Travis," Jonathon whispered as he stood over what appeared to be a chewed-up torso.

Silas opened his mouth, but found himself unable to speak.

"Look over there," Jonathon said, pointing.

Silas squinted, but easily spotted a large tyrannosaur leaning forward and eating something on the ground.

"I think it's a safe guess to say the rest of him is somewhere over there," Jonathon whispered.

Silas swallowed and felt the blood rush away from his face. He felt sick. Then he heard a sound somewhere to his left, it sounded like a twig snapping. He squinted and looked into the foliage for some sign of movement; he was just about to give up when he saw it.

"Jonathon," he whispered, panic in his voice.

"What?"

"Look," he replied, pointing.

Jonathon stared for almost a solid minute and didn't see anything. He was beginning to think his friend was getting paranoid when finally he saw it too. A large eye blinked, and once he caught sight of the eye, the rest of the *Velociraptor* seemed to materialize among the surrounding plants. It was very well camouflaged and nearly impossible to see. It was only fifty feet away, and it was standing deadly still.

"*Velociraptor*. They're probably all around us waiting for the right moment to attack. Follow me...very slowly," Jonathon commanded. He began taking steps backward. Silas followed his lead and found himself desperately wanting his hunting rifle.

"What are we going to do?"

Jonathon clenched his jaw and thought. The truth was, he really didn't know what to do. What he did know is that they had very little time to figure it out. The animals were pack hunters and they no doubt were all around them. All he could think of was the bloody massacre of the *Stygimolochs* they'd witnessed earlier.

"The best thing for us to do is pretend like we don't even know they're there. We've got to find somewhere to hide, and fast. Just walk as calmly as you can."

They walked for what seemed like an hour, although in truth it was probably only fifteen minutes. Jonathon felt as if every step would be his last. He listened hard for any sound of movement in the foliage, and occasionally, he did hear a twig snap. Silas appeared calm on the outside, but Jonathon suspected he was a basket case on the inside. And who could blame him? Suddenly, Silas tugged on Jonathon's shirt sleeve.

He turned to see what the matter was and Silas pointed toward a large hill to the west.

"What about it?"

Silas seemed puzzled by the question and shook his head. "You don't see it?"

Jonathon looked again. "What are you talking about, I don't—" And then he saw it. "Is that a cave?"

"I think so. Do you think we can hide from them there?"

Jonathon mulled it over. He didn't know what would keep the raptors from just following them into the cave. Furthermore, there may be something else bigger and nastier living in the cave. On the other hand, what choice did they have?

"Let's go," he whispered.

***

After a few minutes in the cool darkness of the cave, Lucy's eyes adjusted to the lack of light. Several feet past the entrance, the cave opened up into a large chamber. There were a few holes in the ceiling of the chamber that allowed piercing shafts of daylight to beam down onto the floor in the center. It was there that she spotted a large, round pool containing the bluest water she'd ever seen. The water literally sparkled when the light hit it.

"The fountain of youth," Angus whispered, awestruck. "It's absolutely beautiful." He looked at the others and smiled like a kid on Christmas morning. "We've found it! I can't believe we truly found it? Do you know what this means, Ms. Baker?"

Lucy had to admit the sight before her was pretty incredible and it certainly felt magical. However, she would not allow Angus the pleasure of knowing she felt that way. "It's pretty, Angus, but please think about this before you drink any of the water."

The toothy smile disappeared from the old man's face. "Think about what? Ms. Baker, this water will give ever-lasting life, Osvaldo is the proof," he replied, gesturing toward him.

"Yes, that's right," she snapped back. "Osvaldo is the proof. He told us himself that living forever is not all it's cracked up to be. It's more of a curse than a blessing." Lucy felt as if she was wasting her breath, but she pushed the thought aside. Angus Wedgeworth was an evil man and the world didn't need men like him to live forever. She doubted that talking him out of it was possible, but she had to try.

"Angus, if you drink that water, then you will never die naturally. However, everyone around you will eventually die. I know that you're so self-absorbed you really don't care about that, but at some point you will."

She wanted to say more, but the old man's expression was smug. He clearly wasn't getting anything she was saying. Osvaldo suddenly spoke up.

"And do not forget that you *can* die. If you sustain a mortal injury, you will die just like everyone else. But that is the only way."

Angus stared at him a moment then laughed. "I've gotten by almost eighty years without killing myself. I think I've got that part pretty well mastered."

"Yes, but when you live as long as I have, you will begin to contemplate things that you would never ordinarily think about."

Angus looked toward the fountain with a longing eye, and then turned his attention back to Osvaldo. "What do you mean?"

"What I'm saying is that you will eventually get to a point where living isn't what you want anymore. You will want to die, and after a long time, you will begin to consider taking matters into your own hands."

Angus blinked and didn't seem to comprehend what he was being told.

"Suicide, you old fool," Lucy chimed in. "He's saying that one day, many years from now, you will consider suicide."

Angus laughed, completely dismissing what he was being told. "Somehow, I highly doubt that," he said. He began to walk toward the fountain then stopped abruptly, turning back to the others. "I meant what I said earlier, Ms. Baker. I want you to reap the benefits of this prize with me."

Lucy snorted and looked away. "No, thank you."

Angus shrugged and turned back toward the sparkling pool of water. As he drew nearer to it, he could even smell the sweet liquid. He felt his mouth watering, and it was as if the fountain literally cried out for him to take a drink.

Lucy, Osvaldo, and Armando could only watch as the old man knelt down, his aged knees popping as he did so. He leaned forward and put his entire face into the blue water.

Lucy shook her head in disbelief. *I can't believe this is actually happening.*

Angus took in large gulps of water, and he immediately felt the icy liquid hit his stomach and branch outward throughout his entire body. He pulled his face out of the water and sat still for a moment, allowing the magic water time to do its stuff. His body began to tremble, but the feeling he experienced was pleasant.

Osvaldo had experienced the same sensations hundreds of years ago, but seeing someone else go through it made it seem as if it were yesterday. He too remembered what it was like to feel the wave of energy expand throughout his body, then the brief fear that followed when the trembling began. But he also knew that mere seconds from now, Angus would appear more youthful and full of energy. He closed his eyes and remembered what that was like, how wonderful it seemed at first. Osvaldo opened his eyes as another terrifying memory suddenly crashed through his mind. *There were dinosaurs in the cave after I drank from the fountain. Small feathery dinosaurs.*

Angus turned his back to them all and rubbed the moisture away from his eyes. Suddenly, he felt as if he could run in a marathon with ease. He pictured himself running all the way back to *Bethany,* leaving the others on this wretched island to die. Another smile appeared on his face, and he turned to look at them.

Lucy couldn't believe what she was seeing. Angus, the old man, suddenly wasn't old anymore. He looked more like thirty than seventy-five. The wrinkles on his face had faded away and his silver hair turned a dark brown. And his eyes. They were no longer watery and pale. They became a deep blue and now they glared at her in an unsettling way.

"I feel...alive," Angus said as he clenched both fists. "How do I look?"

"You look...younger. Much younger," she replied, unable to contain her disbelief.

"Are you sure that you don't want to take a drink?" he asked, gesturing toward the fountain.

She stared at the water behind him. It *did* look good, and she was terribly thirsty. The blue water seemed to be begging her to come and take a drink.

"Don't do it," a loud voice called out behind her.

She turned to see who was there and a wide smile swept across her face when Jonathon emerged from the veil of darkness; Silas was behind him.

"Jonathon! You're alive!" She ran to him and leapt into his arms. She immediately noticed the injuries to his abdomen and leg. He was beaten, bloody, and bruised all over. "Are you alright? You look terrible."

"I'm fine, trust me I'm fine. I'm just glad you're alright." He hugged her tightly; he was just relieved that she was alive and unhurt.

For the first time in what seemed like ages, Lucy felt a tremendous amount of relief. Then something else troubling occurred to her.

"Where is Annie?"

"She's fine," he assured her. "I'll explain later. We've got to deal with her uncle right now."

"Yes, of course. Angus found the fountain of youth," she said quickly. "This is why he wanted to explore the island."

"Yeah, I've been watching for a few minutes," he replied. He released her then began marching toward Angus. "You're a lunatic," he growled, jabbing a finger into the man's chest. "As you can see, I've had a rough couple of days because of you. Men have died! And for what? So you can live forever while the rest of us drop dead around you? "

"It is regretful that life was lost," Angus replied, with phony emotion.

Jonathon drew a clenched fist back and threw a punch across Angus's jaw. He stumbled to the ground, blood pouring from his mouth. He looked up at Jonathon, rage burning in his blue eyes. "You shouldn't have done that," he snapped.

"You're a young man now, do something about it," he growled in reply.

Angus reached into his jacket pocket and pulled out his revolver. He stood up quickly and planted the barrel of the gun against Jonathon's forehead.

"Will this suffice?" he asked. He released a sinister chuckle.

"Angus, please no!" Lucy pleaded.

Jonathon directed both his eyes at the barrel of the gun and suddenly felt incredibly foolish. How could he have been so stupid? He knew the man had a gun.

Silas took a step toward them. "Angus, put the gun down!"

"I'm afraid I can't do that," he replied. "Jonathon deserves this. I should've never brought him along."

"You shouldn't have brought any of us along," Jonathon replied, trying to swallow his fear.

"It's ironic that I've just experienced a rebirth of sorts, and you are on the verge of experiencing death," Angus said. "I didn't want it to be this way, really I didn't."

"It doesn't have to be this way," Lucy pleaded.

Osvaldo stood motionless, seemingly uninterested in what was going on. He was scanning the shadows for movement. He'd looked in every corner and saw nothing. He was just about to give up looking when finally he caught a glimpse of something. A familiar silhouette emerged from the deepest point in the chamber. Soon, he caught a glimpse of another, then another. Soon, he saw six dinosaurs altogether creeping toward them.

"Stop with this madness!" he yelled. "We have other problems now," he said, gesturing toward the shadows.

Angus kept the gun pointed at Jonathon, but he turned to see what Osvaldo was referring to. He saw several dinosaurs, roughly five feet high, moving in their direction. As one stepped into a beam of light, he saw red-and-white feathers covering the dinosaur's head.

"Jonathon, what is that?" he asked calmly.

He turned away from Angus, ignoring the gun still pointed at him. "It appears to be a *Troodon*," he said, turning to Lucy for confirmation.

She nodded. "They have binocular vision; yes, I think you may be right. But they have feathers!"

"Yeah," he replied. "They look kind of like big chickens." Jonathon stared at the dinosaurs in amazement; he seemed to forget all about Angus.

"Jonathon, I hate to break up your little moment here," Silas said. "But, are those things gonna eat us?"

Silas's question snapped him back into reality. Most experts believed the *Troodon* to be an herbivore, but at the same time, they were considered highly intelligent in relation to other dinosaurs. More so than even the *Velociraptor*. Jonathon didn't think that they were moving toward them to eat them; however, if they were unwanted guests, he could certainly see the animals attacking them simply to remove them.

"I don't think they want to eat us," he said.

Silas breathed a sigh of relief.

"But," he continued, "I *do* think they mean to harm us. They don't want us here."

Angus suddenly felt fearful and he turned the gun off of Jonathon and pointed it toward the dinosaurs.

"Angus, don't do that," Jonathon snapped. "You'll just piss them off. You can't kill all of them."

Angus couldn't believe his luck. He'd made it so far. Finally, he drank from them fountain and received the gift of eternal youth. Now, he was on the verge of having that gift ripped cruelly away from him.

"I didn't go through everything I've gone through to die now," he said coldly. He turned away from them and began to walk toward the mouth of the cave.

"Where do you think you're going?" Silas barked.

Angus stopped momentarily. "I'm leaving. They clearly don't want us here."

"It's not that simple," Jonathon replied. "They're animals. They'll probably chase after us."

Angus laughed heartily. "Who said that *all* of us were leaving? I'm going to go and the rest of you will stay here while I escape."

Silas felt a rage unlike any he'd ever experienced before. His blood pressure had risen sky high and all he wanted to do now was kill his former friend.

"You're a real piece of work, Angus," he growled. "I can't believe how much you had me fooled."

"Silas, I'm sorry that you feel that way," he replied. "I sincerely wanted you to receive this gift with me."

"I've got a gift I'd love to give you too," Silas snorted and clenched his fist. "Put that gun down and I'll be happy to give it to you."

"Let him leave," Jonathon said calmly.

Silas spun around in disbelief. "Are you nuts? You want him to get away while we die?"

"I don't want him anywhere near me anymore. Chances are pretty good he won't make it back to the ship anyway," he replied.

Silas was about to protest further when he noticed Jonathon give him a subtle wink. He didn't know what Jonathon had in mind, but he knew he had to trust him.

"Good riddance, Angus," he said finally.

Angus replied with a wave and a theatrical bow, and then he turned and pranced out of the cave to enjoy the rest of his life. He couldn't help but smirk as he stepped into the jungle again. He'd outsmarted them all. Sure, there were dangers out here and he had to be extremely careful on the trip back. But he was now young and full of energy. He also had the gun. Most of the dinosaurs they'd encountered ran when they heard gunshots. All he had to do was steer clear of the tyrannosaur and he would be alright.

It was going to be a long and dangerous walk back. He stopped a brief moment to check the revolver so he was absolutely sure the weapon was fully loaded. He smiled when he got confirmation that the gun was good to go. It was basically his ticket out of there, and it comforted him greatly to have it. With the gun clasped tightly in his right hand, he began walking again in the direction he knew would lead him back to the ship. No sooner had he taken his first step, something moved in the bushes nearby. The sound made it seem large, but at first glance, he saw nothing. A large, round eye that reminded him of a cat's eye blinked in the foliage where he was looking. The *Velociraptor* began to move carefully in his direction. Angus clenched his jaw and raised the revolver toward the animal's head.

"You picked the wrong meal today buddy," he whispered as he pulled back the hammer.

He never saw the other raptor approach him from behind. It was only when the animal sank its dagger teeth into the back of his neck that he knew it was there. He tried to open his mouth to scream, not so much from the pain, but to release the overwhelming anger that suddenly overcame him. Eternal life was being ripped away from him only mere minutes after he'd captured it. He wanted to scream, but it was useless as he felt his larynx crush under the hundreds of pounds of bite pressure the raptor was designed to inflict. The one in front of him continued to approach very slowly. It seemed to be happy and content to watch him die before it began to feast upon his flesh. Angus was an extremely easy kill. The second *Velociraptor* held its grip on his throat, and Angus knew his jugular vein had been severed when he saw blood literally spraying from the gaping wound.

He tried desperately to inhale, just to take one more sweet breath of life before his became extinguished forever. It wasn't air he felt fill his lungs, but liquid instead. Finally, the *Velociraptor* released him and Angus fell flat on his back. He gazed up at the sky above and felt intense regret as everything began to darken around him. The last thing he saw before total darkness took over were more *Velociraptors* peering down at him from above his dying body. He closed his eyes just as they all began to lunge at him in unison. Fortunately, his body spared him the physical and emotional pain of being eaten alive.

***

"Forget about Angus," Jonathon said sternly. "We've got to deal with the *Troodons* right now. We'll get Angus later."

He was amazed and somewhat proud of how calm he'd managed to sound. He thought of the pack of *Velociraptors* outside, and if his hunch was right, Angus would be enough to keep them busy while they made their escape from the cave. *If we make our escape from the cave,* he thought. The others stared at him attentively, waiting for his next command.

"What do we do about them?" Silas asked, an unusual quake in his voice. He was clearly terrified.

Jonathon thought hard for some sort of response, but all he could do was look on as all of the *Troodons* closed in around them.

"You've dealt with these things before?" he asked Osvaldo with desperation in his voice.

Osvaldo nodded. "They were here the last time I visited this cave. I narrowly escaped with my life that day."

"Well, don't be bashful," Jonathon said. "Feel free to share with all of us how you made your escape."

"They were far fewer in numbers than they are now," he replied. "I don't know that we will be able to run past them."

Jonathon closed his eyes tightly as he could think of only one option. He pulled Lucy tightly against him, knowing full well he would be unable to bear the sight of her getting ripped apart by the savage animals. He thought of young Armando. The boy was just beginning his life. This wasn't the way it was supposed to end for him. There was only one thing left to do.

"Lucy, get out of here," he whispered.

"What?"

"You heard me. Get out of here," he said again. He looked at the other three. "You guys go on and get out of here. You make darn sure you get Lucy off this island. I'll distract them."

"No," Lucy snapped angrily. "I'm not going anywhere without you."

Jonathon jerked her around to face him. The *Troodons* jumped back at the sign of aggression and looked on curiously. "Lucy, we don't have time for this. I'm gonna get them to go after me while the rest of you run out of here. And don't stop running until you get far away from this cave because I know there are *Velociraptors* outside too."

Lucy shook her head, her eyes glazed over with both fury and sadness. Then they began to well up with tears. She knew there would be no talking him out of this.

The *Troodons* began to hiss loudly and continued to slowly tighten their circle around the invaders of their cave.

"Don't be silly, Jonathon," Silas growled. "I've got thirty years on you. You kids get out of here. I'll hold them off. I always knew sooner or later wild animals would be the end of me. I just never thought it would be dinosaurs," he said with a forced chuckle.

"We will both stay with you, Jonathon," Osvaldo said. "We will stay by your side while Lucy and Armando escape."

Jonathon held up his hands. He knew they had only precious seconds left before the *Troodons* attacked. "No thanks, guys. I've got to do this. Lucy and Armando will need your help to get back to the beach."

Osvaldo and Silas seemed to completely ignore him as they took their places next to him. "No more time to argue, Jonathon," Osvaldo said. "It's time."

Jonathon knew there was nothing left to say. He hugged Lucy again tightly and looked over at Armando. "You get her out of here, kid, I'm counting on you."

Armando nodded, and then looked at his grandfather. He fought back tears.

"Goodbye, Armando," Osvaldo said softly.

As soon as the words passed his lips, Osvaldo did something totally unexpected. He reached out and slapped the *Troodon* nearest to him on the nose and darted away toward the back of the cave.

"All of you run away now!" he yelled.

Jonathon couldn't believe what he was seeing. "What are you doing? This wasn't the plan!"

"Grandfather, no!" Armando cried out in horror.

Osvaldo continued to run as fast as he could deeper into the cave, all of the dinosaurs immediately gave chase after him. "Run now! I don't know how much longer I can keep them distracted. This is what I want!"

Those were the last words Osvaldo ever spoke as the pack of *Troodons* swarmed over him and the man disappeared beneath the chaos.

Jonathon began to shake with anger as the realization of what had just happened began to set in. Osvaldo sacrificed himself so that the rest of them could escape. It was a noble gesture, and although Jonathon felt a tremendous amount of respect for the man who so willingly gave his life, this wasn't the way it was supposed to happen.

Suddenly, he felt a firm grip tug on his forearm. He looked over and found that it was Silas. "The man made his choice. Don't let him die for nothing!"

Jonathon nodded and grabbed Lucy by the arm. He began to run and tried his best to drown out the gruesome sounds of the massacre behind him. He heard Armando screaming in agony. Silas had grabbed the young man and literally threw him over his shoulder to get him out of there.

The four of them ran out of the cave and didn't stop until they found the two ATVs Jonathon and Silas had left. Jonathon collapsed on a large patch of clover and it took a few minutes to regain his breath. Lucy fell beside him and rolled over on her back. She finally got an opportunity to process what had just happened and she wept uncontrollably.

Jonathon crawled next to her and he tried to think of something to say to comfort her. Then he thought of Armando who was now curled up in the fetal position on the ground. He was shaking, and possibly in shock. Who could blame the kid after what he'd just seen. Even Silas seemed to be struggling to accept what had just happened.

Jonathon gave Lucy a soothing kiss on her forehead and redirected his attention to Armando. He drew near and put a comforting hand on the young man's shoulder.

"Your grandfather is a hero," he began. "He's the bravest man I've ever met."

Armando looked up at him; his eyes were full of pain.

Lucy crawled over to Armando and put her arms around him in a maternal way. "Armando, your grandfather is now free of his curse." She continued to sob, but her words were soothing. "I don't think he saved just us. I think he was trying to save himself too."

Armando sat motionless, but he appeared to be listening.

Silas took a seat on a nearby log, his eyes were red and tears streamed down his face.

The four of them rested for around twenty minutes, each of them working out Osvaldo's death in their own way. Jonathon had been ready to move on long before that. He wasn't sure if Angus had slipped away or not, but if he had, it was only a matter of time before him and the ship departed. There wasn't any more time to waste.

He coaxed them all onto the ATVs. He and Silas piloted the vehicles, while Lucy and Armando were passengers. As they drove back, Jonathon almost had the sense that dinosaurs and the island itself had finally had their fill of torturing them. The ride back was pretty much uneventful, and although the countless herds of dinosaurs still remained in the valley watching them with obvious curiosity as they motored across the landscape in retreat, Jonathon didn't spot a single animal that appeared to be threatening to him. The majestic animals had apparently survived extinction thanks to the fountain of youth. It was a power that for literally millions of years, only they possessed. All of them at some point had drunk the magical water. He wondered if there were other pools of it on the island that had not yet been seen with human eyes. He thought of the *Troodons* and how aggressive they were. Although he could never be sure, it certainly seemed that they were protecting the powerful fountain that rested in the heart of their island home. Many paleontologists believed that the *Troodon* was the most intelligent of all the dinosaurs. Jonathon just couldn't help but wonder if they had underestimated the intelligence of the *Troodon*. Maybe they were fully aware of the fact that their species, and many of the other less intelligent dinosaurs, had somehow cheated death when the rest of the world had not. They were the last of their kind, and no doubt they felt the power of the fountain when they drank from it just as Osvaldo and Angus did. It was an incredible thing to consider, and Jonathon even chuckled to himself when he thought of just how far out his imagination was taking him.

When they finally arrived at the large shipping container, Annie began to shed tears of joy. Maybe they were tears of joy since she saw that Jonathon and the others were alive. Maybe it was because she was on the verge of giving up and accepting that her own life was going to end. Maybe it was a little of both, but the only thing Jonathon was sure of was that she was clearly excited to see them. After a brief embrace with Lucy, they continued across the beach until they finally caught sight of *Bethany*. The large ship was the most beautiful thing any of them had seen all day. Jonathon knew before he even got on board the ship that it was deserted. He couldn't help but smile when, for the first time, he realized that Angus didn't make it. The man was either dead, or wandering around aimlessly through the jungle. He wasn't sure which fate was worse.

When they reached the ship's bow, Jonathon and Silas made Armando and the ladies wait in the small boat while they climbed on board to make sure there weren't any flying reptiles waiting for them this time. Silas took time to drag Captain Blackstone onto the deck next to what was left of Denny and he covered them with a canvas tarp. He and Jonathon had no intentions of filling in the others on what was under the tarp, but they figured it would be pretty easy to figure out. There was too much blood all over the deck and bridge for them not to be able to figure it out. When they finally did board the ship, Jonathon quickly ushered them into the bridge and locked the door.

Silas took control of the ship, and Jonathon suddenly felt anxious to see the sun again. The ship rocked back and forth in a much more pronounced fashion than it had when they arrived days earlier. The ocean seemed choppier, but no one on board seemed to care. They were all overcome with exhaustion and no one said a word when *Bethany* finally broke through the other side of the fog. The sun bathed the ship in warm, golden rays that seemed to welcome them back to the normal world they were familiar with. Jonathon walked out on deck and made his way to the stern. He took a seat and watched the horizon until the misty island disappeared. He wondered if he or anyone else would ever see it again. Deep down, he hoped no one ever did. Of course, the last thing he wanted was for more lives to be lost, but the main reason was because he felt that the dinosaurs had overcome extinction. Clearly, they had earned their place in the world. If the rest of the planet learned of its existence, the dinosaurs would never know freedom again. He suddenly felt a tremendous responsibility to keep the island a secret. The unfortunate truth was that he didn't know if it would be possible. There were more of Angus's people that knew of the island's existence. He immediately thought of Eric Gill, Angus's pilot he'd met on board the Gulfstream. There would be questions to answer when they returned. Jonathon knew he would have to think of some good answers. Then he thought of the fountain of youth. *Did Eric know of its existence?* There was no way to know for sure, but he decided it was best to not mention it. If Eric brought it up, then it would be discussed. If he didn't know about it, then Jonathon decided he never would. He didn't want to give him, or anyone else, a reason to venture back to the deadly island. He cringed when he considered what would happen if the world found out about the island, the dinosaurs, and the fountain of youth. The world wasn't ready to know about the island. If anyone did return, more lives would certainly be lost.

CHAPTER 25

One Week Later...

Eric Gill sipped soda through a straw as he watched his hired help finish loading what was left of his supplies on *Bethany*. When Jonathon and the other survivors had returned to Fort Lauderdale a week earlier, the stories they told were frightening to say the least. Eric did his best to seem genuinely happy for their safe return, but the truth was he was fuming mad. He'd learned the awful news that Travis and Frank were dead. That was a mess he really didn't want to deal with, but fortunately for him, he didn't know of any family the two had besides Angus. On the other hand, the demise of Captain Blackstone and Denny was a different story. They *did* have family that would miss them being gone. Eric would allow Angus's lawyers to handle that. There were waivers the good captain and his first mate had signed when they agreed to do the job. Then Jonathon told him the unfortunate news that Angus was missing in action. He even hinted around that he believed the man was dead, but he was adamant that there was no way he could confirm it because he had no body. Eric listened with sincere interest as Jonathon told him an interesting tale about how Angus, Travis, and Frank held Lucy hostage and left the others for dead. It was all Eric could do to keep from smiling as he listened because he knew all along that something like that was a possibility.

The news that the Puerto Rican, Osvaldo, had died mattered very little to him. He figured that was eventually going to happen anyway. He knew better than anyone how Angus acted when he didn't get what he wanted. Angus never accepted the word "no" and anyone who ever tried to butt heads with the old man always got the horns. Jonathon and his buddies learned that the hard way.

Annie didn't seem very upset about her missing uncle when she returned. Eric knew they'd never been close, but judging by her mood, Angus hadn't cut her any slack just because she was a part of his family. Eric did what he could to accommodate her, but in the end, he knew it was useless. Word would get out to other members of the Wedgeworth family. People would begin to ask more questions. *Thank God for those lawyers!* They could deal with that mess too.

Jonathon had made it very clear that returning to the island was not something for Eric or any other employee of Angus Wedgeworth to consider. He told him how frightening some of the dinosaurs that roamed the island were. Eric kept his thoughts to himself, but the whole time he believed some of the stories he'd been told were embellishments. He wondered if there was some other reason that Jonathon wanted him to stay away from the island. *The prick probably wants to go back with some of his own people and claim that he discovered it,* he thought. He shook the thoughts from his head. There was no reason to dwell on what Jonathon's intentions were. Eric had his own agenda at the moment.

Angus Wedgeworth was his boss, and he'd been a faithful employee for fifteen years. He was almost certain the man was still alive somewhere on the island. The man was too mean to die. The only thing that puzzled him was that Jonathon had made no mention about the fountain of youth. Eric guessed that he still wasn't aware of it, and he certainly was not going to volunteer the information. The fact of the matter was that *if* Angus was alive, (and Eric believed he was) then he would be waiting on *him* to come get him. As far as he knew, Angus didn't have any other employees that knew of the existence of the island, the dinosaurs, or the fountain of youth. If Angus was alive, he would fully expect Eric to come for him. If he sat around and did nothing, then there would be hell to pay if Angus found a way back. And knowing the old man the way Eric did, he knew that someway, somehow he would find a way back. He would be as good as dead if he didn't try to find him. Of course, he couldn't do it all alone. He'd hired four college kids to accompany him "while he went to pick up a friend from an island." He didn't have to tell them much more than that once they found out how well they were getting paid. It was easy to find one of the locals to pilot the ship for him; once again, money made all the difference. Now as the sun began to set, the only thing left to do was board the ship and begin the voyage.

Once on board, Eric walked across the deck to a large wooden crate. He grabbed a crowbar that was lying on top of the crate and began to pry the lid open. Inside, there were several assault rifles and countless rounds of ammunition. He'd tried to tell Angus repeatedly they needed to bring more guns. All the old man could think about was the fountain of youth. He would not make the same mistakes. One of the tall, lanky college kids strutted over to where he was. Eric quickly slid the lid back over the crate and turned to face him.

"I think we're all set, Mr. Gill," he said.

Eric smiled. "What's your name, kid?"

"David, my friends call me Dave though."

"Well alright, Dave. Are you excited about the trip?"

Dave's face lit up and answered the question before he even spoke. "Yes, sir. I can't wait. I've always wanted to travel a lot when I grew up.

This is a good start. I've never been out on the ocean. To be honest, I'm kind of nervous about it."

Eric frowned. "Nervous? About the ocean?"

Dave seemed embarrassed; he ran his fingers through his bushy, brown hair. "Yeah, I know this is going to sound really silly, but it's not really the ocean that bothers me. It's what is *in* the ocean."

Eric raised his eyebrows. "And just what are you referring to?"

"Well, there are sharks, and giant squids. There's a lot of stuff in the water that is larger than this ship. That makes me a little nervous," he said sheepishly.

Eric smiled, and shortly after his smile turned into laughter.

"What's so funny?"

"Kid, trust me when I say the monsters in the water should be the least of your worries."

"Okay...I guess," Dave replied, and he looked at Eric as if he thought the man he was speaking to was on drugs or something. The kid strolled away and began helping his buddies move some of the gear down to the cabins.

Eric walked over to the railing at the bow of *Bethany* and leaned forward. He stared into the water and thought of the sharks and giant squids Dave had spoken of. "You ain't seen nothing yet, kid," he whispered.

THE END

SEVEREDPRESS

f facebook.com/severedpress

🐦 twitter.com/severedpress

CHECK OUT OTHER GREAT
DINOSAUR THRILLERS

WRITTEN IN STONE
by David Rhodes

Charles Dawson is trapped 100 million years in the past. Trying to survive from day to day in a world of dinosaurs he devises a plan to change his fate. As he begins to write messages in the soft mud of a nearby stream, he can only hope they will be found by someone who can stop his time travel. Professor Ron Fontana and Professor Ray Taggit, scientists with opposing views, each discover the fossilized messages. While attempting to save Charles, Professor Fontana, his daughter Lauren and their friend Danny are forced to join Taggit and his group of mercenaries. Taggit does not intend to rescue Charles Dawson, but to force Dawson to travel back in time to gather samples for Taggit's fame and fortune. As the two groups jump through time they find they must work together to make it back alive as this fast-paced thriller climaxes at the very moment the age of dinosaurs is ending.

HARD TIME
by Alex Laybourne

Rookie officer Peter Malone and his heavily armed team are sent on a deadly mission to extract a dangerous criminal from a classified prison world. A Kruger Correctional facility where only the hardest, most vicious criminals are sent to fend for themselves, never to return.

But when the team come face to face with ancient beasts from a lost world, their mission is changed. The new objective: Survive.

 SEVERED**PRESS**

CHECK OUT OTHER GREAT DINOSAUR THRILLERS

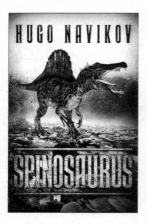

SPINOSAURUS
by Hugo Navikov

Brett Russell is a hunter of the rarest game. His targets are cryptids, animals denied by science. But they are well known by those living on the edges of civilization, where monsters attack and devour their animals and children and lay ruin to their shantytowns.

When a shadowy organization sends Brett to the Congo in search of the legendary dinosaur cryptid Kasai Rex, he will face much more than a terrifying monster from the past.

Spinosaurus is a dinosaur thriller packed with intrigue, action and giant prehistoric predators.

LAND OF DEATH
by Eric S Brown & Alex Laybourne

A group of American soldiers, fleeing an organized attack on their base camp in the Middle East, encounter a storm unlike anything they've seen before. When the storm subsides, they wake up to find themselves no longer in the desert and perhaps not even on Earth. The jungle they've been deposited in is a place ruled by prehistoric creatures long extinct. Each day is a struggle to survive as their ammo begins to run low and virtually everything they encounter, in this land they've been hurled into, is a deadly threat.

CHECK OUT OTHER GREAT DINOSAUR THRILLERS

JURASSIC ISLAND
by Viktor Zarkov

Guided by satellite photos and modern technology a ragtag group of survivalists and scientists travel to an uncharted island in the remote South Indian Ocean. Things go to hell in a hurry once the team reaches the island and the massive megalodon that attacked their boats is only the beginning of their desperate fight for survival.

Nothing could have prepared billionaire explorer Joseph Thornton and washed up archaeologist Christopher "Colt" McKinnon for the terrifying prehistoric creatures that wait for them on JURASSIC ISLAND!

K-REX
by L.Z. Hunter

Deep within the Congo jungle, Circuitz Mining employs mercenaries as security for its Coltan mining site. Armed with assault rifles and decades of experience, nothing should go wrong. However, the dangers within the jungle stretch beyond venomous snakes and poisonous spiders. There is more to fear than guerrillas and vicious animals. Undetected, something lurks under the expansive treetop canopy . . .

Something ancient.

Something dangerous.

Kasai Rex!

29676601R00114

Made in the USA
Lexington, KY
02 February 2019